UNDER THE

COLOR

OF LAW

Also by Michael McGarrity

MICHAEL McGARRITY

A Kevin Kerney Novel

UNDER THE
COLOR
OF LAW

DUTTON

DUTTON
Published by the Penguin Group
Penguin Putnam Inc., 375 Hudson Street, New York, New York 10014, U.S.A.
Penguin Books Ltd, 27 Wrights Lane, London W8 5TZ, England
Penguin Books Australia Ltd, Ringwood, Victoria, Australia
Penguin Books Canada Ltd, 10 Alcorn Avenue, Toronto, Ontario, Canada M4V 3B2
Penguin Books (N.Z.) Ltd, 182–190 Wairau Road, Auckland 10, New Zealand

Penguin Books Ltd, Registered Offices: Harmondsworth, Middlesex, England

Published by Dutton, a member of Penguin Putnam Inc.

First Printing, July, 2001
10 9 8 7 6 5 4 3 2

 REGISTERED TRADEMARK—MARCA REGISTRADA

LIBRARY OF CONGRESS CATALOGING-IN-PUBLICATION DATA
McGarrity, Michael.
    Under the color of law : a Kevin Kerney novel / Michael McGarrity.
        p.   cm.
    ISBN 0-525-94604-7 (alk. paper)
    1. Kerney, Kevin (Fictitious character)—Fiction. 2. Police—New Mexico—Santa
Fe—Fiction. 3. Santa Fe (N.M.)—Fiction. 4. Police chiefs—Fiction.   I. Title.

PS3563.C36359 U64 2001
813'.54—dc21   00-069406

Printed in the United States of America
Set in Goudy
Designed by Eve L. Kirch

PUBLISHER'S NOTE
This book is a work of fiction. Names, characters, places, and incidents are either the product of the author's imagination or are used fictitiously, and any resemblance to actual persons, living or dead, business establishments, events, or locales is entirely coincidental.

This book is printed on acid-free paper.

In memory of Eugene Manlove Rhodes, and for Richard Bradford and Tony Hillerman, three masterful New Mexico writers who have inspired me over the years with their wonderful stories.

Acknowledgments

Thanks go to Chief John Denko, Deputy Chief Beverly K. Lennen, Sergeant Gary Johnson, and Officer Stephen Altonji of the Santa Fe Police Department, who enhanced my understanding of their organization and gave willingly of their time to assist me in my research.

The problems attributed to the department in this book are fictional and should in no way reflect upon the professionalism of the men and women who serve their community.

Thanks also go to Marshal Ken Iskow of Red River, New Mexico; Tom Claffey of Santa Fe; Joann and Paul Davis and their daughter Anita, of Ramah, New Mexico; and Brother George Hetzel and Brother Brian Dybowski of the College of Santa Fe, all of whom cheerfully provided me with valuable information.

UNDER THE
COLOR
OF LAW

Alonso Herrera, nicknamed Cloudy by his fellow Santa Fe police officers because of his piss-poor attitude and constant complaining, cursed as he rolled his unit to a stop in front of the metal security gate at the front end of a dirt driveway. He didn't like working day shifts, didn't like driving through snow and slush, and didn't like checking on some rich-bitch citizen an out-of-state relative was worried about.

He opened the window and punched the call button on the speaker box. An early-morning storm had left two inches of snow on the ground, and the cold wind felt raw against his face.

Fuck February, Herrera thought.

The absence of tire tracks in the driveway probably meant that Mrs. Phyllis Terrell wasn't at home. He would have to hoof it up the driveway and get his feet wet and his shoes dirty, just to report he'd been unable to make contact with the occupant.

He reviewed the notes he'd scribbled when dispatch had assigned him the call. He was looking for Mrs. Phyllis Terrell, age fifty-two, five four, blond and blue, weight 120, health excellent.

When Terrell had failed to show up on an early-morning flight from Albuquerque to Washington, D.C., her sister, who had been waiting at the airport for her, immediately called the house only to get an answering machine.

The sister, Susan Straley, had then called the shift commander, made a big deal about how Terrell was an ambassador's wife, and asked to have an officer sent to check on the woman.

Ambassador to what, Herrera wondered. Santa Fe had more than its share of media celebrities, movie stars, trust funders, and rich arty-farty types, but the politicians who lived in the city were the local garden variety, not prominent national figures.

After buzzing again with no response, Herrera got out of his unit. The ex–chief of police had purchased white patrol cars for the department, which always looked like shit in bad weather. He hated driving a dirty unit, and today his vehicle was splattered with mud and road slush.

Herrera couldn't even begin to count the wasted hours he'd spent in this neighborhood. The high-tech security systems in these houses went off whenever some damn rodent ran across a floor or a lightning storm came too close.

He keyed his handheld radio, reported he would be on foot at the Terrell residence, and climbed over the four-foot gate. A snarling dog came out of nowhere. Before Herrera could retreat, it nipped hard at his leg. He shook it free, his trousers tearing as the dog let go. The mutt backed up, snarled again, and started another run at him. Herrera squirted it with pepper spray and scrambled back over the gate. The dog yelped, went prone, whined, and started working both paws at its eyes, trying to clear out the spray.

Herrera looked down at his leg and lifted the torn flap of fabric. His skin had been broken by the animal's teeth. He decided he hated fucking dogs and thought about shooting this one, but instead called for animal control.

The dog had wandered off by the time Matt Garcia, the animal-control officer, arrived. After getting his snare from the truck, he looked at Herrera's leg. The puncture wound wasn't deep and the blood had stopped running.

Garcia raised his eyes to Cloudy's pinched, sour-looking face. "What breed of dog was it?" he asked.

"How the hell should I know?" Herrera said. "Big, about sixty pounds. At least knee high. Short hair. Black with a white chest. It just looked like an ugly mutt."

"You better hope I find it, and it has a current rabies vaccination," Garcia said. "Otherwise, you're not gonna like what happens next."

"I don't want to hear that shit," Herrera said with a worried glance at his leg. "Go find the damn dog."

"Don't you want to help round him up?" Garcia asked with a grin.

"Just do your job," Herrera snapped.

He watched the young man swing easily over the gate and trot up the steep driveway that had been cut into the granite rock of the hillside. He sucked in his thick gut and decided to add animal control officers to the list of people he didn't like, which up to now had only included his ex-wife, any and all civilians, and his asshole shift commanders.

While Garcia scrambled around trees and over rock outcroppings calling for the dog, Herrera turned his attention to the Terrell house. At least six times larger than his small subdivision tract home, it sat a hundred feet above him, sited to take advantage of the valley view and Atalaya Mountain across the way. It had a deep portal bordered by a high patio wall that was under construction.

He heard a dog bark and switched his gaze to the driveway in time to see Garcia turn a corner, yanking the muzzled mutt along by the handle of the snare.

"You gotta go up there," Garcia called in a shaky voice as he approached.

"What's wrong?"

Garcia stopped at the driveway gate. He was flustered. "There's a dead woman inside the house lying next to the front door with a pair of scissors stuck in her chest. Some guy came out of the back of an RV parked by the garage and ran off when he saw me."

"Shit," Cloudy said, reaching across his chest for the microphone to the handheld that was clipped to his shirt. "You went in the house?"

"I just followed the dog," Garcia said. "The patio door was open."

"Describe the woman for me."

"Dead, for Chrissake," Garcia said. "I didn't stop to take a close look."

Herrera stared at the dog. "Does that piece-of-shit mutt have a current rabies tag?"

"Yeah, you're in luck," Garcia said.

"Walk him around to the road, put him in your truck, and stand by."

"I've got three pending calls," Garcia said.

"Not anymore you don't," Herrera said. He keyed the microphone and called in the homicide.

Lieutenant Salvador Molina, special-investigations commander, peered inside the open patio door of the Terrell residence. The victim lay on her back approximately three feet inside the house, with her feet pointing south toward the door. A blood pool darkened a thick Oriental rug. Dog tracks and human footprints wandered erratically across the floor of the expansive living room.

The expression on Phyllis Terrell's face seemed peaceful. It was a strong, attractive face with even features. She wore expensive diamond studs in her ears, and a larger single diamond on a gold chain around her neck. The scissors protruding from Terrell's chest looked like the type Molina's wife used whenever she tried to sew something.

Molina heard footsteps on the flagstone patio behind him. He'd been waiting for the crime-scene unit and the medical examiner to arrive, so he didn't look back. "This area is off limits," he said. "Go in through the garage door."

"What have you got so far, Lieutenant?" Kevin Kerney asked.

Molina stiffened and turned. Kerney, the new Santa Fe police chief, looked past him at the body on the floor.

Kerney had been appointed at the first of the year over the muttered dismay of many officers who didn't like having a cop-killer for a boss no matter what the reason. The incident had happened last fall while Kerney was serving as a deputy chief of the New Mexico State Police. The official story was that a dirty cop had started a gunfight he couldn't finish, but some on the force didn't buy it.

Kerney had been cleared by an independent internal-affairs investigation. But his resignation soon after the event fueled the flames of speculation. Now people were saying that the chief had managed to get hired through some political string-pulling.

If true, another good old boy had been made police chief by the mayor and city manager, which was enough to cause Molina to think about starting a short-timer's calendar. He had eight months and sixteen days left before he could retire with a maximum pension.

"We've got a mess, Chief," Molina said. "The crime scene was contaminated by an animal-control officer who chased the dog that bit Officer Herrera."

"So I've heard," Kerney said. "What's the status of the investigation?"

"The crime-scene unit and the ME are rolling. I've got four detectives doing a room-to-room plain-view search. A Mexican national has been living in an RV parked next to the garage. The RV was leased from a local company by Mrs. Terrell on a two-year contract. My guess is the man was hired to build the patio wall, and maybe some other stuff that needed doing, and Terrell provided him with a place to stay during construction. We found his personal belongings and clothes, plus some letters from Mexico addressed to a Santiago Terjo. I've got U.S. Customs running a records check on the name to see if he's a legal or not."

"Have you confirmed that this is Phyllis Terrell?" Kerney asked.

Molina nodded. "From the photo on a driver's license we found in her purse."

The dead woman on the floor wore charcoal wool slacks, a turtleneck sweater, and a pair of expensive leather walking boots. Kerney noted the diamond jewelry. "Have you ruled out robbery as a motive?"

"Pretty much. Her purse is on the kitchen counter with her airplane ticket in it, along with two thousand dollars, credit cards, and a wallet. Her travel bags were packed and ready to go."

"What time was her flight from Albuquerque?"

"Seven-twenty," Molina said.

"So, she was up, dressed, and ready to leave by six, at the latest," Kerney said.

"That would be my guess," Molina said.

To take advantage of the views the double doors to the patio were glass. Kerney looked out at the mountains that bracketed the small valley. Tucked away a few miles from the plaza, it was an area few tourists visiting the city ever saw. Once farmed by Hispanic families, the neighborhood was now an upscale address with multimillion-dollar retirement and vacation houses perched on the hillsides.

"Would you open your door to a stranger at that time of day?" Kerney asked, turning back to Molina.

"No way, Chief."

"Is this the door the dog came in?"

Molina nodded. "Yeah. Matt Garcia said it was wide open."

"Does anything bother you about the scene?"

Molina shrugged. "It's too early to say."

"You're probably right. Mind if I take a look inside?" Kerney asked.

"You're the chief," Molina said.

"Thanks. I'll go in through the garage."

Lieutenant Molina watched Kerney walk away with his distinctive limp. He remembered when Kerney had been the department's chief of detectives. A gun battle with a drug dealer had supposedly ended his career with the Santa Fe PD. But after a long period of recuperation Kerney had returned to law enforcement, serving briefly as a sheriff's lieutenant and a Forest Service ranger before joining the state police as an investigator. Within weeks Kerney had been bumped up to a deputy-chief slot, which raised a lot of eyebrows in cop shops throughout the state.

Sal wondered what Kerney had in mind for the department. Over the last five years three previous chiefs had been brought in to kick butt, take names, and reorganize the department. Not one of them had given a rat's ass about what sworn personnel thought, needed, or would be willing to do to clean things up and improve the department.

If Kerney followed suit, he might well have a rebellion on his hands.

He watched Kerney turn the corner. Since starting the job, the chief had come to work every day dressed in civvies. Today Kerney wore a well-tailored sport coat, shirt and tie, dress slacks, and a very choice pair of cowboy boots. A lot of officers were grumbling about Kerney's clothes; they said that not wearing the uniform showed a lack of respect for the department. To them it wasn't a good sign of things to come.

Personally, Sal didn't care what Kerney wore, as long as he did the job professionally and treated people fairly. Whether he would or not remained to be seen.

Kerney had been known as a good boss when he was chief of detectives. But Sal knew that there was only one constant about cops who moved high up the food chain: They changed. Sometimes radically and usually not for the better. He would wait and see which direction Kerney was headed.

Kerney turned the corner of the house, reviewing what he'd seen so far. Molina had established the entry point to the crime scene at the security gate, using Herrera as the log-in officer. He'd strung several rolls of bright yellow police-line tape up the driveway to mark the route to be used to get to the house, which would make any tracks found outside the path easier to identify. Paw prints and two different sets of footprints in the snow had been flagged for the crime-scene unit to photograph. The victim's body and the area around it was off limits and under Molina's watchful eye to keep it preserved, protected, and free from any further contamination.

Good enough for starters, Kerney thought as he entered the house through the garage. But Molina's reticence to speculate about the crime scene bothered Kerney. Maybe Molina felt ill at ease making guesses with his new boss. Still, Kerney wondered why the lieutenant hadn't raised a question about the murder weapon. Scissors weren't normally used in premeditated murders. In fact, they were much more typically associated with crimes of passion or acts of domestic violence. Which, along with the absence of robbery as a motive, could mean the killer was known to the victim, perhaps well known.

The detectives inside the house didn't stop working as Kerney looked around. Behind the great room were two master suites, each with an attached study, separated by a long gallery hallway. The open kitchen adjacent to the great room was within a few short steps to a formal dining room. Another hallway led to an attached, stepped-down guest suite with a private patio containing a marble water fountain.

In Mrs. Terrell's bedroom a detective was visually examining the linens on the unmade bed. In her study, which had built-in shelves filled with framed photographs of family and friends, an officer was reading through the scattered papers on top of a mission-style desk.

Kerney said nothing to the detectives, greeting each one as he passed by only with a friendly nod. He had no intention of disturbing the chain of command by making suggestions, issuing instructions, or asking questions. The Terrell murder was the first major felony case fielded by the department since Kerney had assumed command, and he'd come solely to observe.

The layout of the second study and master bedroom mirrored Mrs. Terrell's suite, minus any personal touches. No one was working the area, so Kerney took his time. There were books on the shelves, tasteful art on the walls, and a very choice modern sculpture on a tall stand in the corner of the study. But nothing in sight signaled daily use or ongoing occupancy by a family member.

Kerney slipped on a pair of plastic gloves and opened desk and dresser drawers. All were empty. The walk-in closet contained some dry cleaning on hangers draped in clear plastic, consisting of two men's suits and some starched white dress shirts. On the floor were a half a dozen sealed packing boxes, each labeled with the contents, purportedly consisting of books, photographs, and odds and ends.

Curious about what might have been removed from the suite and packed away, Kerney decided to break his self-imposed rule not to interfere with the investigation. He took out a pocket knife, knelt down, and slit open the box labeled "Photographs." Packed in bubble wrap was an assortment of framed pictures of Ambassador Hamilton Lowell Terrell with foreign leaders, ex-presidents, and other dignitaries, all of them personally inscribed. But it was the photograph of Terrell wearing the uniform of an army major general that brought Kerney to a full stop.

Kerney had been an infantry officer in Nam during the latter stages of the war. His first brigade commander had been a colonel given to tongue-lashing junior officers, bullying his staff, and bullshitting the brass. Known as the Snake by his troops, Colonel Terrell had moved on to an ARVN airborne advisory assignment a month after Kerney arrived in-country, much to everybody's relief.

Kerney had all but forgotten about the Snake.

He studied the photograph of his old commander, wondering how such a backstabbing, heartless, self-serving officer could possibly become an ambassador, let alone a two-star general.

The thought was so naive it made Kerney smile. The world was filled with ruthless people who achieved high rank and prestigious positions, and over the years it had been Kerney's misfortune to serve under his fair share of them.

He repackaged the photos, stripped off the gloves, told one of the detectives he'd looked through a box of photographs, and left the house. Outside, he glanced inside the RV and then walked around the residence, staying on a meandering flagstone path. When completed, the patio wall would encircle the structure except for a generous parking area near the front entrance. In all it would enclose a half acre. Some sections had already been finished and landscaped, other sections were barely under way, with nothing more than trenches dug for footings that curved and dipped in harmony with the terrain.

It was a major undertaking and not inexpensive by any means.

Kerney returned to the patio and watched the arriving crime-scene techs and the ME walk up the driveway. The view across the valley was spectacular. Early-afternoon sunlight made the snow glisten on Atalaya Mountain, and the Sangre de Cristo Mountain Range was frosty white.

Kerney checked his watch. Things were moving much too slowly. Why hadn't Molina pulled in more manpower? Nearby neighbors needed to be canvassed. Why wasn't a field search of the property under way? Why hadn't Santiago Terjo's tracks in the snow been identified and followed to see if he might be hiding nearby? Had the whereabouts of the ambassador been determined?

His jaw tightened. As much as he wanted to stand back and let Molina run the investigation without interference, the victim's prominence argued against such an approach. This was a case where every wrong move or screw-up would be placed under a media microscope.

He would wait for Molina to finish briefing the techs and ME before talking to him.

Across a deep arroyo that cut into the hillside an SUV climbed a paved road and turned into the driveway of the closest house. While the distance was too far for Kerney to see clearly, the person who got out of the vehicle looked to be a woman wearing a parka, cap, and blue jeans.

She opened the back of the SUV and a large dog hopped out.

For a moment the woman stood by the vehicle staring in the direction of the Terrell residence. Then she started down a footpath into the arroyo and walked quickly in Kerney's direction, the dog following eagerly along.

Using a path that intersected the Terrells' driveway, Kerney hurried to cut the woman off. He intercepted her as she scrambled up the side of the arroyo through wet snow.

"What's wrong?" the woman asked breathlessly as she came to a stop. The dog, a Labrador, gave Kerney's pant cuffs a quick sniff and kept going. "I saw the police cars at the end of the driveway. Has there been a burglary?"

"Can you control your dog?" Kerney asked.

The woman whistled once. "Cassidy, stay."

The dog sat, tail wagging, and smiled at the woman.

Wisps of dark brown hair showed from under the wool cap pulled down over the woman's ears. Her worried brown eyes wandered from Kerney's face to the Terrell residence, partially hidden by pine trees along the path.

"What happened?" she asked

"Tell me who you are," Kerney said.

"You go first," the woman said.

"I'm a police officer," Kerney said, displaying his shield and ID. "Let me walk you back to your residence."

The woman didn't move. "If there has been a burglary, Phyllis will want to know about it."

"Are you friendly with Ambassador and Mrs. Terrell?" Kerney asked.

"You're not answering my question," the woman replied, as she tried to step around Kerney. "I'm going up there to find out what happened."

Kerney blocked her way. "You can't enter a crime scene. Let me escort you home."

The woman bit her lip. "Can you really force me to stay away?"

"Yes, I can."

She gave Kerney an unhappy look, whistled once for Cassidy, then turned, and backtracked into the arroyo. Kerney followed as the woman climbed quickly and easily up the far side of the arroyo.

Inside the house the woman turned off the burglar alarm by the front door. Cassidy scooted past Kerney and made a beeline for a dog bed. He retrieved a rubber ball, brought it to Kerney, and dropped it on the floor, ready to play.

"Sweet dog," Kerney said.

The woman, who had shed her parka and cap, stood with her hands on her hips and said nothing. Slender and of average size, she had attractive features accentuated by lips which suggested that, under normal circumstances, a ready smile came easily. Kerney guessed her to be in her early forties.

"Tell me your name," Kerney asked.

"Alexandra Lawton. Look, I know Phyllis is out of town. She will want to know what has happened."

"I take it the Terrells are friends as well as neighbors," Kerney said.

"Phyllis has been a friend since she built her house two years ago."

"What about Mr. Terrell?"

"He doesn't live here. He moved out shortly after the house was built. They've been separated ever since."

"Do you know Santiago Terjo?"

"Of course I know him. He's worked for Phyllis for over a year."

"Doing what, exactly?"

"Landscaping and construction. Phyllis is creating an extraordinary garden bit by bit inside the patio wall. It keeps growing in scale as she designs it. It's turned into quite a project."

"Would you know where I might find Terjo?" Kerney asked.

"If he's not working or in the RV, mostly likely he'll be at the stables, caring for the horses. He's not a thief. He's worked for me upon occasion, and he's entirely trustworthy."

"Where are the stables?"

"I'll show you." Lawton led Kerney through the living room,

which was filled with northern New Mexico antiques, inviting, comfortable easy chairs, and a grand piano, into a sunroom that had a panoramic southwest view of the valley.

"Phyllis bought two acres in the valley, right across from her driveway, to keep her horses nearby," Lawton said, reaching for a pair of binoculars on an occasional table between two rattan chairs.

She handed Kerney the binoculars. "Look over the house on the far side of the road just a little bit to the left, and you'll see the stables and corral. If Santiago's pickup is there, he's most likely tending to Priscilla and Gigolo, Phyllis's mare and gelding."

Kerney looked; the truck was parked in front of an open stable door. "He doesn't leave his vehicle at the house?"

"Never. In fact, the RV is kept at the stables unless Phyllis is out of town. Then it's moved up so Santiago can keep an eye on the place while she's gone."

"Does Mrs. Terrell have a dog?" Kerney asked.

"No, but Santiago does. It's a Rottweiler–German shepherd mix, named Zippy. What was stolen?"

"We're not sure, Ms. Lawton."

"Well, I'm going to call Phyllis in Virginia. She's visiting her sister. She needs to know what happened."

"Please don't bother. When did you last see Mrs. Terrell?"

"She came for coffee here yesterday afternoon."

"How was her mood?"

"Excellent. She was looking forward to her trip. She always flies back to celebrate her sister's birthday. They're very close."

"Does she have any current houseguests?"

"Not since the holidays."

"I'd like to use your phone so I can have a detective come over and take a statement."

"Aren't you a detective?"

"I'm the police chief."

Lawton paled. "You wouldn't be here to investigate a simple burglary."

"No, I wouldn't. Mrs. Terrell has been murdered."

"Oh, my God," Lawton said, sinking into a rattan chair.

Kerney called Lieutenant Molina on his cell phone, filled him in, and asked for one detective to come to Lawton's house. He ordered an immediate search for Terjo at the stables, and told Molina to stand by at the Terrell residence for his return.

Lawton cried quietly while Kerney kept the binoculars trained on the stables. Soon two detectives and a uniformed officer moved in on foot. They crossed the road, used trees and shrubs for concealment, and split up at the small open meadow in front of the stables. Keeping low, the detectives sprinted to their positions, one at the front and one at the back of the stables, while the uniformed officer found cover behind Terjo's truck, his sidearm drawn and ready.

Kerney focused the binoculars on the detective standing to one side of the stable's front doors, but the distance was too great for him to see any mouthed orders. A few minutes passed before a figure emerged from the darkness of the stable, hands held high. The detective quickly put the man facedown in the snow and cuffed him as the uniform moved in, his weapon aimed at the back of the man's head.

The doorbell rang and Kerney turned to find that Lawton hadn't moved. Although her tears had stopped, the expression of disbelief remained. Cassidy was at Lawton's feet, his chin resting on her knee. She absentmindedly stroked the dog's head.

"I'll get it," Kerney said, and Lawton nodded dully in agreement.

Kerney let the detective in. Molina had sent over Amos Cisneros. He gave Cisneros the gist of his conversation with Lawton, and took the overweight, still wheezing man to the sunroom, thinking he'd have to tighten up the physical-fitness requirements for commissioned personnel.

"Do you know how I can find Ambassador Terrell?" Kerney asked after introducing Cisneros to Lawton.

"No," Lawton replied. "He's a delegate on a trade mission to South America. He's out of the country a great deal of the time."

"Does he still have ambassador rank?" Kerney asked.

"I don't know what his official status is."

"It may take some time for Detective Cisneros to interview you."

"That's fine," Lawton said, smiling weakly. "Please excuse my tears. I really cared for Phyllis. She's been a good friend."

"I understand."

On his way back to the Terrell residence Kerney framed the most diplomatic way he could ask Lieutenant Molina about the lack of resources at the crime scene. He caught Molina's eye. The lieutenant stepped away from the medical examiner and joined him at the edge of the patio.

"Who did your people arrest?" Kerney asked.

"Terjo," Molina replied. "We'll take his preliminary statement here and then interrogate him at headquarters. Thanks for the heads-up, Chief."

"You seem a little short on manpower, Lieutenant," Kerney said. "Can I call in more people?"

"You don't need my permission, Lieutenant."

Molina paused. "Yes, I do. There's a standing order in effect: Only the chief can authorize additional personnel for major felony investigations."

"That makes no sense."

"It's what your predecessor wanted."

"Why?" Kerney asked.

Molina shrugged and ran a hand through his thinning hair. "Cost containment. My unit goes over budget every year. Nothing I said would change his mind. It didn't seem to matter that I don't have a crystal ball that lets me predict violent crimes on an annual basis."

"The order is rescinded," Kerney said. "Get the help you need up here pronto. And in the future, get in my face if there's something that keeps you from doing your job. Are you clear on that?"

Molina smiled broadly. "You bet I am, Chief."

"Let me know when you plan to interrogate Terjo," Kerney said. "I'd like to watch."

"Ten-four."

"Has Terrell's sister or husband been informed of her death?" Kerney asked.

"Not yet. We haven't gotten an answer from the State Department on the ambassador's exact whereabouts."

"Inform the sister, but keep the local media in the dark for as long as possible. If any newspaper reporters show up, refer them to me. I'll be at headquarters."

Looking relieved, Molina hurried away to make his calls. Kerney walked down the driveway, kicking himself mentally. Since coming on board weeks ago, he'd met with each commander and supervisor personally, had spent a good deal of time observing operations, and was still digging through reams of department documents.

To avoid the possibility of reacting to personal agendas carried over from the last administration, Kerney had wanted to be completely up to speed before asking senior staff to recommend any organizational reforms. Now that would have to change. He couldn't let past stupidities stand in the way of good police work.

At the driveway gate Officer Herrera thrust the crime-scene log into Kerney's hands. Kerney studied the officer as he scrawled his name. Herrera was short and skinny through the chest. Not even the Kevlar vest worn under his uniform shirt bulked him up enough to hide his lack of muscle. He had a potbelly and gray humorless eyes.

"How's the leg?" Kerney asked, glancing down at Herrera's torn uniform trousers.

"It's nothing, Chief."

"Glad to hear it. Tell me something, Officer Herrera: Why didn't you accompany the animal-control officer when he went looking for the dog?"

Herrera ran his tongue under his upper lip and clamped his jaw shut.

"Say what's on your mind, Officer."

"I'm not a dogcatcher, Chief."

"No, you're not," Kerney said, thinking Herrera might not be much of a police officer either.

As Kerney walked past the animal-control truck, the young man inside the cab rolled down the window.

"How long do I have to wait here, Chief?" Matt Garcia asked. "Cloudy said I have to give a statement."

"Who's Cloudy?" Kerney asked.

"Officer Herrera."

"Give your statement to Officer Herrera."

Matt shook his head. "He says it's up to the detectives to take it. I'm backed up on five calls and my supervisor wants to know when I'll be released."

Kerney motioned to Herrera. He approached slowly with his chin up and a sour look.

"Take this man's statement," Kerney ordered, "so he can go back to work."

"Right away, Chief."

Kerney turned on his heel to hide his frustration, went to his unit, and drove through the valley, glancing at the expensive homes—some new, some old adobes that had been restored and enlarged—that peppered the hillsides and the river bottomland. Interspersed among the symbols of new wealth were a few remaining modest houses. They were sure to be gobbled up or demolished pretty soon by newcomers seeking a prestigious Santa Fe address.

With the money he'd realized from the sale of the land Erma Fergurson had left him, he could easily build a trophy home and move into the neighborhood.

The thought was totally unappealing. Instead, Kerney had a realtor looking for a section of land in the Galisteo Basin twenty minutes outside of Santa Fe, where he could build a ranch house and keep some animals.

A ranch house with a nursery, he reminded himself, thinking of his wife, Lieutenant Colonel Sara Brannon, pregnant and on active duty while attending the U.S. Army Command and General Staff College at Fort Leavenworth, Kansas.

In January they'd spent a weekend together at Fort Leavenworth. Sara had toured him around the post on a cold, clear Kansas morning, walking him across the parade grounds, pointing out the Victorian houses where George Armstrong Custer and Douglas MacArthur had lived. She showed him the building where F. Scott Fitzgerald had written his first novel. He got to see the old French cannons that looked out over the Missouri River and the monumental Buffalo Soldier statue that honored African-Americans who'd served in segregated units during the Indian campaigns.

After the tour they'd snuggled up in a lovely bed-and-breakfast and tuned out the world. It had been a wonderful weekend, and Kerney had returned to Santa Fe knowing that Sara's commitment to her career as an army officer was as strong as her commitment to their marriage. He wondered if that would ever change.

Sara was due in Santa Fe on the weekend. Kerney hoped that the Terrell murder investigation wouldn't get in the way of her visit. As it was, they had little enough time together.

Radio traffic told Kerney that detectives were responding quickly to Molina's call for more manpower. The street narrowed and curved on the approach to the plaza, past rows of tightly packed houses, creating the feeling of a village lane in a Spanish town.

Kerney pulled to the curb and waited. Five unmarked units running a silent code three passed by in a matter of minutes. That should give Molina the resources he needed. Hopefully, the lieutenant would put the personnel to good use.

Kerney made a mental note to learn more about Officer Herrera and drove on.

Chapter 2

Although the city hadn't been hit with a lot of snow, a foot of new powder crowned the ski basin, and traffic along Cerrillos Road was heavy with day trippers from Albuquerque on their way to and from the slopes. At the Airport Road intersection Kerney turned off and headed for the nearby police headquarters, remembering the time when the old Blue Mountain Ranch and a vast stretch of rangeland along Cerrillos Road had defined the southern limits of the city. Now that open space was gone, filled up by a large shopping mall, an auto park with four dealerships, and commercial clutter that stretched along the roadway almost to the Interstate.

Since starting the job, Kerney had tacked extra time onto his twelve-hour days to explore the city by car and get familiar with his jurisdiction. The growing south-side sprawl continued along Airport Road, where a mixture of strip malls, new residential subdivisions with houses on tiny lots, and boxy apartment buildings had sprung up at an astonishing rate. Santa Fe was fast losing its unique identity and Kerney doubted anything could stop it.

He entered police headquarters, where the receptionist, a young woman with a lackluster complexion and a bit too much blush on her cheeks, sat up straight in her chair and smiled a polite greeting that showed no warmth.

Kerney had grown used to the wariness most of the staff displayed when he came around. But he didn't like it, and he wondered how long it would take for it to ease.

He climbed the stairs to the administrative wing. The vacant deputy chief's office reminded him that he needed to act soon on filling the number-two slot.

Helen Muiz, Kerney's personal secretary and office manager, greeted him with a sheaf of telephone messages.

"Anything urgent?" he asked.

Helen shook her head and took off her reading glasses. "Not yet. But I think you'd better tell the city manager about the Terrell murder before he hears about it from an outside source."

Kerney smiled. A thirty-five-year veteran of the department, Helen had been Kerney's secretary during his tenure as chief of detectives, and had served as the office manager for the past three chiefs. Now a grandmother in her late fifties, Helen didn't look the part. Full bodied, taller than average, with large round eyes that radiated a sharp sense of humor, Helen was the best-dressed civilian employee in the department. Today, she wore a pearl-gray wool gabardine suit and a silk plum-colored blouse.

She could retire at any time on a full pension, but chose not to do so. Kerney was delighted to have her running the office.

"You always give me such good advice," he said.

"Which, if I recall correctly, you usually need," Helen replied.

"Probably. Find the order requiring the chief's approval to assign additional detectives to a major crime investigation and type up a memo rescinding it for my signature."

"That will make Sal Molina happy. Have you decided to stop rubbernecking and start driving?"

"You have an insubordinate personality, Mrs. Muiz."

"Isn't that why you're glad I'm here?"

"No comment," Kerney said lightheartedly. "Don't bother to get the city manager on the line. I'll call him myself."

"How egalitarian of you," Helen said with a laugh. "Shall I prepare another memo directing senior staff to answer their own phones and place their own calls whenever possible?"

"Why not?"

Helen's smile broadened. "I knew having you as the chief would be fun."

"I'm glad I've made at least one employee happy," Kerney replied.

Through the one-way observation window Kerney watched Santiago Terjo as he sat alone in the interrogation room. Neatly dressed in jeans, work boots, and a heavy cotton shirt, Terjo was clean shaven and had dark curly hair that drooped over his forehead.

"According to Customs he's legal," Sal Molina said, referring to the notes from his preliminary interview with Terjo. "Born in Hildalgo del Parral—wherever that is. Age thirty-eight. No wants, warrants, or priors. He's got a wife and three kids in Mexico, and a girlfriend and one baby here in Santa Fe."

"What kind of story did he give you?" Kerney asked.

"He says he moved the RV from the stables to the house yesterday after work before going to his girlfriend's house, where he spent the night. He last saw Terrell alive at about six o'clock in the evening when they talked for a few minutes about what she wanted done while she was gone. According to Terjo, Terrell was alone at the time."

"Does the girlfriend confirm he was with her?"

"All night. Her name is Rebecca Shapiro, originally from New York. Someplace on Long Island. She's a jewelry maker who works out of her house. Shapiro said Terjo didn't leave until seven-thirty this morning."

"Is she lying?" Kerney asked.

"Not likely," Molina replied. "She independently confirmed the events of their night together. Terjo came over, helped Shapiro make dinner, and then they ate. He played with his daughter, Aspen, age one, until her bedtime. After that Terjo gave Shapiro a Spanish lesson—she's trying to learn the language. Then they watched a little television and went to bed."

"Does she know about Terjo's wife and children in Mexico?"

"Yeah. She says she's perfectly comfortable with her relationship with Terjo. Isn't into the marriage thing."

"What happened in the morning?" Kerney asked.

"Terjo leaves his dog, Zippy, at the stables when he stays with Shapiro because she's allergic to animals. In the morning he stopped by to feed him and let him out. He left his truck behind and walked up through the arroyo to the house, so Zippy could do his business. Then he put the dog in the RV and went to work."

"Doing what?"

"Taking out some trees in front of a rock outcropping on an upper slope behind the house. Terrell wanted the area cleared because she was planning to have Terjo build a pergola and an outdoor fireplace on the site, and the trees blocked the view."

"Did anybody see Terjo working?"

"One neighbor heard the sound of a chain saw, and another neighbor coming down from his hilltop house saw Terjo at the site. The detective who examined the area said the trees were freshly cut."

"Why did Terjo run?"

"He came down to the house to get something to eat and let the dog out of the RV. Supposedly, Mrs. Terrell gave him standing permission to raid the refrigerator whenever she was away. He went into the house through the main entrance. That's when he saw Terrell's body. He got scared, panicked, and went back to the RV just about the time Matt Garcia was chasing Zippy up the hill. He saw Garcia and took off. He said he thought Garcia was the murderer."

"It's a good story," Kerney said. "Do we have any physical evidence from the crime scene?"

"No prints on the scissors," Molina replied. "But we've found some pubic and head hairs and a small fluid stain on Mrs. Terrell's bed sheets. Also, we have one set of footprints that don't match up with the victim, Terjo, or Matt Garcia. They're from a size-ten hiking boot. The tracks start at the front side of the patio, drop down the hill, and end at the road."

"Anything else?"

"Yeah. Seven Baggies of marijuana, hidden in the stables. Terjo says he knows nothing about it. But I think he ran away so he could move his stash."

"Have you asked Terjo to provide head and pubic hairs for comparison purposes?"

"He agreed to it in writing. I took him to the hospital on the way here and had a nurse take samples. The lab has them. We're still waiting on results."

"You've found no other physical evidence?" Kerney asked.

"Not yet," Molina said.

"If the precipitating event was a lovers' quarrel or a burglary gone bad, there should be."

Molina nodded. "No prints on the scissors and no sign of forced entry does seem to make it look a little too neat and tidy. I've been thinking that maybe the murder was staged."

"For what purpose?"

"If you can tell me that, Chief, then I'd have a motive."

Kerney studied Terjo through the glass. The man was nervous, rubbing his hands together and constantly shifting his weight in the chair. "Terrell and her husband were separated. Maybe Terjo knows something about Phyllis Terrell that can help us answer that question," he said.

"I think he'll cooperate," Sal said. "He already knows how much time he's facing on a possession-with-intent-to-sell conviction."

"If you can make it stick." Kerney nodded in Terjo's direction. "Let's see what he says."

*   *   *

Santiago Terjo had seen enough television cop shows to figure people were watching through the mirror and talking about him. He slumped against the back of the metal chair and tried to remain calm. But the longer he waited alone in the small room the more his hands got nervous and his gaze wandered toward the mirror.

He'd lied to the police lieutenant about the marijuana, and about his family in Mexico. In truth, Terjo had no wife and children. If the cops found out he'd assumed his dead brother's identity, Terjo could go to prison first and afterward get deported. Then there would be no more money to send home every month for his only sister-in-law, Lupita, her children, his parents, or his aunts and uncles.

Three years ago Santiago, his brother, had died from a stomach illness while home for a visit. Ignacio, who had much the same features as his brother and was only a half inch taller, had used Santiago's green card to enter the United States and find work.

Because Santiago had worked in Texas, Ignacio had decided to go to New Mexico, where the switch wouldn't be discovered. It had worked perfectly. To Rebecca, Mrs. Terrell, and everybody he'd met in Santa Fe, he was Santiago.

How could he convince the cop it wasn't his stash they'd found in the stables, even though it was? He always brought marijuana back with him from his visits to Mexico, but only for his personal use, not to sell. Usually he brought enough to last for six or eight months, sometimes a whole year.

Terjo coughed and swallowed the phlegm in his throat. It scared him to think he could be charged with drug dealing and maybe sent to prison for a very long time. Before the cops arrested him at the stables, he'd used a rag to rub the Baggies clean of any prints. That should help, but what if they found some seeds or stems in the RV, which was likely? How could he explain that?

He needed to come up with a convincing story. He tried to think of something the police lieutenant might believe.

*   *   *

"Sorry to keep you waiting," Sal said as he entered the interrogation room and placed a tape recorder on the table.

"Who's watching me through the mirror?" Terjo asked.

"My new boss," Sal said, easing himself into the chair across from Terjo. "I think he wants to make sure I know how to do my job. Help me out and cooperate, Santiago. I don't want to look bad."

"I already told you everything."

"Give me a minute," Sal said. He turned on the recorder, identified himself, and gave specifics of who he was interviewing, why, and when.

"There, that's out of the way. What did you say before I turned the machine on?"

"That I told you everything," Terjo said, giving Molina a friendly smile.

"But we haven't talked about the scissors," Sal said.

"The scissors?"

"They're expensive German-made, just like my wife's."

"*Así?*" Terjo replied, pulling at an earlobe.

"So, I'm wondering if you ever saw Mrs. Terrell use those scissors, or scissors like them."

"I don't think so," Terjo said. "But she has a lot of stuff she doesn't really use much."

"Maybe she used them as kitchen shears," Sal said. "Or for cutting string and wrapping presents."

"Maybe."

"Are the scissors yours?" Sal asked.

"No, *pero* I keep some in my toolbox."

"We found those." Sal rubbed his chin. "Do you think the killer brought the scissors with him?"

Terjo shook his head.

"You shook your head," Sal noted.

"Nobody does that."

"I agree. Most people don't carry scissors around with them. That tells me something."

"What?"

"The killer was someone Terrell knew and let into the house."

"A lot of people come to the house, making deliveries, visiting."

"I have the list of names you gave me. Does anyone special come around a lot?"

"Alexandra Lawton. She is Señora Terrell's neighbor."

"Killing someone with scissors is something a woman is more likely to do," Sal said.

"She would never do such a thing."

"You must know Ms. Lawton pretty well to call her by her first name."

"She asked me to do so."

"Maybe you used the scissors as the murder weapon."

"I have no reason to kill Señora Terrell. She has been very good to me."

"Does Lawton have a boyfriend?"

"Who knows? It is not my business."

"Have you seen her with men?"

"Sí, but they are strangers to me."

"What about Terrell? Did she have men friends who came to visit?"

"I don't spy on my boss."

"Did you know that Terrell and her husband were getting a divorce?"

"I knew."

"An attractive woman like Mrs. Terrell must have had a boyfriend or someone she was seeing. After all, she'd been separated from her husband for nearly two years."

"I know nothing about that."

"Your English is very good," Sal said.

"I studied it in school as a child."

"How far in school did you go?" Sal asked.

Terjo tensed and stalled momentarily, mentally counting the number of years his brother had been in school. "Eight years."

"And they taught you English?" Sal asked, leaning closer, breaking into Terjo's space. "I didn't think Mexican schools did that very much."

"Everybody wants to learn English so they can come here," Terjo said defensively.

"What was the name of your school?"

"It is gone. The government closed it many years ago."

"You must have been a good student."

"I learned more English when I came to this country."

"I'm thinking maybe Lawton killed Mrs. Terrell because of jealousy," Sal said.

"*Por qué?*"

"Because you were sleeping with both of them."

"That's not true."

"Somebody had sex in Terrell's bedroom before the murder. Was it you?"

Terjo rubbed his nose. "I would never do that."

"The hair samples we took will tell us," Sal said.

"Then you'll know what I say is true."

"I hope so, for your sake," Sal said. "Still, we've got this marijuana thing to deal with."

"I think maybe some kids left it there," Terjo said, the tone of his voice rising slightly.

"Kids?"

Terjo spoke quickly. "Sometimes they use the stables when I'm not around. They get in through the open stalls to the corral. A couple of times they even broke into the RV."

"I see."

"I've found empty beer cans and used rubbers in there before."

"In the RV?"

"Yeah, and the stables."

"How did they get into the RV?"

"Sometimes I forget to lock it."

"When was the last time this happened?"

"Maybe two weeks ago."

"Did you call the police and report it?"

"No. Nothing was stolen, *nada*."

"Did you report any of the prior incidents?" Sal asked.

"No."

"Do you know the kids by name? Where they live?"

Terjo cleared his throat. "No, *pero* I'm guessing it was kids. *Mira*, I never saw them."

Molina shook his head sympathetically. "Too bad. If you'd reported the break-ins, maybe this drug-dealing charge wouldn't be hanging over you."

Terjo lowered his head. "It's not my grass."

"Did Mrs. Terrell ever talk about her husband?"

"Just to say he was a very important man who does much work for the government."

"Nothing more than that?"

"Sometimes she would seem upset after talking to him on the telephone."

"Upset about what?"

"I don't know."

"Did Mrs. Terrell have a lover?"

"She would never talk to me about personal things like that."

Sal pushed. "Did she have a lover?"

Terjo looked away before responding. "I don't know nothing about that."

"Let's go over again what you did last night," Sal said, backing off with a smile.

"I gotta stay here?" Terjo asked.

"For now," Sal replied. "Start with what you were doing just before you spoke to Terrell for the last time."

Molina used his notes to move Terjo through the events he'd previously reported. He finished up and got to his feet. "Did you tell one of your amigos how easy it would be to break into Mrs. Terrell's house and rip her off while she was gone?"

"I would never do such a thing."

"Maybe your friend came at the wrong time, Mrs. Terrell caught him in the act, so he decided to rape and kill her."

"That's loco."

Molina turned off the recorder and extracted the cassette. "Just tap on the door if you remember something else you want to tell me, or if you want to change your story."

"I told you everything. I want to leave now."

"If you left, I'd start to believe you don't want to cooperate," Sal replied. "You wouldn't want me to think that, would you?"

"I'll wait," Terjo said with a sigh.

"He stuck to his story, Chief," Molina said as he walked with Kerney to the second-floor landing, "and it didn't sound rehearsed to me."

"He's lying about something," Kerney said. "Why and what are the questions?"

"I'll talk to the girlfriend."

"Canvass her neighbors to see if they saw Terjo entering or leaving her house. And query the Mexican authorities and see what they have on him."

"We could wait weeks for a reply."

"I want him locked up at least overnight. Book him on the drug-dealing charges."

"Our probable cause is weak," Molina said.

"Granted, but it buys you time to push him a little harder. Let's find out what he's covering up."

"Anything else, Chief?"

"Assuming Terjo isn't involved in the murder, that leaves us only with the victim's profile to go on."

"We're talking to Terrell's friends and acquaintances right now," Molina said.

"Good."

Helen Muiz signaled to Kerney from the doorway to the administrative wing. He waved and she stayed put. "Do you need anything else from me, Lieutenant?"

"Some clarification would help, Chief. How deeply involved in the investigation do you want to be?"

"I want to know everything that goes on."

"I meant personally."

"That depends," Kerney said.

"On how well me and my people do our jobs?"

"Exactly. You've got five open murder investigations that haven't been cleared. That's five out of six during the past year. It is not a cheerful statistic. Don't add the Terrell homicide to the list."

Molina fought off a desire to explain and squared his shoulders. "If you want me to put in my retirement papers, tell me now."

"That's not what I want. At this point you have my goodwill, Lieutenant. Whether or not I come to appreciate your abilities is up to you. Do the job and I'll stay off your butt."

"That's straight enough," Molina said, stomping away.

Helen Muiz eyed Kerney speculatively when he approached.

"What have you got for me?" Kerney asked

Helen flipped open her notebook and started talking. Ambassador Terrell was due to arrive by corporate jet at the Santa Fe airport in several hours. The mayor, governor, and a State Department official had called asking Kerney to extend every courtesy to the ambassador. Several newspaper reporters were in the lobby clamoring for a briefing.

"Have them stand by in the downstairs conference room and ask Lieutenant Molina to issue the standard statement that we're not releasing any information presently," Kerney said.

Helen nodded. "And the FBI has arrived," she said. "Special Agent Applewhite is waiting in your office."

Kerney knew all the local special agents and Applewhite wasn't a name he was familiar with. "Wanting what?"

"She didn't say."

Kerney made a face.

"Welcome to the Crystal Palace," Helen said.

"The what?"

"The chief's office was dubbed the Crystal Palace a couple of administrations ago. It is not a term of endearment."

"No, of course not," Kerney said.

Somewhere in her thirties, Special Agent Elaine Applewhite wore a cardigan sweater over a white turtleneck top and a pair of blue jeans. The outfit didn't hide her sturdy-looking frame. She had a sharp chin, an oval face, a small, turned-down mouth, and empty eyes that reminded Kerney of the thousand-yard stare he'd seen on the faces of soldiers in Vietnam. A bright new red ski parka hung neatly over a chair at the small conference table that butted against the front of Kerney's desk.

"Make yourself at home," Kerney said as Applewhite arranged herself in a chair. He moved to his desk, sat, and waited.

Applewhite adjusted her position to face Kerney head-on. "The wife of a Federal official has been murdered, Chief Kerney. The Bureau has jurisdiction in the matter."

"Are you here to assume oversight?"

"That's not my role," Applewhite replied. "I understand you have a suspect in custody."

"What exactly is your role, Agent Applewhite?" Kerney asked.

Applewhite leaned forward. "We don't have to joust, Chief Kerney. I'm a liaison agent to the State Department. I've been asked to interrupt my vacation and assist you, until a task force arrives from Quantico."

"You're here vacationing?"

Applewhite smiled tightly. "I was."

"Really? Where?"

"Taos. My husband and I are on a week-long skiing trip. He's not too happy about having our plans interrupted, I can tell you."

"I'm sorry to hear it," Kerney said. "Why isn't the local FBI field office handling the case?"

"Because Mrs. Terrell's murder may have national-security implications."

"Such as?"

"I can't go into that."

"Then I assume you're the point man until the task force arrives."

"Not at all. I've been asked to provide you with some background information." Applewhite paused. "Ten years ago Ambassador Terrell divorced his first wife. Within the year he married Phyllis Carol Straley Hasell, a woman twenty years his junior. In both her previous and current marriage Mrs. Terrell maintained a rather liberal attitude regarding her marriage vows, and was somewhat indiscriminate about her choice of sexual partners."

"Are you suggesting Mrs. Terrell may have been killed by a lover?" Kerney asked.

"It's a highly speculative notion, but not outside the realm of possibility."

"Are Mrs. Terrell's past and present lovers known to the Bureau?"

"Our background investigations on family members are confidential, Chief Kerney. But I can say that when the Terrells separated, the ambassador provided the State Department and the Bureau with a full, voluntary statement as to the reasons why."

"The ambassador told your department about his wife's lovers?"

"In the interest of national security he felt it was his obligation to do so. On a political note, you need to be aware that Proctor Straley is Mrs. Terrell's father. You may know of him. He owns the El Moro Land and Cattle Company in Ramah, New Mexico. He moved here from Texas and bought the property about twenty years ago. I understand it's quite a large tract of land. He's a close friend of your governor, and quite influential in state and national politics."

"I know who he is," Kerney said. "How did you come to learn so quickly about Mrs. Terrell's murder?"

"The State Department advised the Bureau as soon as your department requested assistance in locating Ambassador Terrell."

"What is your role with the task force?"

"I've been asked to coordinate information sharing between you, the Bureau, and the State Department."

Kerney digested the statement and stared thoughtfully at the woman. Although Applewhite had denied it, Kerney's hunch wasn't wrong; Applewhite was the watchdog sent to keep the local cops reined in until the task force arrived.

"When do your people get here?" he asked.

"Before dawn. We'll be headquartered at the National Guard armory."

"I'll let my people know."

"We'll need full access to whatever information your detectives have gathered so far."

Kerney smiled. "Of course, and I know you'll be equally forthcoming."

"You'll have clearance for all unclassified information," Applewhite replied. "Is the man you have in custody a possible suspect?"

"He hasn't confessed to anything yet. Will the ambassador be willing to meet with my violent-crimes supervisor?"

"In fact, he's asked to speak with you personally upon his arrival. His plane is due in at twenty-one hundred hours. But he may not have any information of value. For nearly the last two years the ambassador and his wife have maintained separate residences."

"So I've heard. Has he been advised of the theory that his wife may have been murdered by a lover?"

"I really don't know what Ambassador Terrell has been told."

"Interesting," Kerney said, getting to his feet. "I take it the ambassador isn't the jealous type."

"Ambassador Terrell can't possibly be a suspect. He was out of the country, meeting with twenty-five high-ranking foreign and domestic diplomats when his wife was murdered."

"You couldn't ask for a better alibi, could you?"

Applewhite gave Kerney an unfriendly look. "I wouldn't be thinking in that direction if I were you, Chief Kerney."

"With national security involved I'll gladly let your people call the shots," Kerney said as he opened his office door. "My department isn't equipped to handle a case like this. I'm assuming your vacation is over."

"For the duration," Applewhite said, holding out a business card as she approached him. "The phone number for my hotel is on the back. Can you hold off on any statements to the press?"

"Whatever you say," Kerney replied. "It's your case."

"We're here to work with you, Chief Kerney."

"You'll have my full cooperation, Agent Applewhite."

Kerney closed the door behind the departing Applewhite, picked up the telephone, dialed Helen Muiz's extension, and asked her to send somebody outside in a hurry to get a make, model, and license number on Applewhite's vehicle.

"Have it done on the sly," he said, "and run a motor-vehicle check as soon as you have the information."

He replaced the receiver and stared through the office window that gave a view across Cerrillos Road to the shopping mall. The dinner hour had arrived and most of the parked cars were clustered near the entrance closest to a family-style mall cafeteria.

He'd tried to match Applewhite's low-key approach to the Bureau's taking over of the investigation, hoping that if he covered some of the basics but dumbed things down a bit he would be viewed as a hayseed police chief who wouldn't cause any problems. But Kerney had doubts about Applewhite's interrupted vacation story. He ran over the conversation in his mind. Aside from establishing FBI control over the case, Applewhite had laid out two key issues: focus on the victim not the husband, and beware the political and security minefields.

Why?

Kerney thought about sharing his suspicions with Sal Molina and dropped the idea. How did Applewhite know a suspect was in custody? Terjo hadn't been charged with a crime as of yet, and a simple wanted-person computer check wouldn't flag him as a murder suspect.

Kerney tapped his finger on the telephone, and checked the time. There was a chance that Andy Baca, chief of the New Mexico State Police and his ex-boss, might still be at work. He dialed Andy's direct, private office number and Baca picked up.

"Working late?" Kerney asked.

Andy answered lightheartedly. "I thought I got rid of you when you took the Santa Fe job, Kerney."

"I need a favor, Andy."

"What's up? Are you in trouble already?"

Kerney summarized the facts of the Terrell murder and recounted his conversation with Special Agent Applewhite.

"You need help from a much higher power than me," Andy said after Kerney finished. "I'm glad the FBI is landing in your lap and not mine. What can I do?"

"I'd like some substantiation of Applewhite's story."

"A certain amount of paranoia is a healthy thing for any police chief to have, Kerney, but you may be stretching it a bit. Aside from the FBI, it's quite likely you'll have antiterrorist specialists, State Department counterintelligence agents, and the CIA camping at your door."

"I think I'm being played for a fool. Applewhite literally handed me a ready-made motive for murder. If this is a cover-up, I want to know it."

"Or you could sit back, cover your ass, and let them run their game. Forget I said that; it's not your style. Okay, how do you want to handle it?"

"Nothing through official channels. Just a quiet check of Applewhite's cover story. I'd like to know when she arrived in New Mexico and with whom. She was supposedly in Taos before getting pulled off a skiing vacation with her husband and sent down here to meet with me. I've got the name of the Santa Fe hotel where she's booked a room, and we're running a license-plate check on her vehicle. I'll fax the information to you when it comes in."

"That's all?" Andy asked.

"I don't want to telegraph my suspicions."

"Why not use one of your people?"

"Not a good idea."

Andy thought about the mess Kerney had inherited from his predecessors: an understaffed department known for petty politics, poor morale, and vicious infighting. "You're probably right," he said. "I'll get back to you."

"Thanks, Andy."

"Keep your head down, Kevin."

Kerney heard the distant sound of an aircraft and looked up at the clear night sky. Against a backdrop of stars he saw the flashing lights of a plane ten miles out, on a straight gradual descent to the Santa Fe Airport.

Because large commercial jets flew into Albuquerque, less than an hour away by car, the airport terminal—a small, rather charming, old-fashioned pueblo-revival building—was quiet at night.

He got out of his unit, walked through the terminal, with its viga ceiling, tile floor, and mission-style benches and chairs, and waited at the outside gate that led to the tarmac. The night air, still and cold, chilled his face, and a quarter moon shed enough light to kindle a shivery glow on the snow-covered ground beyond the runway.

Kerney watched the corporate jet touch down and taxi to the terminal, thinking the chances were slim Terrell would remember him from their brief service together in Vietnam. He preferred it that way and had no intention of raising the old connection.

The outside terminal lights were bright enough to give Kerney a good look at Terrell as he came down the ramp. He wore an expensive wool coat that covered a chunky frame. His face had a tanned, healthy color and his expression looked subdued. There didn't seem to be any sadness in his eyes, though. He came forward without any hint of recognition. For a man in his mid-seventies Terrell appeared vigorous and lively. He carried a leather overnight bag.

"Are you the police chief?" Terrell asked, barely slowing his pace as he approached.

"Yes, I am, Ambassador."

Terrell didn't stop moving. He nodded his head and pointed a gloved hand at the terminal entrance as a signal for Kerney to follow along.

Kerney complied.

"No press," Terrell observed as they passed through the empty terminal. "That's good. Where's your car?"

Kerney guided Terrell to his unit and drove him away. On the road to town Terrell relaxed against the passenger seat, took off his gloves, and rubbed his face with large, heavy hands.

"Tell me what happened," he said.

"Your wife was stabbed once in the chest with a pair of scissors, probably by an intruder," Kerney said.

"Have you caught the son of a bitch?" A touch of emotion colored his voice.

"We're talking to Santiago Terjo about the crime."

"That's a waste of time," Terrell said.

"You think so?"

Terrell stared out the window and said nothing.

"Can you tell me anything that might be helpful?" Kerney asked.

"Phyllis was never a cautious woman when it came to her personal safety."

"Any enemies?"

"My wife didn't make enemies," Terrell said, swiveling slightly to face Kerney. "She prided herself on being gracious to everyone, and she was. Please tell me what you've learned so far."

Kerney did as Terrell asked, saving for last—without revealing his source—Applewhite's imputations about Phyllis Terrell's moral character. It brought a sigh from the ambassador.

"I didn't realize it was such common knowledge in Santa Fe," Terrell said.

"You were aware that your wife had lovers?" Kerney asked.

"She made that very clear to me after we began to grow apart. My wife and I have been married in name only for the last two years. She built a house here so we could have totally separate lives. I came infrequently to visit and only on family business. We were moving amicably toward a divorce settlement."

"Do you know any of the men who have been involved with your wife?"

Terrell shook his head. "I've been asked not to discuss anything of substance with you or your detectives until it is determined if my wife's murder has any connection to my official capacity."

"What can you tell me about the trade mission?" Kerney asked.

"Very little. It is a confidential, joint enterprise of various federal departments that has operated quietly with White House approval for the past eighteen months. Our existence, who we're dealing with, and why, haven't been publicly disclosed, and will not be unless an accord is reached."

"The FBI has claimed case jurisdiction for national-security reasons," Kerney said, checking the rearview mirror. "They'll be here in full force tomorrow morning. Meanwhile, the two men who got off the plane after we entered the terminal have been behind us since we left the airport."

"Yes, I know. I'm staying at the Hotel San Marcos."

"And your traveling companions?" Kerney asked. "Where will they be staying?"

"I have no idea, Chief Kerney. But they will be at my wife's house shortly on official business. Please have your people give them full access. You do understand that my conversation with you is strictly off the record."

Kerney made a turn onto a narrow street that led to the downtown plaza and the nearby hotel. The car behind continued on, out of sight. "Under pain of federal prosecution?" he asked.

Terrell's hand was on the door latch as Kerney pulled to a stop in front of the hotel. "I'm sure it won't come to that. Thank you for the briefing. I'll be in town for a few days. There are people to notify and arrangements to be made. Perhaps we'll talk again."

"I'll be available," Kerney said.

As Terrell passed through the lobby door, Andy Baca called on Kerney's cell phone and requested a quick meeting in the Wal-Mart parking lot. He wouldn't say why but sounded a little peeved. Kerney gave him a five-minute ETA and drove hurriedly through the empty downtown streets, wondering what was up.

As he cruised through light traffic on Cerrillos Road, Lieutenant Molina made radio contact, asking for clearance to allow two FBI agents access to the crime scene.

"Let them in," Kerney said, "and meet me in my office in twenty minutes so I can bring you up to speed."

"Ten-four," Molina grumbled after a slight hesitation.

At Wal-Mart, Kerney spotted Andy's unmarked unit at the side of the building away from the parking lot lights and got in beside him.

"I got a telephone call right after I spoke with you," Andy said.

"Applewhite?" Kerney asked.

Andy shook his head. "The U.S. attorney. Supposedly he wanted to let me know about the task force and make sure the resources of my department would be made available to the FBI."

"How polite."

Andy grunted. "Yeah, right. When was the last time you ever heard of the FBI using a U.S. attorney as a front man for a task force investigation?"

"Never. What did he really want?"

"After he chatted briefly about national security implications and the need for discretion, he gave me Applewhite's name as the FBI contact person and asked me to call her at her hotel. So I did. She basically gave me the same line that she fed you, minus any aspersions about Mrs. Terrell's sexual escapades."

"So, you get a reassuring call from the U.S. attorney within minutes of our conversation. What a coincidence."

"Your phone is tapped," Andy said.

"Either that or they're using a telecommunications-intercept system through the National Security Agency, which means they probably know we're meeting right now."

Andy brushed a hand through his thinning hand. "Jesus."

"Drop the Applewhite fact check," Kerney said. "You don't need to get involved."

Andy smiled slyly. "Too late. I did it myself just to be obstinate. Her story checks out. I verified the car rental, the date she and her husband arrived by plane in Albuquerque, when they checked into their rented Taos condominium, and the time today that she reserved a hotel room in Santa Fe. But what I found interesting was that everybody I talked to, once I connected with the right people, had the information I needed at their fingertips. No paper shuffling, record searching, or computer scan."

"Oops," Kerney said. "Tomorrow should be a very interesting day."

"I know a retired special agent who might be willing to give me some background on Applewhite," Andy said.

"Let it go. If they're listening to my conversations, they're probably listening to yours. Best for them to think I'm satisfied that all is as it seems. I picked Terrell up at the airport and drove him to his hotel. He brought two company men masquerading as FBI."

"You're sure?"

"That's my guess."

"Want some advice?" Andy asked after a pause.

"Sure."

Andy pulled at the collar of his off-white uniform shirt. "Start wearing your blues, Kerney."

"Do you think that will impress the feds?" Kerney asked with a laugh.

"No, but it might make your troops start to think you're proud to be their chief."

"You know how I feel about uniforms."

"Then you should have been an accountant instead of a cop."

Kerney studied Andy's serious expression. "What have you heard?"

"The same gripe that dogged you when you were my chief deputy. I put up with it because I knew what you did was far more important than whether or not you wore a uniform on the job. But now you're the chief of a department, and you damn well better dress like one. Wear the uniform."

Andy was right and Kerney knew it. "I'll spit-shine my shoes and polish my brass in the morning," he said as he opened the car door.

"Call me if you get into a firefight with the feds," Andy said.

"If that happens, it will be too late to call," Kerney said.

"All of this could turn out to mean nothing."

"You never know," Kerney replied.

Chapter 3

About the only thing Cloudy Herrera liked about working days was that the shift started at six in the morning and usually nothing much happened for an hour or two. Assigned to the north patrol, Cloudy expected he'd catch some false burglary alarm calls and take spillover assignments on the south side of the city where the units stayed busy with shoplifting, assault, auto theft, vandalism, and traffic accidents. So far his radio had been quiet.

At a stop-and-rob convenience store just off the Interstate, Cloudy bought an extra large coffee, left it on the counter, and went to empty his bladder in the public restroom. As he zipped up, his call number came over the handheld radio. Cloudy keyed the microphone clipped to his shirt and responded.

"Unattended death at the College of Santa Fe," the dispatcher said. "See Brother Jerome Brodsky at the Christian Brothers residence hall."

Cloudy acknowledged and checked the time. It was five minutes after seven. "ETA four minutes," he added, hurrying to his unit.

Morning traffic was still light and he could get to the campus running with lights only in plenty of time. Halfway there he remembered he'd left his coffee behind on the counter, which had cost him a buck and some change. That didn't make him happy, but the thought passed when he realized he didn't have a clue where the Christian Brothers' residence hall was located on the campus. He called dispatch and asked for directions.

Two dead bodies in two days, a first in his three years on the force. He parked in front of the old World War Two barracks where the brothers lived. There better not be any damn dogs around, he grumbled silently, thinking about his ruined uniform trousers.

He announced his arrival and the shift sergeant came on the horn to say he was rolling and would be there in two.

"Ten-four," Cloudy replied, staring at a tall, older man in long black robes who came hurrying down a pathway to a gate, his expression dazed and shaken.

Kerney passed the National Guard recruitment billboard, turned off the frontage road that paralleled the Interstate, and drove toward the new armory. He parked and listened for a minute to the radio traffic about an unattended death at the college before entering the building. Inside a female staff sergeant dressed in army fatigues directed him to the conference room where the FBI task force had set up shop. He entered the room to find Lieutenant Molina at a conference table large enough to seat the Joint Chiefs, the National Security Council, and the whole White House cabinet. With Molina were every on-duty detective, an eight-man FBI crew, and Special Agent Applewhite, who assisted a man at the head of the table as he quickly scanned through a document folder. The two men who'd accompanied Ambassador Terrell to Santa Fe were not present.

The surprised look on Sal Molina's face as he considered the sight of Kerney in uniform almost made Kerney smile. Molina's reaction alone made wearing the blues worth the effort.

The man with Applewhite looked up, nodded at Kerney, rose, and came around the table to greet him.

"Chief Kerney," Charlie Perry said. "It's good to see you again."

"Hello, Charlie." Kerney shook Perry's hand, thinking back to his summer as a seasonal ranger in the Gila Wilderness, where he'd met Perry, who'd been undercover at the time, investigating a militia group in Catron County. He'd butted heads with Perry, who had treated him as a washed-up ex-cop, hamstrung his attempts to link the militia to a lucrative game-poaching operation, and forced him off the job—all out of pure ego. But with the help of a state game and fish officer named Jim Stiles, Kerney had still managed to punch a big hole in the militia's leadership and make some rock-solid arrests.

"Seems you've resurrected your career since last we met," Perry said.

The sarcastic bite came from Perry's choice of words, not his tone. Kerney studied the younger man's face. Trim and lean, Perry matched Kerney's six-one height. Perry had missed one long neck hair when shaving. It curled below his Adam's apple just above his shirt collar. Another jutted out on the side of a nostril. Judging by his past experience with the man, Kerney assumed Perry was too vain to realize he needed glasses.

Perry stared back at Kerney cockily, his brown eyes showing a touch of disdain.

"Looks like you've moved up in the food chain yourself, Charlie," Kerney said. "Let's get to work."

"We're ready when you are," Perry replied, gesturing at the table.

After introductions Applewhite passed out folders and Perry guided the group through the documents, which laid out very little about Phyllis Terrell's personal history or her extramarital affairs, and gave a brief résumé on Hamilton Lowell Terrell, who after his retirement from the army had served as ambassador in both Panama and Ecuador, and who now carried the rank of ambassador without portfolio. Included in the paperwork were the names of three men who allegedly had been Mrs. Terrell's lovers during the past two years, and some supplementary information on the considerable net worth of the surviving members of the Straley family, including the victim's father and sister.

"This is all you're going to give us?" Molina asked when Perry closed the file and put it to one side.

"You have the names of two local men who may have been sexually involved with the victim," Perry replied. "That should be enough to keep you and your people busy."

"And the third guy down in Ramah?" Molina asked, consulting his notes. "Scott Gatlin."

"I have an agent on the way there now," Perry replied. "We'll handle it."

"What about the papers and items that were removed from Mrs. Terrell's residence last night?" Molina asked.

"Nothing of value to the investigation was taken," Perry said.

"I'm supposed to trust you on that?" Molina snapped back.

Perry fiddled with his pen before replying. "The ambassador's personal property was secured at his request and consisted of nothing more than photographs, books, and memorabilia."

"Then why wasn't I allowed to inventory the contents last night before the boxes were removed by your two agents?"

"Because, as I just said, it had no bearing on the case," Perry replied.

"I want to do a full-scale search of the residence," Molina said.

Perry reached for another folder. "Agent Applewhite asked the ambassador to sign a permission-to-search form late last night. He was more than willing to do so."

Perry passed it down the table, watched Molina read it, and then turned his attention to Kerney. "I'd like Agent Applewhite and another agent to assist in the search, if that's all right with you, Chief."

"No problem," Kerney said.

Perry smiled thinly. "Good. Then there's only a few more issues to cover. Susan Straley has arrived from Virginia and Proctor Straley is on his way to Santa Fe now. My people will conduct the necessary interviews. Also, I've called a press briefing at noon to release the name of the victim, announce the formation of the task force, and read a prepared statement from the ambassador."

Perry's smile widened. "Unless you'd rather handle it, Chief Kerney."

"Go for it, Charlie," Kerney said, looking at the tidy, neat rows of agents flanking Perry at the far end of the table. "But tell me, what will the rest of the task force be doing while we're searching the house and interviewing Mrs. Terrell's boyfriends?"

Perry stood up. "I'm unable to discuss that, but I'll keep you informed to the extent that I can. Let's get to it."

Outside, Kerney waited for Sal Molina to appear. Sunlight and an unseasonably warm day had melted the remaining snow on all but the foothills and mountains, and the intense blue sky seemed limitless. On the Interstate a steady stream of vehicles moved in both directions.

Molina came out the door in a hurry, cell phone in hand. "That unattended death at the college was a homicide, Chief. A priest had his throat cut."

"Do you have any more specifics?"

"That's all I know. I can only spare one detective."

"I'll back him up," Kerney said.

"Great."

"Contact the Armed Forces Record Center in St. Louis. See if they'll release a copy of Ambassador Terrell's service jacket."

"You don't buy the killed-by-a-lover theory?"

"Right now I don't buy any theory. Since the feds have locked us out of the trade-mission slant, let's take a look at Terrell through the back door. Put someone on a computer, have him surf newspaper archives, and find out what Terrell did between the time he retired from active duty and his appointment as an ambassador. I want it as specific and complete as possible."

"You got it."

"And I want Proctor and Susan Straley interviewed by our people after the feds are finished with them."

"That will raise the feds' eyebrows." Molina watched as Kerney rubbed his chin and looked at him thoughtfully. "Anything else?"

Kerney hesitated before responding. He had to start trusting his senior officers, otherwise he would never find out who he could count on. "Find out who told Applewhite that we'd picked up Santiago Terjo for questioning. The information had to come from within the department."

"You want Internal Affairs to handle it?"

"No, you do it. Concentrate on the detectives, officers, and technicians who were at the crime scene."

Molina inclined his head toward the door. "What in the hell was going on in there with you and Agent Perry?"

"It's old business," Kerney said. "Make sure you put Applewhite and her partner under constant observation during the house search. I don't want anything else disappearing from the residence. Take photographs while you're there. If Applewhite questions it, say it's department policy. Get me a few good shots of her."

Applewhite came out the door with another agent before Molina could ask what in the hell was going on.

"We're ready to roll, Chief," she said, with a nod and a smile in Molina's direction.

"Lieutenant Molina will guide you to the house," Kerney said as he stepped away to his unit.

After World War Two the College of Santa Fe, an independent institution founded by four Christian Brothers in 1859, had relocated from a site near the plaza to the surplus Fort Burns Army Hospital at the edge of town. Now besieged by urban sprawl and bordered by major roads, the campus was more or less tucked away from view except for the main entrance off St. Michael's Drive.

Over the past twenty years the college had built a reputation for its liberal arts, performance, and fine arts programs.

Kerney drove past the flashy new garnet-red Visual Arts Center, an ultramodern building of exceedingly sharp angles, rows of geometrically square and rectangular windows, stiff jutting cornices, and pyramid domes, to the old army barracks, where two squad cars, an unmarked unit, a crime-tech vehicle, and an ambulance were parked.

Officer Herrera once again stood guard, positioned at the gate to the courtyard entrance with clipboard in hand next to a sign that read, "Christian Brothers Residence."

Kerney wondered if Herrera was good at anything other than checking people in and out of crime scenes. He had his doubts.

He sat in his car for a long minute looking at the barracks, which sported new roofs and siding, but clearly proclaimed a wartime heritage. Although brown and dormant, the courtyard was a showcase of ardent gardening and careful landscaping, with curving walkways, carefully pruned shrubs, a grass lawn, mulched flower-beds, and ornamental trees. Around the perimeter of the buildings mature pine and cedar trees overarched the roofs and provided screening.

Kerney wondered how long it would be before the college tore the barracks down, and hoped it never happened. Not every structure worth saving had to be an architectural marvel, and there was something to be said for preserving a few reminders of a time when the country had been defended by millions of citizen soldiers.

"Did you see the body?" Kerney asked as he signed in with Herrera.

"Just for a minute," Cloudy answered. "Then Sergeant Catanach arrived and stationed me out here."

"Did you detain any witnesses?"

"Like I said, Chief, the sergeant took over."

Kerney looked into Herrera's dull gray eyes and decided to trust the hunch that popped up. "Did anyone from outside the department come by the Terrell crime scene yesterday?"

"Yeah, an FBI agent stopped by just before I was relieved. Some woman. I don't remember her name. Applegate, or something like that."

"What did she want?"

"Just to know what was happening with the case."

"And?" Kerney prodded, trying to keep a scolding tone out of his voice.

"I filled her in."

"What did you tell her?"

"That we had a suspect, the Mexican guy."

"Did she ask permission to inspect the crime scene?"

"No."

"Did you document the conversation?" Kerney asked.

"What for?" Herrera said with a shrug.

Kerney forced a smile. "Contact Lieutenant Molina, tell him what you told me, and write up a supplemental report. Have it ready for me before I leave."

Herrera shrugged again. "Okay."

Sergeant Tony Catanach was in the dining room where he had assembled the brothers, who sat clustered together silently at two tables. Kerney scanned the group: all the men were middle aged or older; but some were dressed in casual civilian attire, while others wore clerical garb. Several had their heads bowed in prayer.

Catanach gave an approving glance at Kerney's uniform and stepped into the hallway. A young man in his early thirties and a five-year veteran of the force, he was a newly minted sergeant who took his job seriously.

"I was just about to start taking statements, Chief," he said.

"Bring me up to speed."

"The victim is Father Joseph Mitchell, a Maryknoll priest. His throat was slashed. Entry may have been gained either through an unlocked window or a door."

Along the corridor of the nicely remodeled barracks a series of doors gave access to the dining room, a library, a large lounge, an entertainment room, and a chapel.

"Where's the body?" Kerney asked.

Catanach inclined his head toward the row of hallway windows that looked out on the courtyard and an adjacent two-story barracks, connected to the common area by a passageway. "The brothers' bedrooms are across the way. Father Mitchell had a first-floor room right inside a door that leads directly to the courtyard. The screen was off his unlatched window, but all the others are still in place. Nobody can remember if the entrance closest to Mitchell's room was locked or not. The brothers aren't real concerned about security. There isn't any sign of forced entry, and if you walk around you'll see four more doors that also could have been used by the killer to gain entry."

"Have you got everyone here?"

"No," Catanach said. "There are twelve residents, if you count Father Mitchell. Seven are in the dining room and four of the brothers are in their offices canceling their classes. They'll be back in twenty minutes. I've asked them not to discuss Father Mitchell's death."

Catanach consulted a pocket notebook. "Robbery may have been the motive, Chief. A laptop and desktop computer were taken, along with a tape recorder, a camera, and a VCR. Detective Sloan is in the room waiting for the body to be removed."

"What do you know about the victim?"

"Not much, yet. He was a visiting scholar-in-residence working on a research project. Brother Jerome Brodsky, chair of the social science department, supposedly knows the most about Father Mitchell. He'll be back in twenty."

"What else?" Kerney asked.

"Check out the knife wound, Chief. One deep cut at the jugular. No hesitation marks, nothing sloppy, and no cuts on the victim's hands to indicate any struggle with his attacker. I'd say the priest was probably asleep at the time."

"I'll take a look and be back to help take statements," Kerney said.

Bobby Sloan, a thirty-year veteran of the department, pulled back the sheet covering Father Mitchell's body. "A clean kill," he said to Kerney. "This wasn't done by your typical addict looking to steal something so he could fence it and score. The incision is deep-est right at the jugular. The killer knows his anatomy."

Kerney agreed, the angled wound was clean, sharp, and long, slicing through the jugular, an axillary vein, and the larynx. The cut had been made where a trained assassin would strike with a knife, and the edges of the wound were close together. Blood had flowed freely.

Kerney scrutinized the dead man's face. His gray hair was cropped short and receded at the temples. Age lines around the mouth and eyes and a fullness to the cheeks suggested the priest had seen the passage of five decades, maybe more.

"Seen enough?" Sloan asked.

Kerney nodded.

Sloan flipped the cover over Mitchell's face and gestured to the two paramedics who waited in the hall with a collapsible gurney. The men stepped inside and removed the body while Kerney and Sloan stood to one side.

The sleeping room was small, no more than a hundred square feet, with a tiny adjacent bathroom. The furniture consisted of a twin bed, a bedside table, a student-size writing desk, and an al-most empty bookcase—all obviously postwar items bought at sur-plus. In one corner a built-in shelf and rod served as a clothes closet.

"We've searched the room, photographed, and vacuumed," Sloan said. "The techs are dusting every door to the building for prints," Sloan said. "There are no toolmarks on the doors or win-dows suggesting forced entry. The ground froze last night, but we've found no footprints outside the window."

"What was on the bookcase?" Kerney asked.

"Before he left for his office, Brother Jerome said it was mostly empty. But you know, Chief, with two computers you'd think there would be a box or two of floppy disks around. There weren't any in the room."

"Any personal items?" Kerney asked.

"Nothing in his clothes. But we did find some letters from his mother in Houston. He had a Louisiana driver's license with a New Orleans address that checked out to be a Catholic seminary. New Orleans PD is making contact."

Only a few investigators from Kerney's earlier tenure as chief of detectives still remained with the department, and Sloan was one of them. From past experience Kerney knew him to be reliable, hardworking, and a straight talker. Somewhat older than Kerney, Sloan had a missing tooth near the front of his mouth and an unconscious habit of probing it with his tongue.

Through the window Kerney saw Officer Herrera lounging against the fender of his squad car, smoking a cigarette, watching the ambulance drive away.

"Tell me about Herrera, Bobby," Kerney said.

Sloan snorted. "As a cop he's worthless, Chief, and as a person he's piss-poor company. The last chief didn't have the balls to can him. His uncle is on the city council. Serves on the finance committee."

"I see."

"You need anything else from me?" Sloan asked.

"Continue with the crime-scene work-up," Kerney replied. "I'll help Catanach take the witness statements."

"That's a big help," Sloan said. "How do you like being back with the department, Chief?"

"I'm glad to be back, Bobby."

Sloan grinned. "Just don't sweat the small stuff, Chief. Most of us know what we're doing."

"I'll keep that in mind."

Along with the clerics in residence two women employees worked as housekeepers and cooks. Sergeant Catanach had rounded them up with the brothers and was in the dining room conducting interviews. Kerney took over the lounge, a large room with a stone fireplace, comfortable easy chairs, and an overflowing wall of bookshelves, and began taking statements.

Kerney learned very little about Father Mitchell from the people he interviewed. An historian working on a compendium of late-twentieth-century military aid to South American countries, Father Mitchell had been in residence slightly less than a year. He rarely discussed his work and when engaged in conversation about it responded very vaguely. The brothers knew Mitchell had served as an army chaplain, had taught for a spell at a Midwest Catholic college, and held an advanced degree from an Ivy League university. He'd been murdered a week short of his fifty-ninth birthday.

Brother Jerome, chair of the social science department, was the last faculty member to return from his office. A tall, reserved, intelligent-looking man in his early sixties, dressed in a clerical robe, he sat across from Kerney with his hands folded in his lap. Only the rapid blinking of his eyes gave a hint of his dismay and shock about Father Mitchell's murder.

"You found Father Joseph," Kerney said.

"Yes. He'd missed morning prayers and didn't appear for breakfast. I thought he might be sick."

"What time was that?"

"About seven o'clock," Brother Jerome said. "There was so much blood I knew he was dead as soon as I stepped into the room."

"The door was unlocked?"

"Yes, and all his personal possessions were missing. I gave a list of what I knew he kept in his room to the sergeant."

"How long was it before you called to report the death?"

"Within a few minutes. Almost immediately."

"Did you see anybody nearby?"

"I saw no strangers, if that's what you mean, and everyone else had been to prayer and breakfast."

"Your colleagues seem to know very little about Father Joseph."

"He kept to himself and we respected his privacy. I may know a little more, since I granted Father Joseph's request for a visiting scholar's appointment."

"So far all I've learned is where he earned his advanced degrees, where he recently taught, and that he served a hitch as an army chaplain," Kerney said.

"Father Joseph retired as an army chaplain with the rank of major about a dozen years ago. He was stationed all over the world. He took his master's in history at a university in Georgia while on active duty, and completed his PhD after he retired."

"What else can you tell me about his professional life?" Kerney asked.

"His research interest was military history. Much of it he did on the Internet."

"What brought him to Santa Fe?"

"He was gathering oral histories from some significant primary and secondary sources. Mostly retired military officers living in the state, I believe."

"Did Father Joseph mention any names?"

"Not to me. But he spent a fair amount of time conducting interviews."

"Did he talk about his personal or family life?"

Brother Jerome shook his head. "Only in the most general of terms. We shared a few reminiscences one evening shortly after he arrived. He has a widowed mother who lives in Houston. And his only younger brother died while serving as a military attaché at an embassy in Latin American some time ago. He wouldn't say more about it and never seemed willing to discuss it again."

"Did you ever try?"

"Yes. Father Joseph said it was just an everyday sort of tragedy in today's America."

"How would you characterize Father Joseph's political views?" Kerney asked.

"Very liberal. Are you looking to do a bit of witch hunting, Chief Kerney?"

"That's not how the question was meant. Understanding Father Joseph may help me catch his killer. This could be the act of an everyday criminal. On the other hand it could be connected to something in Father Joseph's past. Did you learn anything about the younger brother?"

"He was career military, I believe. A colonel in the army."

"Did Father Joseph speak to you of any personal or family problems, conflicts with others, or worries he might have had?" Kerney asked.

"No. He seemed very content and at ease with himself and others. He was a fine man and a good priest."

"What about contact with students?"

"He had no teaching responsibilities," Brother Jerome replied, "although he may have had some casual association with individual students."

"Did he keep any papers or documents outside of his room, or show you his work in progress?"

"I never saw his manuscript or research notes. He did have a briefcase he carried with him whenever he left the residence."

"Did Father Mitchell have a car?"

"Yes, he drives a brown Toyota. It should be parked outside."

"We found no briefcase in his room," Kerney noted.

"I see," Brother Jerome said. "Would you like to look for it?"

"If it's not a bother."

"By all means."

No briefcase was found during the search of the residence hall, and nothing turned up in the car search. After checking in with Catanach and Sloan, Kerney left the residence hall to find Officer Herrera hurriedly finishing his supplemental report.

Cloudy handed over the paperwork and had Kerney sign the crime-scene log.

"Is your report complete?" Kerney asked.

"Yeah. There wasn't much to say."

At his office Kerney entered the information he'd gathered from his interviews into the computerized paperwork system. He finished and looked over the list of stolen items. The perpetrator had cleaned out all the priest's research plus two computers. Two trips would have been necessary to cart it away, which heightened the chance of discovery. No professional thief would risk getting caught unless the stolen items had more than a monetary value. It upped the probability that Father Joseph had been silenced by someone who wanted to avoid exposure or keep a secret. But of what?

He accessed the Terrell case file and read through the forensic notes that had been posted earlier that morning. Semen had been found on the bed sheets, along with some pubic and head hairs not from the victim, which didn't match the samples taken from Santiago Terjo. Autopsy findings showed Phyllis Terrell had engaged in sexual intercourse no more than a few hours before her murder. DNA analysis confirmed Terjo wasn't Terrell's bed partner, at least not on the night of the murder.

He scrolled through the supplementary report menu and pulled up Sal Molina's notes on Terjo. The man had stuck with his story during Sal's second full-press interrogation. But Kerney still felt Terjo was holding something back. Maybe the night spent in jail would induce him to be more forthcoming.

He shut down the computer and switched his attention to Alonso Herrera's personnel file. After a year on patrol Herrera had been transferred to the Crime Prevention Unit. Six months into the assignment he'd requested a return to patrol and had been assigned to a different team. Ratings from his field training officers and supervisors fell in the adequate range and nothing in the file reflected negatively on the officer.

Kerney found Herrera's unusually rapid transfer to the crime prevention unit interesting. From experience he knew junior officers rarely moved so quickly off patrol duty. Normally, it took between three to five years for a uniformed officer to get bumped up to a specialist slot. Occasionally, an exceptionally sharp officer could make the cut in two years, but that was rare. From what Kerney had seen of Herrera, he certainly didn't fit the criteria of an officer on a fast track.

He switched his attention to the supplemental field report Herrera had given him on his way out of the crime scene, first reading for content and then for competency. Because of a patrol-officer shortage on the swing shift, Herrera had been held over at the Terrell residence for several hours, and according to his report Applewhite had appeared about an hour before her arrival at police headquarters. Herrera's penmanship was sloppy, his use of grammar and syntax unbelievably bad, and his spelling bordered on semiliterate.

Kerney buzzed Helen Muiz and asked for a quick meeting. Helen came in, notebook and file folder in hand, and sat with Kerney at the conference table. Today's outfit was a smartly tailored pair of slacks complemented by a cashmere sweater.

"You look very nice today," Kerney said.

"As do you," Helen replied.

"You mean the uniform?" Kerney asked, tugging at the collar with the four stars.

"Yes, and it's about time you started wearing it."

"Should I wear it every day?" he asked.

"Frequently will do," Helen replied. "A response to your FAA inquiry regarding the aircraft identification numbers on the corporate jet used by Ambassador Terrell came in while you were out. The plane is leased by Trade Source Venture International. According to its Web site the company engages in multinational high-value technology start-up enterprises—whatever that means."

"It usually means, give us your money," Kerney replied.

Helen smiled agreeably and referred to her notebook. "I did some digging on your behalf. Trade Source is headquartered in Virginia, but they control a local subsidiary, called APT Performa, which has offices in the business park off Rodeo Road. It's a Los Alamos National Laboratory private-sector technology-transfer spin-off company, that develops state-of-the-art high-tech computer security software bundles."

"Whatever that means," Kerney said before Helen had the chance.

"Exactly. The CEO is a Mr. Clarence Thayer. Trade Source is on the NASDAQ exchange. I've asked a stockbroker friend to send over all the information she has on the company. You'll have it this afternoon."

"You should have been a cop, Helen."

Helen's eyes smiled. "You don't want to hear my response to that comment, Chief."

"Probably not. Give me the back channel scoop on Alonso Herrera."

Helen's expression turned sober. "Do you really want to step into that open manhole right now?"

"That bad?" Kerney asked.

"You know about Herrera's uncle?"

"I just learned who he was."

"Herrera was bounced from his patrol team and sent to the crime-prevention unit in an attempt to keep him off the streets."

"Be more specific," Kerney said.

"Shoddy paperwork, poor attitude toward the public, abuse of sick leave, subpar performance, citizen complaints about the use of excessive force."

"There's nothing documented in his file."

"Not anymore there isn't," Helen replied. "Your predecessor ordered the file purged and Herrera's performance evaluations upgraded to adequate. As a result the department got a nice bump in the annual budget that sailed through the finance committee and the city council without a hitch."

Helen passed the file folder she'd brought in to Kerney. "When you asked me for Herrera's personnel file, I thought we might have this discussion. That file contains copies of the original disciplinary reports and performance evaluations on Officer Herrera, along with some internal memoranda. When I heard that you were to be our next chief, I was glad I saved them."

"You are insubordinate," Kerney said with a laugh.

"Only when it's in the best interest of the department."

An incredulous expression creased Kerney's face as he read the material. He set the folder aside and said, "Herrera starts his days off tomorrow. Prepare an order assigning him to permanent duty in Fleet Management upon his return to work."

"Are you sure you want to do that now?" Helen asked.

"I might as well find out right away if I'm going to survive in this job or not."

"You'll be making an enemy on the city council."

"I'll add him to my list. Captain Otero wrote some strongly worded memos protesting the decision. Is that why he was removed as a field-operation captain and placed in charge of Technical Services?"

Helen nodded. "It tubed his career. He's got a short-timer's calendar in the top drawer of his desk, and he's counting the days until he can take early retirement."

"How close is he?"

"Sixty days."

"Have him come see me," Kerney said.

"May I tell him why? With the old chief the senior commanders never knew what to expect when called to appear at the Crystal Palace."

"Tell him I've a few minor questions about the fleet-replacement schedule. Set up the appointment for late this afternoon, and get me his personnel jacket. I want to take another look at it. I may have found my deputy chief."

Helen grinned.

"What?" Kerney asked.

"Nothing," Helen said lightly as she rose and left the office.

Detective Sloan had accepted Kerney's offer to scout out Father Joseph's military records and make contact with the priest's mother, so he turned to those tasks, first calling the Armed Forces Record Center. Kerney got nowhere with the civilian employee he spoke to. Terrell's records could not be released without his written permission.

He called the retirement home where Mrs. Mitchell resided, and spoke to a caseworker. Mrs. Mitchell, age eighty-seven, was in failing health but mentally alert. Leaving out many of the details, Kerney gave the caseworker the news of Father Joseph's death. The woman suggested it would be best for her to pass the information on to Mrs. Mitchell to soften the impact.

"By all means, please do that," Kerney said. "But Mrs. Mitchell will still need to speak to the police. I'm going to ask the Houston Police Department to have an investigator meet with her as soon as possible."

"Why is that necessary?" the woman asked.

"To learn as much as we can about Father Mitchell, and find his killer."

The caseworker sighed and hung up.

By phone Kerney put in his request to the chief of detectives of the Houston PD, who agreed to get someone on it right away. As an afterthought Kerney asked for any information Mrs. Mitchell might have on the death of her other son, Colonel Mitchell, United States Army, first name unknown.

He hung up and read through Captain Larry Otero's personnel file. Otero had attended a number of traffic-safety institutes, was a graduate of two FBI police-management training courses, and had earned instructorship status in field-officer training, officer survival techniques, and DWI enforcement. He held a BA degree in criminal justice, and up until the prior administration his performance ratings had been excellent.

Aside from his present assignment and his prior position as a patrol captain, Otero's job experience included a tour in Traffic Services as commander, a stint as an Internal Affairs lieutenant, and two years as a sergeant in crime prevention.

At forty-two Otero was seasoned, capable, and knowledgeable about a wide range of department operations, which was exactly what Kerney needed in a deputy chief. He also liked the tone of Otero's clearly written, dissenting memos about the Herrera whitewash. The man had backbone and principles.

It could work out to be a good match, he thought, as he closed the file and checked the time. Charlie Perry's press conference was due to begin soon. Although he knew he had to go, he disliked the thought of watching Perry do the FBI spin-doctor routine that inevitably accompanied such events.

Chapter 4

Charlie Perry opened the press conference reading a two-page prepared statement that had been distributed to the media. Minus the hype about cooperation with local law enforcement, it boiled down to nothing more than that the FBI was on the scene and in charge of the investigation. Kerney hung back while Perry finished his canned remarks and fielded questions.

The reporters, all from area newspapers and Albuquerque television stations, focused their attention on the ambassador's wife, eager to get quotes and sound bites that would guarantee a wire service byline or network news spot.

One young man, a television reporter standing at the back of the room, called out Kerney's name.

Kerney stepped to the microphone and acknowledged the reporter.

"Did you request FBI involvement, Chief?" the reporter asked.

"Whenever a crime is committed against a federal government official or a family member, the FBI has jurisdiction. My department welcomes the Bureau's help and the resources they can bring to the investigation," Kerney replied.

"Do you have any reason, at this stage of the investigation, to believe that the murder was a terrorist act?"

Charlie Perry crowded close to Kerney, impatient to take back the podium. Kerney refused to yield. "At this point all avenues are being explored," he said. "That's why the FBI is here."

"Was the ambassador the target?" the reporter asked.

"I think Special Agent Perry should answer that question."

Perry stepped up to the microphone. "From what we know so far, that does not appear to be the case," he said. "While we don't have a clear motive, it's very possible that Mrs. Terrell was killed by someone known to her. But as Chief Kerney said, it's too early to rule anything out. We'll keep you advised of any new developments."

The conference broke up and the reporters hurried away to write their stories or videotape their lead-ins outside on the armory steps.

Perry pulled Kerney aside. "Were you trying to let that reporter box me in?" he asked hotly.

"Not at all, Charlie," Kerney said innocently, as he walked away. "I just didn't feel like speaking for you."

Ten minutes after Kerney arrived at his office, Andy Baca walked in. He grinned at the sight of Kerney in uniform, but said nothing.

"What brings you up the street?" Kerney asked.

Andy put his hat on the conference table and took a seat. "I picked up some collateral information from my source."

"Who's your source?" Kerney asked.

"Fred Browning," Andy replied. "He headed up the governor's security unit before retiring about six years ago. He now works as chief of plant security for a computer chip company in Albuquerque."

"What did Browning tell you?"

"Don't rush me, Kerney," Andy said with a laugh. "There's some background to this. Browning is a big booster for a society of corporate and industrial security professionals. A sizable percentage of the membership consists of retired FBI and other federal law enforcement types who work in the private sector. The society is headquartered in Alexandria, Virginia, right outside the Beltway and within easy driving distance to Quantico."

"That's chummy," Kerney said.

"Fred serves on the national board of directors. The society recruits from professionals in corporate and industrial security, gaming and wagering, hotel and hospital security, loss prevention and retail sales—you name it."

"Sounds fairly typical," Kerney said.

"Yeah, but I have some suspicions, which I'll get to in a minute," Andy said. "Fred came around several months ago on a membership recruitment drive and suggested my department needed to get on board. He gave me a big pitch about the benefits of the society's professional certification program."

"Did you sign up?"

"I passed the information down the line and left it at that. What's interesting is that Fred also told me that the FBI requires all special agents with national security assignments to be members of the society."

"Are you saying the Bureau stays cozy with the private-sector security boys so they can keep an eye on them?"

"It would be one way to watch for high-tech corporate espionage that could compromise national security."

"Okay, but where are you going with this?"

"I asked Fred this morning if he had a membership directory. There is no Special Agent Applewhite carried on the national roster. However, the special agent assigned as liaison coordinator with the State Department is, and his name isn't Elaine Applewhite."

"Well, well," Kerney said, leaning back in his chair.

"There's one membership group I haven't mentioned," Andy said. "The military. When Applewhite's name didn't pop on the society records, I asked Fred to do a first-name-only search. A Major Elaine Cornell, U.S. Army, is a member. She's assigned to the Defense Intelligence Agency at the Pentagon."

"How many other first-name hits did Browning get?"

"Five. Fred checked the membership applications for each one. Except for Major Cornell none of them has any law-enforcement or intelligence experience. The others work for hospitals, big retail and hotel chains, and one heads up security at a Las Vegas casino."

"If Applewhite really is Cornell, why is an army intelligence officer operating undercover on this case?" Kerney asked.

"My question exactly," Andy said.

"Does Browning know Cornell personally?"

"No, but if we can get him a photograph, he has a friend who does."

"I should have one later today," Kerney said. "Will Browning keep his mouth shut about this?"

"That's not a problem. He was a solid cop, and he's not a big FBI fan."

"Who is?" Kerney said. "What about his friend?"

"Fred says not to worry. The guy is a civilian."

"Good enough," Kerney said. "Can you lend me a few agents?"

Andy raised an eyebrow. "What do you need them for?"

"We caught another homicide. A priest was murdered early this morning at the College of Santa Fe. I'm stretched thin with the Terrell investigation and only have one detective assigned to the case."

"Fill me in."

Kerney told him what had been uncovered so far and his conjectures about the case. "I could use four agents for three days," he said.

"I can give you three for two days," Andy said. "I wish it were more, but I'm short on people myself. Batten down the hatches, Kerney. The news media is going to be riding your butt on these homicides."

"Thanks for the help."

Andy picked up his hat and stepped to the door. "Watch your back with the feds. I'd hate to see that snappy uniform you're wearing get shot up by friendly fire."

"That's a pleasant thought."

Sal Molina entered the office immediately after Andy's departure. He had dark circles under his eyes and his shoulders were hunched with tension. He sat wearily and rubbed his eyes.

"Is the state police entering the Terrell case?"

"No, Chief Baca has agreed to help us out on the Mitchell homicide," Kerney said. "Sloan will get three agents for two days."

Molina smiled. "That's a big help. Sloan has been begging for some more manpower."

"Has he made any progress?" Kerney asked.

Molina shook his head. "He's still putting together a list of people Father Joseph had any contact with on campus. Library staff, students who attended the two masses Father Joseph celebrated at the college when the chaplain was ill, faculty members who met the priest at social functions—stuff like that."

"Any forensics?"

"The techs are fingerprinting everyone with access to the residence hall for comparison to latents lifted at the scene. But it's gonna take time. They've identified about fifty different prints, most of them at the entrances to the sleeping quarters, although there were a few in Mitchell's room."

"Where are you with the Terrell case?" Kerney asked.

"The house search turned up zilch. And the bone the FBI threw us this morning about Terrell's lovers went nowhere: the two men we've interviewed have solid alibis."

"Start with the house search," Kerney said. "How clean was it?"

"Scoured, Chief, right down to the hard drive on Mrs. Terrell's computer. There were no personal letters, no address books, and nothing pertaining to the ambassador at all. About the only thing we got was some records of Mrs. Terrell's financial assets—the woman was worth big bucks—and a few good pictures of Agent Applewhite. They're being processed now."

"And Terrell's lovers?" Kerney asked.

"Solid alibis, like I said. Both men are married. One was the architect who designed Terrell's house, and the other is an attorney she met through a friend. The attorney has been out of town for the last three days pleading a civil case in North Carolina. He was with his client until eleven-thirty last night. He just got back to town after getting a continuance on the trial until next week. The architect spent all night at home. The wife said he got up at three in the morning when the baby started crying. It was his turn. He didn't leave home for the office until nine. We'll probe more, but it doesn't look promising."

"Did you get any insight into Terrell from the men?"

"The architect said Terrell liked to sport-fuck—that she had endurance, a really high sex drive, liked it lots of different ways, and wasn't shy about expressing her preferences."

"Had Terrell broken off relationships with either man?"

"Yeah, with the architect," Molina said. "But from what I gather, it wasn't like she had a relationship with either of them. It was more like a sex-on-demand situation, with Terrell calling the shots, so to speak."

"Any word on Terrell's lover who lives in Ramah?" Kerney asked. "According to the FBI, Scott Gatlin is Proctor Straley's ranch manager."

Molina snorted. "I asked Charlie Perry about that. He said his agent hadn't reported back yet. While we're waiting to hear, I've got people checking on all deliveries and service calls made to the residence in the last six months, and following up on the list of names we got from Terjo. I've asked the postal service to put an intercept on Terrell's mail. I've also expanded the canvass to a wider area and we're reinterviewing the neighbors."

"What's the status on Terrell's sister and father?" Kerney asked.

"Both are still being questioned by Agent Perry's boys. I don't know when I'll have a chance to get to them."

"If you get stonewalled, let me know."

"Terjo walked, Chief. The DA said we didn't have enough to take to an arraignment for either drug dealing or possession."

"Where is he?"

"I don't know. The jail called me after they released him. He left on foot. I've got an officer stationed at the girlfriend's house in case he shows."

"Let's hope he's not hitchhiking his way to Mexico," Kerney said.

"I've alerted the Border Patrol, and I've got units looking for him in the south-side barrios. I'd like to pull in the swing shift gang unit, Chief. They know that area well."

"Do it, Lieutenant, and from here on out don't slow yourself down waiting to get my permission. You're authorized to use all available plainclothes personnel. Cancel days off if you need to."

"I'm not used to having so much latitude, Chief."

"Well, get used to it, Sal."

Molina grinned. "That's not going to be a problem."

"Where's that background information on the ambassador I asked for?"

"We've got a file of newspaper clips that give a résumé version of Terrell's military career and diplomatic appointments, but not much else."

"What were his major duty assignments after Vietnam?"

"He attended the War College, did an extended tour at the Pentagon in the Defense Intelligence Agency, then assumed command of the School of the Americas at Fort Benning, Georgia. After getting his first star he served as deputy commander for army intelligence. In his final posting as a major general he headed up the army's intelligence and security command."

Andy Baca had found a link to army intelligence through Fred Brown, and now Sal Molina added another connection that pointed in the same direction.

"Thanks for the update, Lieutenant," Kerney said. "Keep me informed."

Molina nodded. "Thanks for getting us some help, Chief. I'll give Sloan the word."

Sal left to call Sloan. Kerney put his head against the chair back, stared at the ceiling, and wondered what set of circumstances might tie Elaine Applewhite to Hamilton Lowell Terrell and his murdered wife.

Fred Browning stood in his office at a west-side Albuquerque computer-chip production plant looking at the copy of the photograph Andy Baca had faxed to him. The woman wasn't particularly attractive, but then most female FBI agents and police officers Browning had known over the years didn't look anything like the actresses who played cop parts in movies and on television. He called Tim Ingram and said he was on the way.

"I'm leaving work a little early," Tim said. "Why don't you do the same? Come by the house and I'll buy you a drink."

"It's a deal," Browning said.

In the year since Tim Ingram's arrival in Albuquerque a strong friendship had developed between the two men. Both were divorced, and they spent a lot of free time together, meeting for after-work drinks, taking off for day-long fishing trips on the weekends, and frequently working on state chapter business for the Society of Professional Corporate Security Executives.

Tim had come west from a job with a Virginia high-tech think tank to take over as chief of security for a Department of Defense contractor that did top secret research and development at Kirtland Air Force Base. His job required him to live on the base and he'd been given a choice field-grade officer's housing unit.

A guy with a casual style who made friends easily, Tim liked to throw parties and entertain. Fred had been his guest many times, usually sitting in at a regular Thursday-night poker game, or hanging out on Sunday afternoons at the cookouts Tim organized during the NFL season.

Adjacent to the Albuquerque International Sunport, Kirtland began as a World War Two bomber training facility. After the war, part of the Los Alamos atomic bomb project moved to the base, and over the next fifty-odd years, Kirtland grew into a high-security facility for the storage of nuclear warheads and cold-war weapons development and testing.

Sandia National Laboratory, an Energy Department facility, was housed on the base along with an Air Force Test and Evaluation Center and a Space Technology Center. Although much of the work on the post remained secret, the development of satellite and computer-based systems for verifying arms-treaty nuclear-weapons reduction had received a great deal of press attention over the last few years.

Construction around the main gate to the base slowed Browning's entry. He waited patiently for traffic to move, thinking if anyone could confirm the identity of the FBI special agent as a military officer, Tim Ingram could. Tim had spent countless hours during his years back east in Beltway meetings with defense intelligence types, and he loved to tell funny stories about their ineptitude and dull wits. He particularly disliked pedantic military analysts and knee-jerk FBI bureaucrats.

The air-police guard stopped him as he rolled up to the checkpoint, consulted his clipboard, scanned Browning's driver's license, and waved him through. He drove toward the officers' housing area wondering why Andy Baca, who hadn't told him much, wanted an ID check on an FBI agent.

Maybe it was tied to the murder of the ambassador's wife up in Santa Fe. But then again, New Mexico was home to two national laboratories, several high-security military installations, and dozens of defense contractors engaged in sensitive government work. There was always the possibility that one government spy shop or another had some big investigation going on. Any good cop would want to learn what he could about the people who came snooping around in his backyard.

He parked at the curb and rang the bell. Tim opened up right away.

"Hey," Browning said.

Ingram smiled. About five eight, Tim had a boyish face, curly light brown hair, and the trim frame of a middleweight boxer.

"I'm just about to make myself a drink," Ingram said. "It's been a hell of a week so far. Take off your jacket and join me."

"Gladly," Browning replied, pulling off his suit coat.

In the kitchen he watched Tim pour generous double shots of his favorite whiskey into tumblers.

"So, you've got a friend who wants some back-door information on a fed," Tim said with a chuckle and a shake of his head. He handed Browning a glass and led him into the living room. "That's pretty cheeky, but you've got to love it. Anybody willing to risk stepping on a few FBI toes must be a good guy."

"I thought you'd get a kick out of it," Browning replied.

"What got his antenna up?" Ingram asked as he settled into an easy chair.

"He's got good instincts," Browning said. He sat across from Ingram and put his drink on the coffee table.

"How did he come to tap into you as a source?"

"We go way back," Browning replied. "I tried to pitch him to join the society a few months ago. Told him about the membership and what the organization does. He remembered enough to think I might be able to help."

"Sounds like he's pretty sharp."

"He is."

"If the feds aren't playing straight, he's got a right to know. I'm guessing it's about the ex-ambassador's wife who got iced up in Santa Fe."

"That was my guess too."

Ingram made a face. "Those damn prima donnas. Somebody ought to tell the Bureau we don't have a national police force in this country—thank God. I'd love to know what he's got cooking. I bet it would make a great story. Did your pal give you any specifics at all?"

"Nope, he just asked for a records search of FBI agents who belong to the society. When this agent's name didn't pop up, he asked me to expand the search to all members with the same first name."

"Well, let's see the picture."

Browning reached for his coat jacket, fished out the fax, and handed it over.

"This isn't Major Elaine Cornell," Ingram said.

"You're sure?"

"Positive," Ingram replied snapping a finger against the fax paper. "Compared to Cornell this woman looks halfway decent. I think the major is one of the 'don't ask, don't tell' soldiers."

"Good enough," Browning said, retrieving the fax.

"Stay for dinner." Ingram picked up the cordless phone from the end table and tossed it to Browning. "Call your friend with the news while I get the grill cranked up. You like your steak medium rare, right?"

"Hey, you don't have to feed me," Browning said.

"No bother, amigo," Tim said as he made his way to the kitchen. "Besides, I need some company."

After a few more drinks, a steak and potatoes dinner, and an hour of laid-back conversation, Browning left. Ingram took his cordless phone into the study, used the redial key to access the number Browning had called, and identified its location using a software program on his laptop computer. Then Special Agent Ingram called Charlie Perry and gave him the news.

"What's the state police chief mucking around in this for?" Perry grumbled.

"Not my problem, Charlie. You can tell Applewhite—who in hell came up with that name?—that her cover is intact. Make sure you put a lid on this so it doesn't spread any further."

"Yeah, sure," Perry said. "I know what to do."

Ingram's next call went to the executive who managed the operations of the computer-chip facility. "At the end of the week, downsize Fred Browning," he said. "In the meantime keep him completely out of the loop."

"He doesn't know anything in the first place," the man replied. "Care to tell me why?"

"Double up on production security and be prepared for a complete facility shakedown next week."

"I still need a reason."

"Make one up."

"He'll put up a stink about it."

"Not if you give him a generous severance package *and* recommend him for a new job with another company," Ingram said. "I'll get back to you with the specifics."

"Do we have a leak?"

"Unknown at this time," Ingram answered. "Your new security chief will report to you on Monday. Assessing any security breach will be his first assignment."

"And who exactly is that person going to be?"

"Someone with impeccable credentials."

Ingram's last call of the evening went to a Silicon Valley company vice president. He hung up after making sure Fred Browning would have a job in California with more money and greater responsibilities, at least for a while. That should keep Browning from pondering too carefully the events of the week or jumping to conclusions.

If not, stronger arrangements might be necessary.

Kerney stayed in his office well past quitting time, half expecting to get a phone call summoning him to city hall to explain his decision to pull Officer Herrera off the streets. According to Helen Muiz, Herrera had stormed out of police headquarters at the end of his shift after receiving his transfer papers, saying he had no desire to be a paper shuffler or a desk jockey. She gave Kerney five-to-one odds that Cloudy had gone directly to his uncle, the city councilman, to complain. So far, there had been no repercussions, but that could change quickly.

His meeting with Captain Larry Otero had gone better than expected, and Helen was typing up the promotion order and the personnel paperwork for Kerney's new deputy chief.

Before leaving his office she predicted the deep-freeze reception Kerney had received as chief was about to thaw rapidly. She gave him twenty-to-one odds on it, along with a big smile of approval.

Ten minutes into his talk with Otero, Kerney knew he'd found his second-in-command. The captain was smart, level headed, and a good fit with his temperament and management style. Otero agreed not only to take over supervision of day-to-day department operations, but also to spearhead the completion of the five-year strategic plan that had been left hanging by the last administration.

Andy Baca's call to report that Special Agent Applewhite wasn't an army intelligence officer had left Kerney questioning whether he'd been paranoid or just way off the mark about his gut reaction to the woman.

He still felt uneasy. While he had no reason to doubt the national security implications of the case, he found it hard to understand why Applewhite had fed him a line about her State Department assignment. Kerney knew he would never be given all the facts or reasons, regardless of the outcome, and that galled him.

He was equally bothered by his thirty-year-old recollections of Hamilton Lowell Terrell, aka the Snake, Kerney's first in-country commander. He had not been a man to be trusted.

Under Terrell's command routine patrols were reported as inserts into enemy territory, every skirmish became a major firefight, any setbacks in field operations were blamed on the attached ARVN units, and body counts were always inflated. But old grievances about Terrell probably had no bearing on the present situation.

Because he saw no point to it, Kerney had opted out of attending a task-force debriefing session currently in progress. He already knew that Terjo was still missing and that the special agent sent to Ramah had yet to locate or interview Proctor Straley's ranch manager, Scott Gatlin, alleged to be the third of Phyllis Terrell's recent lovers. He also knew that Sal Molina hadn't been allowed anywhere near Proctor Straley or his daughter Susan, who were sequestered in a Santa Fe hotel suite with FBI bodyguards.

Meanwhile, Detective Bobby Sloan and the three agents on loan from Andy Baca were wading knee-deep through interviews in the Father Mitchell slaying with nothing substantial to report.

Kerney leaned back in his desk chair and looked around the stark office. He'd done nothing to decorate it since moving in, and he wasn't inclined to hang up framed certificates, plaques, or other memorabilia from his law enforcement career as most other police chiefs did. He'd read recently that such a "trophy wall" was standard equipment for corporate VIPs and Capitol Hill politicians.

Now that he was a bigwig, maybe he should get with the program. If nothing else, it would spark some amusing sarcasm from Helen Muiz. And Sara would never let him hear the end of it, he thought with a smile.

Sara was coming in from Fort Leavenworth this weekend. After they toured the land in Galisteo that was up for sale, maybe she'd help him pick out a few prints he could have framed for the office.

Because of his hectic week and the intensity of her class schedule at the U.S. Army Command and General Staff College, he hadn't spoken to her for days. He missed the sound of her voice, the updates about the progress of her pregnancy, and all their exciting talk about building a home and starting a family.

With Larry Otero on board as deputy chief, unless something major broke in the homicide cases, the weekend would be his to spend with his bride.

He'd married Sara less than a year ago, soon after her return from a tour of duty in Korea, where she'd been decorated and promoted for crushing a North Korean assassination plot against the visiting secretary of state.

Although he saw her infrequently, she'd made Kerney feel far happier about his life than he ever could have imagined. The considerable wealth he'd recently inherited from the proceeds of Erma Fergurson's land bequest paled in comparison to the rich texture of his relationship with Sara. He couldn't imagine loving someone other than smart, sexy, feisty Lieutenant Colonel Sara Brannon.

He left his office, signed the paperwork for Otero's promotion Helen had waiting for him on her desk, said good-night, and drove to his cramped quarters, thinking it was time to get serious about building a new house.

The top-floor presidential suite at the Hotel San Marcos consisted of a sitting room, bedroom with master bath, fully equipped and stocked galley kitchen, and study. Furnished with high-quality reproductions of Spanish Colonial pieces and decorated with original lithographs of well-known New Mexico artists, it had corner fireplaces in each room, hand-troweled plaster walls, and Mexican tile accents in the kitchen and bath.

Ambassador Hamilton Lowell Terrell stood gazing out the sitting-room window with his back to Charlie Perry. The narrow street was empty of foot traffic and only a few cars remained parked at the curbs. From his vantage point he looked down on a line of flat-roofed buildings that housed retail shops, all closed for the night. At the corner of the block rose a three-story building. It had two rows of old-fashioned wood sash windows evenly spaced above the ground floor, some with broken glass, others with damaged screens. Although two stores, a gift shop, and a boutique operated at street level, the rest of the building looked empty and unused.

"You're quite certain everything is set?" Terrell asked, turning to face Perry, who stood in the galley kitchen stirring sugar into a freshly poured cup of coffee.

"We should be able to wrap it up tomorrow," Perry said as he dropped the spoon into the sink.

Terrell moved to the kitchen, rinsed and dried the spoon, and put it in the proper drawer. "I don't like this probing by the local authorities into Applewhite's cover."

"That has been contained," Perry said, moving away from Terrell.

"It better be," Terrell said as he dried his hands. "Is Proctor Straley on board?"

Perry sat on the couch facing the fireplace where piñon and cedar logs crackled in a warm blaze, and sipped his coffee. "Along with his daughter Susan. They know about the affair between your wife and Straley's ranch manager. Mrs. Terrell made no effort to hide it, and both were well aware of Mrs. Terrell's appetites."

"Give me the specifics," Terrell said.

"As we discussed, you'll be the grieving husband."

Terrell stared at Perry, a cocky young man he didn't much like. "I know my role. What about the preparations for Scott Gatlin, the ranch manager?" he said.

"It's better if you don't know, Ambassador."

Terrell walked to the fireplace and warmed his hands. "Don't presume to coddle me, Agent Perry."

Perry's smile vanished. "Gatlin has been on vacation, fortunately traveling alone with no set agenda. He's due to return late tonight. He'll be intercepted as he arrives, taken to Gallup to be interviewed, and then released. He'll go home, get drunk, write a suicide note confessing to the killing, and put a bullet in his head."

"Is there anyone staying at the Straley ranch?"

"No, and there aren't any nearby neighbors."

"How will you make the confession stand up?"

"Threatening letters from Gatlin to your wife, vowing to kill her if he couldn't have her, were recovered by the FBI last night at her residence. A packet of letters written by Mrs. Terrell to Gatlin demanding that he stop harassing her will be found among his personal effects. Gatlin will be portrayed as a fixated, mentally ill stalker who killed his ex-lover."

"Straley isn't a stupid man," Terrell said, "and my sister-in-law has never liked me. Are you sure this will work?"

"Both of them know Gatlin as a lady's man with a temper and a jealous streak. With the proof we'll provide there should be no reason for them not to buy it."

"Which is?" Terrell demanded.

"That Gatlin raped your wife the night of her murder. If necessary, we'll produce witnesses who saw him in Santa Fe before the crimes were committed."

Terrell nodded. "I hope this Kerney fellow is as inept as you say he is."

Perry snickered. "Kerney? Absolutely."

"I've read Kerney's background file, Agent Perry. His credentials as an investigator are strong, and he's made some impressive arrests over the years."

"I've worked with him before, Ambassador. Believe me, he's a loose cannon. Besides that, he's running a department filled with shit-for-brains detectives."

"I don't think Chief Kerney remembers I was his commanding officer for a time in Vietnam."

"I didn't know that," Perry said.

"You didn't serve in the military, did you, Perry?"

"No, sir."

"Too bad. Ben Franklin once said that there is no such thing as a 'little enemy.' The politicians didn't keep that in mind when we fought in Vietnam. Don't make the same mistake with Chief Kerney, Agent Perry."

"I won't. We'll continue monitoring the situation."

"Very good. See that you do."

Perry left and Terrell moved to the writing desk, turning his attention to funeral arrangements. He thought about Phyllis as he began making a list: private services at the cathedral, burial at the national cemetery, invitations limited to a small group of government officials and the immediate family.

Aware of Phyllis's loose reputation, he'd married her anyway, because it allowed him access to Proctor Straley's sphere of considerable influence. At the time Straley had almost swooned with delight to see his tramp daughter finally so well wed. The great sex she gave Terrell until the marriage soured had been an enjoyable bonus.

Phyllis would be alive today, if she hadn't been so damn nosey.

He paused and looked at his list. A letter of condolence to Proctor Straley from the President was in order. He made a note to call the White House in the morning.

Chapter 5

K erney sat in an office chair and watched the smile on William Demora's face fade as he settled behind his large executive desk and tidied an already neatly stacked set of documents. Last night, without giving a reason, the city manager had called Kerney at home and asked for an early morning meeting. And it was very early indeed; workers at city hall weren't due to show up for another hour.

The city offices were housed in an old school building a block from the plaza. In spite of extensive renovations the wide hallways, far wider than a modern office building would allow for, made it feel like a place for junior high students, not city bureaucrats. Kerney could remember the days when noisy, boisterous kids spilled out of the school to spend lunch hour on the plaza.

"Aside from carrying out the mayor's goals," Demora said, weighing his words carefully, "my job, as I see it, is to act as a buffer between my department heads and members of the city council. In other words, to keep politics from interfering with our daily operations. But I can't always shield my people from controversy. Especially if I find myself caught unaware."

"What's come up?" Kerney asked, maintaining a neutral tone.

Demora ran a hand over his closely cropped salt-and-pepper beard. "The issue of your appointment of Captain Otero as deputy chief has raised some concern among several council members."

It wasn't the issue Kerney expected, but he held back his surprise and stayed silent.

"I thought we had an understanding that you'd run key appointments through my office first," Demora said.

"No," Kerney said evenly. "The understanding was that I would have full authority on all personnel matters and would keep you advised in a timely fashion."

"So why am I placed in the position of learning about Otero's promotion secondhand through the grapevine?"

Kerney checked his watch. "Otero's promotion orders were cut less than twelve hours ago, after city hall closed for the day. You would have gotten a call from me in about an hour. But to answer your question more specifically, the reason you heard about it through the grapevine is because I have inherited a department filled with people who are accustomed to undercutting the chain of command whenever it suits their purpose to do so. Who are the unhappy council members?"

"You needn't concern yourself with them," Demora replied. "I'll deal with that problem. But surely you understand that the police officers' union is a political action group. You can't expect them not to use their influence to raise issues, especially with several strong union supporters on the council."

"Was the issue raised by the union?"

"Yes. They feel that Otero's appointment is a step backward."

Kerney chose his words carefully. "Although the contract gives the union no voice in management issues, I'd be happy to meet with them here in your office to address their concerns."

"I don't think we should open that door to the union," Demora said quickly. "But I . . . The mayor does expect you to concentrate on building employee morale. Your decision to promote Otero seems to be having the opposite effect."

"It's my highest priority," Kerney said. "Every police department needs good morale to do its job of protecting the public and upholding the law."

"How you get to that goal is important, Chief," Demora said smoothly. "Developing constructive and informed input from employees makes them feel empowered."

"Exactly how does the union view Otero?" Kerney asked, trying to move Demora away from his favorite team-building theory of management.

"He's seen as abrasive, argumentative, and authoritarian."

"Is that your reading of the man?"

"I've found him to be confrontational upon occasion. Unnecessarily so."

Kerney thought back to the purged documents about Officer Herrera that Helen Muiz had saved from destruction. None of Otero's memos had showed evidence of distribution outside the department. Had Demora been behind the cleansing of Herrera's personnel jacket and the decision to destroy Otero's career? Captains not slated for promotions were frequently buried in technical-duty slots, far away from the operational-command assignments that were crucial for advancement. Perhaps Demora had assumed Kerney would overlook Otero because of his career-ending posting.

Kerney decided to push the issue. "Can you give me more details?"

Demora ran a hand over a horseshoe-shaped bald spot. "I'd rather not get into specifics, but it was a situation requiring subtle handling, and Otero failed to realize that."

"I see."

"It's not too late to withdraw Otero's appointment. Doing so could win you some allies on the city council."

"Allies would be nice to have," Kerney said. "But caving in to what could be perceived as union pressure might not be wise. When the union contract comes up for renegotiation, they'll be clamoring for a voice in management."

Demora nodded vigorously. "Yes, of course, you're exactly right. Do you have an alternative suggestion?"

"Otero is eligible for retirement in sixty days. If he fails to do a competent job or conduct himself professionally, I'll ask him to put in his papers and retire."

Demora smiled with pursed lips. "Very well. Sixty days, then, and you'll keep me advised of his performance."

"Of course," Kerney said. "And you'll advise me if any additional concerns are lodged about his promotion?"

"Absolutely," Demora replied. His smile widened as he showed some teeth. "It's essential that the two of us maintain a free-flowing communication. There's no need to hold anything back. With that in mind I do want Otero carefully supervised."

"That won't be a problem."

Demora nodded. "I hope not. Now, fill me in on the murder investigations so I can brief the mayor. This isn't the kind of national exposure Santa Fe needs."

"It certainly isn't," Kerney said, holding back on the somewhat snide thought that criminals really should be more sensitive to the chamber-of-commerce vision of a picture-perfect retirement and playground community for the well-to-do and outright rich. The murder of a prominent citizen was unseemly, only served to tarnish the city's image, and caused hand wringing for both the boosters and the local politicians.

He forced down his anger at having his first major decision as chief challenged for the sake of petty politics, and began to explain the status of the investigations.

Growing up poor in Mexico, Ignacio Terjo had learned the hard way the importance of money. His first border crossing into America had driven the point home even more thoroughly. After arriving in Santa Fe he'd gone hungry and had slept under a bridge, covered only by newspapers and cardboard, until he found his way to a homeless shelter. Vowing never to be so needy again, Terjo now kept two hundred dollars sewn in the inside lining of his winter coat or tucked into the watch pocket of his jeans during warm weather.

Wary about his false identity, Ignacio had avoided becoming too friendly with the Mexican nationals who lived on the south side of the city, fearing he might be recognized. Instead, he'd gotten to know some of the locals, found his way to a good job with Mrs. Terrell, and met Rebecca. Life had been good for a while, and now it wasn't anymore.

Released from the county jail, he'd walked to the outlet mall near the Interstate and rented a room for the night at a nearby motel, figuring the police wouldn't look for him there. After a quick trip to the food court at the mall, he'd locked himself inside the room, passed the time watching a Spanish television station, and plotted his escape from Santa Fe. He would go to Tucson where he could blend in easily, find work, and then call Rebecca to tell her that he was all right.

To do it he needed to get to his truck, which was parked at the stables. A city bus stopped at the mall soon after it opened. He would ride the bus downtown, walk from there to the stables, and, if the police weren't there watching, drive away.

He checked the clock on the bedside table. The bus wasn't due to arrive for another thirty minutes.

Outside his room he heard the sound of a car. It started briefly, sputtered, and then died. Again and again the engine failed to catch. He went to the window, pulled back the curtain, peeked out, and saw a woman bent over the car's engine compartment. Before he could release the curtain she turned, saw him, and gestured for him to come outside.

Terjo shook his head.

The woman stepped to the window and knocked on the glass. Terjo studied her. She looked frustrated and distressed. He slid the window open.

"Do you know anything about cars?" the woman asked.

"Yes, a little," Terjo replied.

"Could you please see if you can get it started for me? Please?"

Terjo looked around at the parking lot before replying. He didn't see any police. "Okay."

He unlocked the door and it slammed into his face, knocking him backward. The woman and a man with a pistol forced him face-down on the carpet, handcuffed him, and searched him before yanking him to a sitting position.

Charlie Perry cocked his weapon and put the barrel an inch away from Terjo's right eye. "You've got one minute to tell me who Phyllis Terrell had sex with the night she was murdered."

"And if I do?" Terjo asked, stammering to get the words out.

"You go home to Mexico and you live," Perry said. "But if you ever come back to this country, you die, Ignacio."

"I'm Santiago, not Ignacio."

"Drop the game," Perry snapped. "You're wasting time."

"What about Rebecca and my daughter? I need to see them, *por favor*."

Perry pushed the barrel against Terjo's eyeball. "That's not an option. Maybe we'll have the Mexico authorities throw you in prison as a drug smuggler. Now you have three choices. Pick one."

Terjo pulled his head back and looked through watery eyes at the woman, who stared at him without expression. "His name is Randall Stewart. He lives up the hill from Mrs. Terrell, behind Alexandra Lawton's house. He was with her the last time I saw the *señora* alive. She asked me not to say anything."

"You're a good boy, Ignacio," Perry said as he released the hammer to his weapon and turned to the woman. "Get him out of here."

Agent Applewhite nodded and pulled Terjo to his feet.

"Don't even think about killing him," Perry added.

Applewhite smiled wickedly and marched Terjo out the door.

*   *   *

At the office Kerney worked his way slowly through a large group of smiling officers and civilian employees who'd gathered for an informal celebration of Larry Otero's promotion. Folks who'd been reserved, distant, or hesitant with Kerney praised his selection. Even two senior captains who'd been passed over for the appointment seemed pleased, as did several sergeants and lieutenants who could now think seriously about the possibility of moving up in rank. But the officers active in the police union were conspicuous by their absence.

Helen had bought a bouquet of flowers that sat on the vacant secretary's desk outside Otero's new office. She'd had a metallic silver banner hung above the door that read in bold letters, CONGRATULATIONS. A large coffeepot and pastries arranged on platters filled an office desk that had been covered with a tablecloth.

With his wife and two adolescent children next to him—a gangly, beanpole boy and an attractive, serious-looking girl—Larry Otero stood in the middle of the room surrounded by well-wishers, his face flushed with quiet pleasure. Otero's wife, a petite woman with a toothy smile, held a camera with a flash attachment in her hand.

Kerney stepped over to Otero, who interrupted the flow of conversation to introduce Kerney to his family.

"Will you do the honors, Chief?" Larry asked as he held out a double set of three stars, denoting his new rank.

"With pleasure," Kerney said. He pinned the stars on Otero's collar while Larry's wife took pictures, and the room broke into applause.

After more picture-taking and small talk, the event ended as off-duty personnel from the graveyard shift who'd stayed over for the party went home and the day-shift workers scattered. When Otero's wife left to take the kids to school and go to work, Kerney invited Larry into his office and sat with him at the conference table.

"Did you catch any flak out of city hall about my appointment?" Otero asked uneasily.

"None at all," Kerney said, unwilling to start Otero off in his new job on a negative note.

A smile erased a slight tightness at the corners of Otero's mouth and he relaxed in his chair. His eyes seemed to invite further discussion, but he let the topic slide.

"Are you ready for your marching orders?" Kerney asked.

Otero's smiled widened and he nodded. "Whenever you are, Chief."

"Let's get to it," Kerney said, reaching for the paperwork he'd prepared for Otero.

Randall Stewart's hands were cold and clammy, and a persistent impulse to wash them wouldn't go away. Because he was locked in a room at the National Guard armory, handcuffed with his arms between the slats of a straight-backed chair, sitting in the middle of a room, he couldn't do that. Instead, he waited for the special agent to come back into view.

For twenty minutes Stewart had been bombarded with questions. But now the agent constantly circled around the chair, silently scrutinizing him. Stewart felt trapped and vulnerable.

Charlie Perry had intercepted Stewart as he'd parked his shiny new BMW in front of his stock brokerage office. Tall and slim with a full head of curly dark hair, Stewart was at least fifteen years younger than Phyllis Terrell. Perry disliked the man instantly. His carefully tailored, expensive suit, his fancy car, the premium leather attaché case he carried, the smug look on his face when Perry approached him, all combined to piss Charlie off.

"Phyllis never talked to you about political matters?" Perry asked, stopping behind Stewart's chair, out of sight.

"Never," Stewart replied craning his neck in a futile attempt to look at the agent.

"What about the ambassador?" Perry asked. "Did she talk about him?"

"Only to say she was glad the divorce was going through."

"What about his work?"

"She didn't talk about that."

"Never?"

"I knew he was on some sort of a government trade mission, that's all."

"Did she tell you about the trade mission?"

"No."

Perry stepped into Stewart's view. "Did you ever have any political or philosophical discussions with her?"

"That wasn't the focus of our relationship."

"She didn't seem to care if people knew about her other lovers. Why the secrecy when it came to you?"

"Because we were neighbors, and I didn't want my wife to find out about it. Nor did she."

"And Terjo? Why was he asked to keep the secret?"

"Because he'd worked for my wife upon occasion, and he knew both of us. And my wife was friendly with Phyllis."

"Did you pay him for his silence?"

"I didn't, no. Phyllis may have, but I doubt it. Terjo seemed willing to treat it as none of his business."

"Did Phyllis ever ask you to do any favors for her?"

"Like what?" Stewart asked.

"You tell me," Perry replied.

The agent had clamped the handcuffs painfully tight around Stewart's wrists. "You can't keep me handcuffed like this," he said.

Perry smiled devilishly and leaned close to Stewart. "Does it hurt, Randall?"

"It's a violation of my rights."

"You've got no rights," Perry said. "I could blow your fucking brains out and probably get a personal commendation from the White House. You were in Phyllis Terrell's pants the night she was murdered. That makes you murder suspect number one. As far as I'm concerned you're a stone-cold killer."

"I didn't kill her. Listen, it was just sex, like I told you. There was nothing else to it."

Perry guffawed. "Or maybe she was gonna cut you off, and you didn't like the idea of losing out on some great pussy."

"That's not true."

Perry circled behind Stewart again and patted him on the shoulder. "You know," he said gently, "I want to believe you, Randall. Now, let's try again: Did Phyllis give you anything to hold for her? Documents? Papers? Anything like that?"

"No, nothing. She asked me to mail a letter at the post office the next morning on my way to work, which I did."

"What kind of letter?"

"A manila envelope."

"Who was it addressed to?"

"She didn't say."

"You didn't look at the address?"

"I checked it to make sure I dropped it in the right drive-up box outside the post office. It had a local address."

"What was the address?"

"I don't remember exactly. Somebody at the College of Santa Fe, but I don't remember who."

Perry remained behind Stewart to hide the look of annoyance on his face. He kept his tone even. "Did Phyllis mention the contents of the envelope?"

"No, she just said she wanted to make sure it didn't sit in her mailbox, because she was going out of town and she'd put a hold on her mail delivery until she got back."

Perry patted Stewart's shoulder one more time and uncuffed him.

Randall pulled his arms through the slats, rubbed his wrists, and glared angrily at the agent when he stepped into view. "You can't treat people this way," he said.

"Is that a threat, Randall?"

Stewart looked away and said nothing.

Perry clamped a hand around Stewart's neck. "If you talk to the media, go to the police, see an attorney, or divulge this conversation to anyone, it will be denied and you'll be arrested and charged with conspiracy to commit treason," Agent Perry said.

"This isn't a police state," Stewart sputtered, "and I'm not a traitor or a criminal."

Perry sneered. "I know that. But believe me, I'll use all available resources to make everybody, including your mother, your wife, and your children think you are. And when I'm finished, you won't have a job, a family, or a life that's worth squat. Do I make myself clear?"

"I can't believe this is happening to me," Stewart said.

"It could've been a lot worse," Charlie replied, lifting Randall Stewart to his feet.

"I need the bathroom," Stewart said, feeling a wetness in his underwear.

"First make and sign a voluntary statement," Perry said, gesturing at a gray army-issue table against the wall. He looked down at the spreading stain at Stewart's crotch. "Then you can tidy up before you go back to the office."

Two solid hours of discussion passed before Larry Otero left to spend the rest of the morning moving into his new office. Kerney turned his attention to the updated field notes on the murder investigations. Sal Molina had worked his people hard, but not much had been accomplished. In spite of the dozens of field interviews no suspects had emerged in either killing. Terjo was still missing, Father Mitchell's briefcase hadn't been found, and the FBI had refused Molina's request to interview Ambassador Terrell, Proctor Straley, and his daughter Susan.

The corporate information about APT Performa that Helen had promised to get yesterday afternoon had finally arrived this morning. He paged through the company's annual report and learned that the firm produced civilian computer security programs using technology originally developed at Sandia and Los Alamos National Laboratories for nuclear-disarmament monitoring. That could mean the company created firewall protection systems, cyber-snooping programs, or some other rarefied software designed to safe-guard network data.

How APT Performa figured into Ambassador Terrell's trade mission—if it did at all—remained an unanswered question. Maybe Trade Source Venture International, APT Performa's parent company, had flown Terrell back from South America on its corporate jet purely out of compassion for the ambassador's loss. Or because it was just good business sense to do a favor for a high-ranking government official. A reasonable person would figure it was some combination of the two and let it go at that. But how would that explain the two CIA types who got off the jet with Terrell at the airport and immediately cleaned out the crime scene?

Kerney set the material aside and paged through the graveyard-shift commander's report. Before dawn, patrol officers had noticed unmarked FBI vehicles assigned to the task force stopping at various motels along the Cerrillos Road corridor. The officers had queried their commander asking if a wanted-person sweep was under way. After checking with Lieutenant Molina the commander had ordered his officers not to provide any assistance.

Kerney called Sal Molina's extension, got him on the line, and asked for a briefing.

"I talked to Special Agent Perry about it, Chief," Molina said. "He had his agents out looking for Terjo."

"Did you suggest to Perry that this is a joint operation?"

"Yeah, I did. I asked him to team up the agents with the gang-unit detectives who were working the south-side barrios. Perry didn't want to do it."

"Why didn't you call me?"

"There didn't seem any point, Chief. I read him out about it, and he told me he was shutting the search down. I asked to be alerted if any officers spotted his agents again, but apparently he meant what he said."

"Or he'd already found Terjo."

"Shit, I should have thought of that."

"Don't worry about it. If he has Terjo, we couldn't have taken action anyway."

"Can I say something, Chief?"

"Go ahead," Kerney said.

"As far as I'm concerned, you picked the right man to be your deputy."

"I'm glad you feel that way."

Kerney disconnected and Helen buzzed him on the intercom to announce that Special Agent Perry was waiting outside. Perry came in, glanced around the unadorned office, and gave Kerney a wiseass smile.

"Going for the spare, clean look, Kerney?" he asked. "Or have you signed on as chief for the short tour? Maybe all that money you inherited has given you second thoughts about staying on the job for very long."

Perry swung a chair out from the conference table and sat. Kerney stayed put behind his desk.

"You had everybody on your team out last night looking for Terjo," Kerney said.

"Didn't I tell you about it? Sorry about that. It must have slipped my mind. Anyway, your Lieutenant Molina didn't seem to want the help, so we gave it up."

"You didn't find Terjo?"

Perry shrugged. "No. Anyway, Terjo isn't an issue anymore. We've closed the case."

"How did you manage to do that?"

"Scott Gatlin, Proctor Straley's ranch manager, wrote out a confession and committed suicide last night."

"Really?" Kerney said. "What else do you have besides the confession of a dead man?"

"Letters that Terrell wrote Gatlin asking him to stop harassing her. Letters Gatlin wrote to Terrell threatening to kill her if she didn't stop sleeping around. Witness reports that he'd come up to Santa Fe a number of times and stalked Terrell."

"So the jealous lover stalks and kills the object of his desire," Kerney said. "Very interesting. Any physical proof?"

"We sent some of the semen stains and hair samples your people collected at the Terrell crime scene to our lab. They'll run a DNA comparison with samples from Gatlin. We should have preliminary results this afternoon. I've asked for a quick turnaround."

"Whatever happened to the concerns about national security?"

"Apparently it isn't an issue, Kerney. But we'll continue to pursue that possibility for a while longer."

"Care to tell me how?" Kerney asked.

Perry stared at the four stars on Kerney's collars and tried not to smirk at the half-assed, over-the-hill investigator with a bum leg who'd cozied up to the local politicians and gotten himself appointed chief.

"You don't really need to know," he finally said. "But I'll be in town with Agent Applewhite for a while longer. We'll touch base with you if we require any assistance."

"Where is Agent Applewhite?" Kerney asked. "I haven't seen much of her."

"She's busy. Just give your people the news that they can close the Terrell case, and pass on my thanks for their cooperation."

"I'll sure do that." Kerney stood up and reached for his hat. "Where's Gatlin's body?"

"In Ramah."

"Let's go see."

Perry laughed. "Don't waste your time."

"It's no bother." Kerney put on his hat and stepped to the front of his desk. "You can ride with me."

"There is nothing for you to do there," Perry said. "Don't start playing games with me and going behind my back, like you did with the Catron County militia."

"Why don't you want me to see Gatlin's body, Charlie?"

"Wise up, Kerney, or you'll get burned, big time."

"Don't you think this is all too quick and easy?"

Perry stood up and leaned in close to Kerney. "I don't like you, never have. But I'll say this once and you'd better listen: This time you could lose a lot more than that shitty little seasonal job you had with the Forest Service."

Kerney tossed his hat on the desk. "It's been a pleasure working with you again, Charlie."

"Yeah, right," Perry said. He dropped a folded paper on the conference table. "That's a copy of the official FBI statement to the press. I'm releasing it in an hour. Want to be there?"

"I'll pass," Kerney said. "It's your party. Have a good time."

Sal Molina had gone back out in the field. Kerney got him on the radio and told him the Terrell case had been closed by the FBI. Molina wanted specifics.

"Not over the radio," Kerney said. "We can hook up later. Go to Perry's press conference. It starts in an hour. That way you'll know what I know."

"Ten-four."

Kerney read over the graveyard report that noted the last motel the agents had been seen at during their early-morning search for Terjo on Cerrillos Road. He got in his car and started checking the remaining motels from that point on along the strip, looking for Terjo.

February had suddenly turned unseasonably warm and the snowpack on the mountains was fast disappearing, along with the tourists who had traveled north to Taos looking for better skiing conditions.

Between stops Kerney wondered what was keeping Agent Applewhite so busy. She hadn't coordinated anything, as far as he could tell. Why would she be staying on in Santa Fe with Charlie Perry when she was supposed to be returning to Taos to resume an interrupted vacation with her husband? He wondered if it would be worth his time to try to get a line on the husband.

His last stop was at a motel near an outlet mall. He parked and tried to talk himself into taking Charlie Perry's advice and dropping the whole mess. He stared at the mall, and tried to think of other things.

Surrounded by acres of parking, the mall had a facade that combined elements of an oversized northern New Mexico hacienda with what appeared to be medieval castle battlements. The building consisted of retail shops around a large open-air courtyard, which shoppers entered through an enormous gate decorated with stylized buffalos, bracketed by two mock watchtower turrets. The watchtower motif continued around the perimeter of the structure, jutting up at different elevations. The walls had been stuccoed in two different colors, one of which, ugly mustard, reminded Kerney of dirty diapers.

The thought of dirty diapers made Kerney smile. Although it still felt unreal, in a little more than six months he would become a father. With Sara far away and seeing her so infrequently, to Kerney the relationship had felt more like a passionate love affair than a marriage. The baby would change all that, but Kerney wasn't sure how. Of course, Sara would return to active duty after her maternity leave, but then what? She was exploring the possibility of landing an assignment in New Mexico after finishing up at the Command and General Staff College. But there was no guarantee she could swing it.

The idea that his wife could be stationed far away at an army post with their child while he stayed behind in Santa Fe held no appeal.

Through no fault of his own Kerney had missed out on raising one child, a son born to his college sweetheart, Isabel Istee, who'd kept the birth a secret from him for over twenty-five years.

While Kerney was in Vietnam as an infantry lieutenant, Isabel had returned to the Mescalero reservation in the Sacramento Mountains to give birth and raise her son as a single parent. She lived there still, as did her son Clayton, who was a tribal police officer, a husband, and the father of two small children.

The recent shock of discovering that he was both an instant father and grandfather still stunned Kerney on occasion. He pushed the random thoughts away and focused on Applewhite. It shouldn't be all that difficult to confirm her Taos vacation ski story, and it would ease his mind if it were true.

He made contact with Sal Molina. "How did the press conference go?"

"Unbelievable, Chief," Molina said. "Are you buying it?"

"For now. Applewhite's husband is supposedly in Taos."

"Yeah, I know. She made a big deal to me about how her vacation got screwed up by the Terrell case."

"Find out if she made any calls to her hubby."

"This doesn't sound like you're buying Perry's spin, Chief."

"It's just my natural curiosity at work, Lieutenant."

"It may take some time to track down her cell-phone provider," Molina said.

"Do it quietly and without radio transmissions."

"Ten-four."

Kerney went into the motel and talked to the desk clerk, who glanced at the stars on Kerney's uniform shirt collar and nodded his head vigorously at Terjo's photograph.

"Yeah, he was here. Two FBI agents came looking for him earlier. A man and a woman."

"And?" Kerney prompted, thinking that he'd been wrong about Applewhite. She'd been given some work to do after all.

The man lifted a shoulder. "I didn't see what happened. Nothing, I guess. There wasn't a commotion or anything like that."

"Did you give them a room key?"

"No, they said they'd come back if they needed one."

"Had Terjo checked out?"

"I don't know. He paid in cash. People who do that usually just leave the key in the room when they go."

"I'd like to see the room. Has it been cleaned?"

The man consulted a housekeeping schedule. "Maybe. There's a girl working that wing now. She'll let you in. Room one sixty-three."

The housekeeping cart stood on the walkway in front of the open door to Terjo's room. The bed had been stripped by an older, tired-looking Mexican woman who was running a vacuum cleaner. She switched off the machine when Kerney entered and dropped her head as if to avoid trouble.

Kerney spoke to her in Spanish. "Was the room slept in?"

"Yes."

"Was it messy?"

"No more than any other room."

"Were there any signs of a fight or a struggle?"

"No." The woman reached into an apron pocket and held out a key ring. "But I did find these on the carpet next to the night-stand."

Kerney took the keys, inspected them, thanked the woman, and left.

Terjo had left behind his truck keys, which wasn't what a man who should've been on the run and had stayed in town overnight would do. Terjo had to have been thinking of getting his truck and maybe borrowing some money from his girlfriend.

Kerney jiggled the keys in his hand. Charlie Perry's story about not finding Terjo was pure bullshit. He wondered where Perry had Terjo stashed.

Charlie's reasons for the heavy warning to drop the case were now completely clear: everything related to the Terrell murder was being systematically sanitized.

Kerney knew it was probably in his best interest to accept the FBI's party line, walk away from the game, and get on with the task of running his department. More than enough important issues were nipping at his heels demanding attention. He also knew he couldn't let things slide that easily.

*   *   *

Ignacio Terjo leaned forward to ease the discomfort of the muscle spasms and loss of feeling in his arms. His hands were handcuffed behind his back and after two hours of sitting in the backseat of the sedan, he was tense and agitated. He twisted his head to get limber, but it didn't help.

The woman driving the car wouldn't talk to him, although she had the rearview mirror at an angle so she could see him clearly. He stared out the window at the desert and mountain landscape to distract himself from the pain. They were traveling south toward Mexico on the Interstate, maybe three hours away from the border. Until they reached Las Cruces, which was a very short distance from El Paso, there would be only a few towns and small cities along the route.

The buzz of a cell phone made Terjo switch his attention back to the woman. He watched as she answered, listened, and disconnected after acknowledging the call. Still, she said nothing to him. Finally, after another half hour, she spoke.

"We'll be stopping soon," she said,

Terjo nodded and watched a low-flying helicopter parallel the car and pass out of sight.

They left the Interstate ten miles further on at an exit where nothing but a dirt road cut through brown sand hills. After a few miles on the rutted road the car topped a small rise. Terjo saw a helicopter on the ground. Two men waited at the front of the aircraft canopy.

"Why is that here?" Terjo asked.

"To take you the rest of the way to Mexico," the woman said as she stopped the car.

"I have to make water first," Terjo said.

"No problem."

Outside the vehicle the woman took the handcuffs off and pointed at a nearby mesquite tree. "Over there," she said.

Terjo walked to the tree with the woman close behind. He unzipped his pants and relieved himself. One of the men opened the hinged helicopter door and took out what looked to be a folded black blanket.

"Finished?" the woman asked.

Terjo nodded and zipped up. Before he could turn around, Agent Applewhite raised her handgun and shot him in the back of the head.

Chapter 6

Late in the afternoon Bobby Sloan released two of the state police agents who'd assisted in his investigation and held a debriefing session with the senior agent, Lalo Escudero. Escudero, an old friend who'd tipped more than a few beers with Sloan over the years, sat in the cubbyhole that served as Bobby's office reading off the list of people who'd been interviewed over the last two days. At his desk Sloan checked off the names one by one.

"That's it," Escudero said, looking at the sprawling stacks of files, reports, and paperwork on Sloan's desk. "How in the hell do you find anything in that mess?"

"It's all organized," Sloan said. "As far as I can tell, we've talked to every faculty member, student, and staff member at the college who had any contact with Mitchell."

"Including a few whose only interaction with the priest was sharing a table with him at the college library or using the men's room at the same time he was taking a leak," Escudero noted.

"So, nobody's lying, or withholding information?" Sloan asked.

"So it seems," Escudero replied. "Supposedly it's not unusual for an academic researcher to stay tight lipped about his work."

"Yeah, yeah, I heard that from every faculty member I talked with," Sloan said. "I'm thinking about personal stuff Mitchell might have talked about. You know, his hobbies, his years in the army, what he liked to read. Anything like that."

"The man kept to himself," Escudero said.

"Why?"

"Hell if I know," Escudero said. "Maybe that was his personality."

"Or he was hiding something," Sloan said, stifling a burp.

"Maybe. But other than the robbery, you've got no motive for the murder. Nobody had a grudge against him, he wasn't embroiled in any controversial campus politics, and nobody disliked him."

Sloan looked at the blank piece of paper he'd placed on his desk for note taking, removed his reading glasses, and rubbed his eyes. "So say he wasn't killed by somebody on campus," he said.

Escudero rolled his eyes.

"What?" Sloan demanded.

"Either way, you've got robbery as a motive."

Sloan shook his head. "Come on, Lalo. Robbers are the sloppiest killers on the fucking planet. They get surprised by the victim, panic, pull off a couple of caps, bolt, and leave most of what they wanted to steal behind. We get prints, find witnesses, get a make on a vehicle, cruise the pawnshops, and make a bust."

"Okay," Escudero said. "Mitchell was retired army and his research project involved interviewing ex-military types."

Sloan elaborated on Lalo's guess. "Are you saying officer X or sergeant Y dusted Mitchell because of his research?"

"That would explain the professional kill," Escudero replied. "The killer could have been one of those special forces types."

Sloan covered his mouth, burped, and noted the idea on the paper. "Let's say Mitchell gets whacked because of his research. Something from the past he was writing about, maybe gonna publish. Now the robbery starts to make sense. The killer wasn't sure what Mitchell had or where it was, so he cleaned out everything."

"Or he knew exactly what he was looking for and staged the rest of the rip-off to throw us off the track."

"That, I don't buy," Sloan said, suppressing a burp. "The perp didn't waste time killing Mitchell. I doubt he wanted to risk getting caught lugging a bunch of unnecessary stuff away."

"Okay, what's the motive?" Escudero replied, pausing to let Bobby finish another belch. "Revenge?"

"More likely fear of exposure," Sloan replied, "if it was related to Mitchell's research. But what if the perp killed him for something that didn't have diddly to do with the army? Maybe it was personal. Maybe the priest was a pedophile and the church was hiding him away."

"What we know about the victim doesn't tell us much," Escudero said, watching Bobby burp again. "Maybe you should forget about figuring out the motive for now and concentrate on the victim."

"Yeah," Sloan said. "You'd think if the perp didn't know exactly what he was looking for, he would have left something behind about Mitchell's research that would give us a clue."

"No good motive, no hard evidence, no known suspects," Escudero said. "Your case is a piece of shit, Bobby. When do you want our paperwork?"

"Tell me about it. Tomorrow will do." Sloan let out a long belch and patted his stomach.

"We're finished talking, right? I want to get out of here before you start blowing farts."

"It's just gas," Sloan said.

"You sound like a bullfrog in heat," Escudero said. "You gotta stop eating that junk food."

Sloan grimaced. "Thanks for the advice and the help."

"Any time."

Lalo left the cubicle and Sloan picked up the page of notes he'd just made and let the paper float down to the desktop. Was Mitchell killed for revenge? Was Mitchell killed to cover up some past crime? Was he killed because of what his research had uncovered?

He hated this kind of homicide. The chances were good it would go unsolved unless someone stepped forward with solid information or another crime occurred that could be tied conclusively to the murder, with sufficient evidence to target a suspect.

He rocked his chair back and reached down for a thick three-holed binder on the floor. Although forms and reports were now computerized, Sloan still used a homicide casebook to keep his material organized. He thumbed through the pages, stopping to look once again at the two yellow Post-it notes he'd found as page markers in Father Mitchell's Bible.

Mitchell had written "INSCOM" on one Post-it and "video" on the other. Sloan had no idea what INSCOM meant. Maybe it was a stock-market abbreviation, the name of a corporation, or an acronym of some sort. He would try and track it down.

No videotapes had been found in Mitchell's room, so maybe that note was a reminder to return a borrowed or rented movie. There were several video players and televisions in the common areas of the Christian Brothers residence hall. Although it was probably a dead lead, tomorrow he would ask around to see if Father Mitchell was a movie buff, and check the video stores near the college on Cerrillos Road.

But maybe it referred to something else. Mitchell supposedly was taking oral histories of retired veterans for his research. Was he making audio or video recordings?

Sloan decided not to get excited about the idea until morning. He started writing his report, and his gut rumbled as the gas built up. He needed to stop by the drugstore and get something for it on his way home.

Kerney's last meeting of the day was with Tobias Maestas, the lieutenant in charge of training. Maestas, a low-key, competent officer, sat stiffly across the conference table and with a pained expression on his face described how Kerney's predecessor had gutted the annual in-service training budget by taking himself and a few high-ranking cronies to expensive out-of-state law-enforcement seminars and conferences.

As a result, unless new money could be found or existing funds transferred from another budget category, firearms instruction and range requalification testing with the department's newly adopted Smith & Wesson .45 caliber semiautomatic would have to be curtailed until the start of the new fiscal year in July.

Kerney heard Maestas out, thinking that every new day on the job seemed to bring another surprising revelation of past mismanagement. He glanced at the weapons-training cost estimate and the instruction schedule Maestas had prepared and closed the file.

"We have six unfilled patrol officer positions," Kerney said. "I'll ask Chief Otero to transfer the funds you need out of personnel costs into the training budget. Go ahead and set it up, Lieutenant."

Maestas smiled as though he'd won the lottery, thanked Kerney, packed up his paperwork, and left. Almost immediately, Sal Molina stuck his head inside the open door.

"Got a minute, Chief?" he asked.

"Sure," Kerney replied.

"We've cleared last summer's drive-by shooting. The Albuquerque PD picked up our suspect on a fugitive warrant early this morning during a DWI traffic stop. He's booked into the county jail."

"That's good news."

"I couldn't find a record of any calls made by Applewhite to Taos," Molina said. "I even checked to see if she'd placed calls to some nearby resort communities like Red River and Angel Fire. I struck out there too."

"Let it go, Lieutenant. The case is closed." Kerney held out the hand-delivered FBI report.

In it was a copy of Gatlin's handwritten confession and the initial DNA test results confirming that the pubic hair and semen stains found at the crime scene were from Gatlin.

Molina shook his head as he read the paperwork. "This is bogus, Chief. How many rape-murders do you know about where the perp quarrels with his victim, lets her dress and pack for a trip, and then stabs her with a pair of scissors?"

"I can buy it," Kerney said. "We know there was no forced entry at the house. We can assume with very little doubt that Terrell knew her murderer. It's also pretty clear by the killer's choice of weapons that the attack was an act of passion or rage that wasn't premeditated. Put that together with the fact that Terrell and Gatlin had been lovers, that prior to the murder Gatlin had repeatedly threatened violence, and you've got a case. Gatlin's confession and the lab findings ice the cake."

Molina dropped the paperwork on Kerney's desk and looked at Kerney with angry eyes. "How does that explain Ambassador Terrell coming to town with two cleaners in tow who remove and erase any pertinent evidence we might have found during a full house search? Then Charlie Perry shows up waving national security in our faces, takes over the investigation, won't give us squat, and watches our every move. Then, big surprise, within two days Perry dumps a neat and tidy solution in our laps that we have absolutely no way to verify."

"Agent Perry made it clear there would be elements to the investigation we would not be privy to. National security matters do not fall within our domain."

Molina leaned forward and put his fists on Kerney's desk. "Let me and my people keep working this case, Chief. You know it's the right thing to do."

Kerney bit his lip and shook his head. "No, Lieutenant, and that's final."

Without another word Molina turned on his heel and stalked out of the office.

Kerney stared at a blank wall and tried to remain calm. Molina was right, of course, and his blistering indictment of Kerney's decision was perfectly reasonable.

He got up, turned out the lights, and walked to a window that gave a view of the shopping mall on the other side of Cerrillos

Road. A van with dark-tinted glass covered with curtains and several roof-mounted antennas had been parked in the lot day and night since Charlie Perry had arrived on the scene. Preoccupied with all that needed doing, Kerney had taken a full day to snap to the realization that he was under electronic surveillance.

He rationalized his slow uptake by thinking he'd never been spied on before, at least not to his knowledge. It gave him no satisfaction. He hoped that Charlie Perry would be lulled to sleep after listening to the tape of his conversation with Sal Molina. What he would do while Charlie was snoozing still had to be thought out.

Charlie Perry waited in his car for the custodian to turn out the lights and leave the college administration building. Earlier in the day, pretending to be gathering information about the college for a cousin, Perry had met with an admissions counselor. During his visit he'd scoped out the exit doors, located the faculty mailroom, and noticed the absence of a security system. Then he'd taken a self-guided walking tour around the campus.

The custodian drove away. Perry put on plastic gloves, walked from his car to a side entrance, picked the lock, and hurried down a long corridor to the mailroom. Using a pocket flashlight he located Father Mitchell's empty mailbox. He searched a bin of unsorted mail and found nothing addressed to the priest. The manila envelope Randall Stewart had mailed for Phyllis Terrell had to be around somewhere, but where?

He checked every mailbox to make sure the envelope hadn't been misrouted, and looked through the outgoing mail bin in the hope it might have been forwarded by the clerk to Mitchell's home address. Nothing.

He found a dog-eared campus directory and paged through it for Brother Jerome Brodsky's office location. Mitchell's resident-scholar appointment had been in the social science department, which Brodsky chaired. Maybe Brother Jerome had picked up

Mitchell's mail. If not, Perry would be forced to go through every faculty office in the department until he found it.

Outside, Perry stood in the shadow of the administration building as a group of students walked by on their way from the nearby library. Night classes had ended over an hour ago and Perry figured the faculty had long since departed from both classrooms and offices. The lone security guard on duty was parked some distance away, next to a dormitory, keeping an eye on female students returning to their rooms.

He hurried across the parking lot and made his way to a row of ratty old army barracks that served as faculty offices. Getting in the darkened building was a breeze, but it took him a few minutes to gain access to the locked suite of offices and another thirty seconds to open Brother Jerome's door.

Perry saw the envelope lying address-side up on the top of Brother Jerome's desk. He grabbed it just as the hinges on the outer suite door squeaked. Lights flicked on in the reception area. He flattened himself against a wall by the door, stuffed the envelope in his waistband, and pulled his handgun. Brother Jerome walked in and Perry tapped him once with the barrel at the base of the skull to put him down, and again a little harder to put him out.

Perry quickly trashed the office, took a laptop computer to make it look like a burglary, stepped over the unconscious body, and headed for the parking lot, his hands sweating inside the plastic gloves.

A squad car with flashing lights, two unmarked units, a campus security vehicle, and a fire department EMT ambulance were parked outside the old army barracks. Inside a small reception area a woozy Brother Jerome sat in a straight-back chair while an EMT tended to him. A useless-looking campus security officer stood nearby giving a statement to a patrol officer. Sal Molina and Bobby Sloan conferred in the open doorway to an office. They stopped talking when Kerney approached.

"What have you got?" Kerney asked.

Molina spoke first. "Brother Jerome interrupted a burglary in progress, Chief. He came back to grade some papers, found the doors open, and got cold-cocked when he walked into his office."

"There's no sign of forced entry," Sloan said. "But just about anyone could have picked the locks on the door to the reception area and the office."

"Or they were left open," Molina added, "which isn't unusual. Sometimes the brothers don't lock up if they're just stepping away from their desks for a few minutes."

"Did Brother Jerome find the entrance unlocked?" Kerney asked.

"Yes," Bobby Sloan said.

"Did he see his attacker?" Kerney asked.

"Nope," Sloan said. "He saw that his office door was open, walked in, and got clobbered."

"How is he?" Kerney asked.

"He's got a mild concussion," Sloan said. "The EMTs are gonna transport him to the hospital for a medical evaluation. Except for a laptop computer he doesn't know what else was taken. But the file cabinet where he keeps his test exams wasn't tampered with, so probably a student didn't do this."

"He was laid out neatly," Molina added. "From the bumps on his head I'd say he was tapped once to put him down, and given a second hit to put him out."

"Not something a typical college kid would know how to do," Kerney said. He looked at the papers, telephone, and desk lamp that were strewn on the floor. A chair had been overturned, and some books had been pulled off a bookshelf. "Okay, let's say the perp panics when Brother Jerome shows up, and knocks him out to avoid discovery. As far as we know, only a laptop is missing. Why trash the office?"

Sloan shrugged. "Maybe the perp was looking for something else."

"Like what?" Kerney said, scanning the office. "The perp has the laptop and there's nothing left in plain view worth stealing. Were any of the offices closer to the entrance entered?"

"Nope," Sloan replied. "The burglar made a beeline for this one."

"Brother Jerome sponsored Mitchell as a resident scholar," Kerney said.

"I thought about that," Sloan said.

"Any thief with half a brain would have waited a few more hours until the campus was quiet before pulling a break-in," Kerney said. "Unless he was desperate to get his hands on something important."

"Like something of Mitchell's that wasn't in his room the night of the murder," Sloan said, eyeing the mess on the floor. "I'd love to make that connection, Chief. If we can tie this to the homicide, then maybe I can get a handle on a motive."

"Assume it for now," Kerney said. "None of us would be here if Father Mitchell hadn't been murdered in his room less than fifty yards away."

"This has a completely different MO than the Mitchell homicide," Molina said.

"I agree, LT," Sloan replied. "But the crimes could still be linked."

Kerney focused on Sloan. "Where are you with the Mitchell case?"

"Running into brick walls, Chief. I've got a few more leads to chase down that don't look promising. I'll know if I've got anything in the morning."

Kerney watched the EMT take a still wobbly Brother Jerome to the waiting ambulance. "As soon as he's able, have Brother Jerome inventory everything in his office."

"I've already got it on my list, Chief."

"Start interviews now. Talk to the brothers, campus security, janitors, library staff—anybody who is usually around after night classes end."

Kerney glanced at Sal Molina. "I want you and Detective Sloan to head up this investigation. Pull in as many people as you need. Soft-pedal it as an aggravated burglary, not connected to the Mitchell homicide."

"Whatever you say," Molina replied.

"As a precaution, let's button down the Brothers' residence," Kerney said. "Put a uniformed officer on-site around the clock starting now. Call me if anything breaks."

Molina held his tongue until Kerney had limped his way out of the building. "This isn't the way I want to spend my time," he said.

"I think the chief may be onto something here, LT," Sloan said, rubbing his aching gut.

"Yeah, maybe, but I'd rather be working the Terrell homicide."

"That wasn't his call to make," Sloan said. "Give the guy a break, he's doing the job."

"You think so?" Molina asked.

"I do."

"Well, he hasn't got my vote yet."

Fred Browning sat in a back booth of his favorite Albuquerque sports bar staring at his double whiskey. Televisions positioned throughout the dimly lit room, all turned to the same station, showed halftime highlights of a West Coast college basketball game while a color commentator blithered. Buff-looking college-age waitresses, dressed in skimpy workout shorts and tank tops, cruised through the crowd taking drink and food orders, with easy smiles and sassy prattle designed to loosen wallets for big tips.

Browning had planned to get slam-dunk drunk, but instead he'd been sipping the same whiskey for almost an hour, trying to sort out why he'd been laid off. A good dozen patrons waited at the front of the room to be seated, and his waitress looked longingly at the four-person booth he occupied as she passed by. He ordered another double and some food, dropped a fifty on her tray when she brought it, and told her to keep the change. Placated and pleased, she walked away, toned buns twitching under her tight-fitting nylon shorts.

Browning's day had turned crappy real fast when the plant manager had dumped him from his job without anything more than bullshit explanation. The promise of a nice severance package and a position with a Silicon Valley company hadn't done much to lift his spirits. With two grown children and aging parents living in Albuquerque, Fred had no desire to leave New Mexico to move to a place that sucked big time—where a one-bedroom apartment cost over a thousand a month in rent and everybody worth less than ten million was considered poor. He'd taken the severance pay and turned down the job.

He looked up from his drink and overcooked hamburger and saw Tim Ingram standing at his table.

"Hey, buddy, I've been looking for you," Ingram said. "I heard what happened."

"Bad news travels fast," Fred said. "Tell me what happened. I'd damn well like to know. Hell, I was doing the job. They had no cause to can me."

"Hell, no, they didn't," Ingram said, easing himself into the booth. "Look, don't take it personally. This is the new world order. All it takes is a little downward blip in the market, a little dip in projected profits, and corporate America decides somebody has to go, loyalty be damned. You don't think management is going to cut back on their stock options just to keep regular guys like you and me working, do you?"

"That makes me feel a whole lot better about myself," Fred said sarcastically.

"I know it doesn't," Tim said, reaching out to snare a french fry off Browning's plate. "Did they give you any idea why you were downsized?"

"Just the usual bullshit about corporate restructuring."

"Why do you think it happened?" Ingram asked.

"About six months ago I started feeling out of the loop. We

opened a new R-and-D production unit and a bunch of new pro-grammers and technicians were shipped in from out-of-state to work on it. Me and my people were given no information, and told only to provide tight physical security for the unit."

"Of course, you challenged the decision."

"Big time. All it got me was a pat on the back for being dedi-cated to my job and an order to back off."

"What do you think is going on?"

Browning shook his head. "I haven't a clue, but the visitors to the unit look like heavy hitters from back east."

"Heavy hitters?"

"Yeah, high-ranking government officials, research scientists—people like that. Best I can figure is they're designing and produc-ing some sort of stealth chip."

Ingram laughed. "A stealth chip. That's funny. What the hell is a stealth chip?"

"I'm guessing it's to instantly track hackers who break into net-works and Web sites."

"How did you come up with that idea?"

"From snatches of coffee-room chatter I've overheard."

"Well, come to think of it, it makes a lot of sense."

Browning shrugged. "Like I said, I'm guessing."

Conversation stopped while the waitress took Ingram's drink order.

"So what are you going to do next?" Ingram asked when she walked away.

"Hell if I know."

"Nothing on the horizon?"

"Yeah, a job in California was offered, but I turned it down. I got family here, a house, all my relatives, and this is where I want to stay."

"Was it a good job?" Ingram asked.

Browning nodded. "Commensurate to my old job with a nice salary boost and all relocation costs paid."

Ingram smiled kindly. "I know you're helping your kids with their monthly mortgages and covering a big chunk of your parents' expenses. Plus, you've got your own bills. That severance package and your police pension isn't gonna take you very far."

"Don't I know it."

"Here's an idea: Take the California job for six or eight months and then come back as my replacement."

"You're planning to leave?"

"Always have been. I've got a lock on a sweet job back east. Big corner office, leggy personal secretary, lots of perks. But I want to finish up here before I make the move. And I get to pick who steps into my shoes. Why shouldn't it be you? In fact, I was planning to talk to you about it in a couple of months to see if you'd be interested."

Browning's expression brightened. "I could handle Silicon Valley for a while if I knew I was coming back."

"Sure you could," Ingram said. "And it would a hell of a lot easier for me to justify your appointment if you're not coming to the job from the unemployment line."

Browning leaned back, let out a sigh of relief, and smiled. "This could work. You're one hell of a good friend."

"Hey, you're the one who'll be doing me a favor," Ingram said, reaching for another french fry. "Is it a deal?"

"My boss left the job offer on the table. I'll call him in the morning and say I've changed my mind."

The waitress set Ingram's drink on the table. He raised it and watched Browning do the same. "Great. We've got the weekend coming up, amigo. How about heading down to the lake for a day of fishing?"

"Sounds good to me."

Browning started eating his hamburger and talking about some new lures he'd bought. Ingram kept the chatter going with smiles and nods.

Browning didn't have a handle on the project, of that Ingram was certain, but his stealth-chip idea wasn't completely off the mark either. If Fred had managed to ferret out any specific information, he wouldn't have survived the night. As it was, the poor son of a bitch was in for a big surprise down the road when he realized he'd been left stranded in Silicon Valley.

Browning finished his burger and drink, and Ingram walked him to the parking lot. He left with Fred's effusive thanks ringing in his ears, thinking the man didn't know how lucky he really was.

Charlie Perry handed Ambassador Terrell the manila envelope and waited in the doorway to the presidential suite.

"Consider your answer very carefully, Agent Perry," Terrell said. "Did you open it and read the contents?"

"I did not, sir."

"Very well. Come in. I want to be brought up to date."

Perry sat in an easy chair and watched as Terrell slipped the manila envelope into a briefcase and locked it.

Terrell turned and said, "You may begin."

"Kerney has shut his investigation down," Perry said.

"You're absolutely sure?" Terrell asked before Perry could continue.

"Positive. He gave his violent-crimes supervisor the order earlier this evening after our report crossed his desk."

"At least that went as expected," Terrell said as he sat across from Perry.

"Terjo is in Mexico. Both Fred Browning and Randall Stewart have been contained and counseled, so to speak."

"Give me specifics," Terrell said.

Perry summarized the ploy Special Agent Ingram had used on Browning, and the gist of his interrogation earlier in the day with Stewart. "It should suffice," he added.

"I hope so," Terrell replied.

"There's no reason to take it any further, for now."

"Agreed. And Father Mitchell's briefcase?"

"It hasn't surfaced."

"You'd better find it."

Perry wanted to point out that none of this would have been necessary if Terrell hadn't downloaded and kept military and government secrets on his personal computer at his Washington home, and used a dip-shit stupid password that even his dead cunt wife was able to break on her last visit back east.

"We're looking," he said.

"That's not good enough."

"We'll find it."

"See that you do. That's all, Agent Perry."

Perry walked down the hotel corridor to the elevators. Ever since the assignment landed in his lap, he'd been trying to figure out what kind of Beltway clout Hamilton Lowell Terrell had that kept him out of jail, protected him from exposure, and sanctioned the killing of two civilians. For the same degree of stupidity in similar situations a Chinese-American scientist from Los Alamos had been kept in solitary confinement for almost a whole year and a former CIA director had been forced to endure public censure by members of Congress.

The only solace in the whole mess was that the Bureau hadn't been asked to do any of the actual killing. At least, not yet.

The elevator door opened and Perry stepped inside the cage, shaking his head at the thought that whatever Terrell had going for him, it was some powerful political voodoo.

Hamilton Lowell Terrell dialed the phone and Applewhite answered on the first ring. "Was our friend able to return to Mexico as he had hoped?" he asked.

"I'm afraid not, sir," Applewhite said. "His travel plans were interrupted."

"That's unfortunate. Perhaps new arrangements can be made."

"They already have been."

"Good news, indeed. However, now those two other friends of ours need assistance setting their itineraries."

"I thought that was already accomplished and under control," Applewhite replied.

"Not to their satisfaction," Terrell said.

"I see. How soon do our friends need to leave?"

"With all due speed," Terrell replied.

"I understand."

He replaced the receiver, went to the bedroom, and looked through the suits and shirts he'd asked the head concierge to have dry-cleaned and laundered.

Tomorrow he would bury his wife. He selected the sober Savile Row three-button, a solid neutral tie, and a white Oxford shirt. That would do nicely.

Chapter 7

The new day broke with a dull, angry sky and a wicked wind that howled out of the mountains without letup. Ambassador Terrell had arranged for his wife's burial at the Santa Fe National Cemetery, and about twenty people were clustered around a coffin by a freshly dug grave, heads lowered as a minister read a prayer, his coattails flapping in the stiff breeze.

Kerney stood apart from the group, taking it all in. He knew the mayor, Bill Demora; the governor; his chief of staff; the state police captain in charge of the governor's security unit; and Frank Powers, the resident FBI special agent. From photographs he recognized Proctor Straley, his daughter, and Clarence Thayer, the CEO of APT Performa. The rest of the people were unfamiliar to him, but as a group they were sober-looking, well-dressed, late-middle-aged males.

The minister droned on. Kerney noted the absence of Alexandra Lawton, Phyllis Terrell's friend, and wondered why the gathering had been limited to so few people. Surely, Phyllis Terrell had friends who would have wanted to participate. Why did everything feel so staged? It said something about the ambassador, but Kerney wasn't sure what that might be.

The winds kicked up and the minister's words were lost in a fierce gust that swirled dirt out of the freshly dug grave and blew it into the mourners' faces.

Kerney studied the faces. Straley and his daughter looked grief stricken. Terrell looked pensive and subdued. The expressions of the others seemed polite, but showed no sorrow.

The minister closed his prayer book, raised his head, and the group began to move away. Terrell shook hands with Thayer and whispered something in the man's ear, then found his way to Proctor and Susan Straley and walked with them to the waiting cars. Frank Powers, the resident FBI agent, led the way.

Terrell passed Kerney by without a look or a word. Below, where the cars waited, television cameramen started filming video.

He watched the procession leave before paying a visit to his godson's grave. He stood in front of the plain military headstone. The windblown dust that whipped his face only partially caused the wetness in his eyes. Sammy had been murdered while serving in the army. Kerney had solved the case with the help of Sara Brannon, who then commanded the provost marshal criminal investigation unit at White Sands Missile Range. Through the bitter loss of a young man he'd known since birth, Kerney had met his wife.

Until this morning it had been several days since he'd talked to Sara. He'd deliberately phoned her just before her classes to avoid any lengthy discussion about his work. They talked about the need to get the land bought and the house built, and how Sara was feeling. She reported the pregnancy was going just fine and suggested Kerney should call her back in the evening when they had more time to talk.

He returned to his unit and through the windshield looked beyond the last long rows of headstones that stopped at a swath of freshly cleared ground recently prepared to accommodate the upsurge in deaths of aging World War Two veterans and their spouses. He dialed a number on his cell phone and the agent in charge of the

State Police Intelligence Unit picked up. Kerney had borrowed the agent's services from Andy Baca.

"How did it go?" Kerney asked, keeping his question vague.

Although the electronic-surveillance van that had been parked across the street from police headquarters had disappeared last night, Kerney remained cautious. He scanned the tree-covered ridgeline above the clearing and saw no sign of the agent.

"Ten-four, Chief," the agent said. "I'll get something for you soon."

"Roger that, and thanks," Kerney said. He disconnected and drove away. Hidden in the tree line, using a camera with a telephoto lens, the agent had been taking photographs of everyone in attendance at the services. It was a long shot, but just maybe somebody invited to the services might provide a clue to what was really going on.

He called Larry Otero, told him he was taking the rest of the morning off and would be back in the office by noon.

"Steven Summer wants to meet with you, Chief," Otero said. "He's Officer Herrera's lawyer. He specializes in human-rights and discrimination cases."

"You handle it."

"I already made the offer. He only wants to meet with you."

"Have Helen make an appointment for him late this afternoon."

"Summer is an ex–city counselor, Chief. He's tight with the mayor, the city manager, and a couple of his cronies are still on the council. He might not appreciate being put off."

"Should I be more accommodating?" Kerney asked.

"I'd make him wait," Otero said. "But then, I've never liked the guy anyway."

"I'll see him at four-thirty."

The doctors at the hospital had kept Brother Jerome overnight for observation. Sloan picked him up early in the morning, drove him to the campus, and gladly settled into a chair while Brother Jerome sorted through the papers on his office floor.

Sloan looked around the office in the light of day. Discounting the littered floor, the room reflected Brother Jerome's fastidious personality. Office decorations consisted of a crucifix hung on the wall; a hand-carved wooden statue of St. John Baptiste de la Salle, founder of the Christian Brothers, placed in the center of the top shelf of a large built-in bookcase; and a few family photographs neatly positioned on a plain rectangular credenza behind the desk. A window broke the march of a row of file cabinets neatly lined up against a wall. There was no evidence of clutter. Even the file trays on top of the cabinets were trimmed out in an orderly line.

Lack of sleep made Sloan light headed, and he eagerly accepted a cup of coffee from the worried office receptionist who stepped in to see if there was anything she could do to help Brother Jerome. Sloan told the woman everything was under control and asked her to keep staff and faculty members at bay until they finished up.

Sloan's long night had been fruitless. Security at the college was minimal. The college had an open campus policy. There was no visitor check-in system, no procedure for recording or flagging unauthorized vehicles, and no thorough security patrols of buildings after normal working hours. He'd learned that about the only thing the lone night-shift security officer did was cruise in a car, keep an eye on the dorms, shut down loud student parties that went on too late or too loud, turn off lights that had been left on in classrooms, and rattle a few doorknobs. As a result Sloan had learned nothing that gave him a clue about Brother Jerome's attacker.

However, he did learn from reading the morning newspaper that somebody on campus, probably the security guard, had leaked the story to the press. The front-page headline read "Professor Attacked at the College of Santa Fe." Not wanting to raise his blood pressure, Sloan had scanned only the first paragraph of the story. But that had been enough to make him fantasize finding the dip-shit security guard and punching his lights out.

Brother Jerome picked up the pile of papers and envelopes, now nicely sorted by size and type, placed it on his desk, and shook his head. "Nothing was taken as far as I can tell," he said. "My lecture notes for today's classes are all here, my grade book hasn't been tampered with, and none of the student term-paper outlines are missing."

"Check again," Sloan said, "just to be sure."

He waited while Brother Jerome sat at his desk, carefully went through the stack, and placed each item to one side after reviewing it.

"One thing," he said, looking up at Sloan. "An envelope came for Father Mitchell yesterday, and it doesn't seem to be here."

Sloan's tiredness vanished.

Kerney's plans to move out of the small guesthouse he rented in the South Capitol neighborhood had been delayed by the workload of his new job. He changed from his uniform into cold-weather civvies, and drove his truck to the end of Upper Canyon Road, where he left it in the parking lot of the New Mexico Audubon Society. The house, which bordered the edge of the Santa Fe watershed and reservoir system, had once belonged to a well-known local artist.

He started up a hiking trail that led into the mountains, but as soon as he passed out of sight of the building, he veered off the path jumped a fence, and entered the restricted area of the Santa Fe watershed. He cut across below the lower reservoir to the hills beyond, where Phyllis Terrell's house overlooked the valley, and made a hard climb up the foothills, his bad knee protesting with each step. He topped out at a circular dirt road that served the expensive houses bordering the watershed, hobbled his way to Alexandra Lawton's front door, and rang the bell.

The door opened. Lawton looked over Kerney's shoulder at the empty driveway and then down at his snow-covered hiking boots and wet pant cuffs.

"You walked up here?" she asked. "Why?"

"I needed the exercise," Kerney replied.

"Please, Chief Kerney, I doubt that was the reason."

"I wanted to talk with you privately and off the record."

Lawton stepped back to let Kerney enter. "Come in."

"Could we talk outside?"

The wind had subsided and wet heavy snowflakes drifted out of a slate-dark sky, covering the teakwood patio furniture. "It's not a particularly pleasant day to sit outside," she said.

"I'll explain my reason if you'll get your coat," Kerney said.

Lawton studied Kerney's expression, nodded in assent, and pulled a parka off the hall coatrack. "This better be good, Chief Kerney."

Kerney waited to speak until Lawton closed the front door. "I wonder if you ever heard Mrs. Terrell talk about being under electronic surveillance."

"That's absurd," Lawton said. "Why would anyone want to spy on Phyllis?"

"The ambassador is engaged in highly confidential government work. Protective services and precautions to keep foreign-service staff and their immediate family members safe from harm are standard protocols in the diplomatic corps."

"But why should they bother with Phyllis?" Lawton asked. "After all, she was living apart from the ambassador, divorcing him."

"A wife, even an estranged one, could still be a kidnaping target," Kerney said, "and the ambassador did visit her upon occasion. State Department officials are vulnerable to acts of terrorism."

"Why don't you talk to the government about this?" Lawton asked sharply.

"I did," Kerney replied, "and got nowhere. You know, the federal government has a good deal of latitude when it comes to protecting high-ranking officials. Frequently, citizens who have personal relationships with people in sensitive positions, diplomats, or their immediate family members, undergo deep background investigations, often without any knowledge that they've been scrutinized."

Lawton shivered, partly from the cold and partly because of Kerney's words. "All they would learn about me is that I'm pro-choice and in favor of banning all handguns. You're pushing my natural skepticism about our government into paranoia. Why are you doing this, Chief Kerney? From what I've read in the papers, Phyllis's murder has been solved."

"That's correct," Kerney said. "But Santiago Terjo is missing. If I can determine that surveillance is in place at the Terrell residence, I can ask for a court order that will allow me to access all recorded conversations. It may be helpful in finding him."

"Santiago missing? Are you quite sure? His truck is parked at the stables."

"Have you seen him over the past several days?"

"I haven't seen him since the day he was arrested. I hope nothing bad has happened to him."

"Let me change the subject, Ms. Lawton. Have there been any problems with the utilities in the neighborhood recently?"

"Around the holidays an electrical transformer had to be replaced. We were without power for several hours."

"Were you given the location of the faulty transformer?"

"No, but I was home when it happened and watched from my picture window when the man came to fix it. It was the one at the bottom of the hill between Phyllis's driveway and my road."

"Was that about the time Ambassador Terrell came to Santa Fe?" Kerney asked.

Lawton nodded. "Yes, a day or two before. I remember Phyllis was in a snit about his visit. She didn't want to see him, but he was insistent."

"Did she go into any detail?"

Lawton shook her head.

"I noticed you weren't at the cemetery this morning."

"I knew nothing about it."

"Do you know of any other neighbors who might have wanted to attend?"

Lawton shrugged a shoulder. "Randall and Lori Stewart might have gone. Phyllis had little contact with the rest of the people who live nearby."

"The Stewarts were friends of Mrs. Terrell?"

"Phyllis and Lori got along well, and sometimes Randall would help her when her computer crashed, or if she needed help moving rocks when Santiago wasn't around."

"The Stewarts live where?" Kerney asked.

"Two houses up the hill. Randall's probably at work. He's a stock-broker. But Lori should be there. She's a fine arts dealer who works out of her home."

"Did Phyllis talk to you about her lovelife or her relationships with men?" Kerney asked.

"She was closed mouthed about the subject of men. But I attributed that to what she was going through with the divorce. In fact, she hardly ever discussed the ambassador or the reasons she was divorcing him."

"She said nothing?"

"Just that she couldn't live with him."

"Why the long, drawn-out divorce negotiations?" Kerney asked.

"Property settlements can be very difficult when a great deal of money is involved. Phyllis wanted to make sure she kept all of hers." Lawton wrapped her arms tightly around her body. "Why am I standing out here freezing, Chief Kerney?"

"Ambassador Terrell most likely has the highest government security clearance possible. Sometimes federal agencies will monitor the conversations of family and friends. It's a good way to make sure classified information isn't being inadvertently discussed."

"Are you saying I'm being spied upon?"

"I doubt it," Kerney said. "But then you never know."

Lawton searched Kerney's face. "This is unreal. I don't like what you're saying at all. What can I do?"

"Call in an electronics expert to sweep your house inside and out. The cost may well be worth your peace of mind." He shook Lawton's gloved hand. "Thank you for your time."

"Unreal," Lawton said again, shaking her head as she went inside.

The woman who opened the door at the Randall Stewart residence had her long brown hair pinned up. She wore bright yellow rubber kitchen gloves. In her forties, she had tired eyes and seemed decidedly unhappy about the interruption. Kerney showed the woman his shield and asked if she was Mrs. Stewart.

"I'm Cynthia Cabot, the housekeeper," the woman replied. "The Stewarts are out of town on a skiing vacation. Where's your police car?"

"I walked up from Ms. Lawton's house," Kerney said. "When did the Stewarts leave?"

"I'm not sure. There was a note on the kitchen table when I arrived this morning. The trip wasn't planned ahead of time, I can tell you that. Mrs. Stewart always lets me know when they'll be gone. This must have been a spur-of-the-moment thing. And they took the boys out of school to go with them."

"Is that unusual?"

"I've worked for the Stewarts for three years and until now, family vacations have always been scheduled during school holidays."

"Do you know where they went?"

"No, and Mrs. Stewart always leaves that information for me in case something important comes up."

"Any idea when they'll be back?" Kerney asked.

"The note didn't say. What's this all about?"

"Just a follow-up to an investigation," Kerney answered.

"The Terrell murder?" Cabot asked.

"A completely different matter. Do the Stewarts call in when they're vacationing?"

"Always. I check the house daily while they're gone, usually in the evening after I've finished with my other clients. If Mrs. Stewart doesn't call while I'm here, I'm sure there will be a message on the answering machine tonight."

Kerney held out his business card. "When they call, ask them to get in touch with me. It's not an emergency, but I do need to speak with them."

Cabot read Kerney's card and gave him a surprised look. "You're the police chief?"

"Yes, I am," Kerney said. He turned before Cabot could probe further and walked away.

Through thickening snow Kerney hiked back to his truck, cranked the engine, turned up the heater, and sat for a minute until the throbbing in his knee subsided. His kneecap had been almost completely destroyed by a drug dealer's bullet, and the surgical reconstruction had left him with a limp and a leg that performed poorly. Over the years he'd maintained a fairly rigorous exercise program to keep his legs in good shape. But the pain never completely went away, and his hike up and down the hills had made it worse.

He used his cell phone to call the electric company and learned that no power outage had occurred in the vicinity of the Terrell neighborhood before or after the holidays. He turned on the windshield wipers and the blades thudded against the wet, heavy snow as he drove out of the parking lot. According to the housekeeper the Stewarts' decision to leave suddenly on an unplanned vacation was completely out of character. He wondered why, and couldn't dismiss the possibility that it was somehow linked to everything else he'd learned so far about the ambassador and his wife.

He drove the loop that passed in front of the Terrell residence, stopped a hundred yards down the road from the driveway, and studied the electric transformer on the power pole through binoculars. Mounted above the transformer a tiny video camera was trained on the security gate and driveway to the Terrell house.

Kerney turned the truck around. He needed to find out who had put the surveillance camera in place. But more important, now that the possibility of hard evidence existed that could identify Terrell's murderer, he needed to get hold of the videotapes.

Brother Jerome had been unable to give Bobby Sloan any information about a return address on the missing envelope sent to Father Mitchell. He did recall that the envelope had been addressed by hand, not typed, and postage stamps, not metered mail, had been used to send it. Brother Jerome also noted that the quality of the penmanship was excellent and that the hand was most probably a woman's.

Without a name the information wasn't much help to Sloan's investigation. While he now had a clear-cut link between the priest's murder and the aggravated burglary, he still lacked both a suspect and a viable motive.

He left the last video store on his list, which, like all the others he'd checked, had no customer record on Father Mitchell, and walked glumly through the snow to his unit. Reduced to chasing down tangential shreds of information, Sloan felt the rhythm of the investigation fading into one of those unsolved murder mysteries that ten years down the road would be featured by the local paper in a Sunday edition.

He went back to the college and started another round of interviews that focused on the burglary of Brother Jerome's office, sloshing through the wet snow from building to building, meeting with staff and faculty members who'd been on campus around the time of the break-in.

He finished up with nothing to show for the effort and walked toward the parking lot, passing a blocky two-story building with a stepped-down entrance that looked like a modern version of an ancient Aztec temple.

The building housed the Moving Images Arts Department and construction of the facility had been funded by a famous old movie actress named Greer Garson, who'd lived outside of Santa Fe on a ranch until her death some time back.

Sloan stopped, went inside, and asked the college student working at the desk if he knew Father Mitchell.

The young man, who had stringy shoulder-length blond hair and a nose ring, nodded his head. "Yeah, he was in here all the time, mostly in the evenings after classes ended. That's when I'm usually here working on my own stuff."

"Did he talk to you about what he was doing?" Sloan asked.

"No, but he spent most of his time in an editing suite, so he must have been producing something. I never saw him in the screening room or in the archives."

"Is there someplace in the building where he might have stored his materials?"

"There are dozens of places like that where we can lock up film, videos, and shooting scripts. All of the postproduction rooms have built-in locking cabinets, and there are lots of storage lockers for students to use all over the building, on a first come, first served basis."

The kid opened a drawer and pulled out a loose-leaf binder. "But since Father Mitchell had faculty status, he probably got an assigned locker. Yeah, here it is. One seventy-six. You go past the production rooms and the soundstage down to the end of the hall. You'll find his locker there."

"Who can open it?" Sloan asked.

The kid shrugged. "Beats me."

"Find out who can open the locker, okay?"

It took ten minutes with the kid calling around and then another ten before a harried-looking female faculty member with big hair showed up carrying a key ring. She immediately asked Sloan why he needed to get into the locker.

Sloan told her to chill out. "There may be evidence in the locker important to Father Mitchell's murder, and I need to search it now."

"Show me your credentials," the woman said.

Sloan flipped open his badge case. "Good enough?"

"Follow me."

At no. 176 Sloan held his breath while the woman opened the locker. In it were a briefcase and a stack of videocassettes. He wrote out a receipt, gathered everything up, thanked the woman, and left the building, oblivious to the full-fledged blizzard that had settled over the city.

Kerney made stops at the electric, phone, and cable companies. He asked about a special law-enforcement request to install a surveillance camera on the utility pole near the Terrell driveway. Clerks studied work orders, pulled files, and shook their heads. Security personnel fanned through court orders and shook their heads. Maintenance supervisors licked their thumbs, paged through smudged paperwork, and shook their heads.

He borrowed an office phone and called all local police agencies within the jurisdiction. No one knew anything.

He stopped at Phyllis Terrell's alarm company. Her contract called for burglary and fire monitoring, gate control, and driveway sensors to warn of vehicle approach. No audio or video services were included.

He drove to city hall, parked in his reserved space, and crossed the street to the post office, an ugly 1960s era building that looked incongruous next to the stately old stone federal courthouse.

Once, on one of her long weekends in town, Sara had asked to see something in Santa Fe tourists didn't know about. After an elegant lunch at a nearby restaurant, he'd walked her to the courthouse and shown her the old wooden telephone booth that stood in the lobby.

Sara had laughed, marveling at the sight of it. Then she had pulled him into the booth, closed the accordion door, and pressed herself against him. The guard sitting at the end of the hall had grinned insipidly at them when they emerged.

Kerney found the resident FBI agent, Frank Powers, in his small third-floor suite at the post office building.

"I get to see you twice in one day," Powers said, unwinding his long legs and getting to his feet to shake Kerney's hand. "Boy, am I one lucky SOB."

In his early fifties, Powers was on his final duty assignment before retirement. Powers and his wife were ballroom-dance fanatics. Kerney and Sara had watched the couple put on quite a show one Saturday night when they'd stopped at a club for an after-dinner drink.

"As the new police chief I thought it was time to touch base with you," Kerney said.

"Yeah, sure," Powers said with a smile. "What do you really want?"

"Did Perry keep you in the loop on his investigation?" Kerney asked.

Powers chuckled sarcastically. "Me? You've got to be kidding. All he asked me to do was give him a ring if you paid me a social call, and be the ambassador's bodyguard at the funeral."

"Well, here I am," Kerney said. "Call him up."

"What for? From what I've heard, the case is closed, the task force is disbanded. That means I'm once again free to assist local law-enforcement representatives such as yourself without dropping a dime on you."

"Can I hold you to that?" Kerney asked.

"Unless I hear otherwise, you can. Why do you ask?"

"Perry is staying in town for a couple more days just to make sure everything's tidied up."

"I didn't know that," Powers said.

"Do you know anything about the surveillance camera at the foot of Phyllis Terrell's driveway?"

"You've got the wrong agency, Kerney. You need to talk to the State Department. Call the Bureau of Diplomatic Security."

"You know nothing about it?"

"If Ambassador Terrell needed enhanced security at his wife's Santa Fe home, that's who would handle it."

"I don't think Phyllis Terrell knew anything about the surveillance."

"What makes you say that?"

"The Terrells were planning to divorce. They'd been living apart for almost two years. The ambassador rarely visited. Phyllis Terrell was known to have entertained several lovers at her home."

"Well, then, there you have it," Powers said. "The ambassador hired himself a private investigator to spy on his wife."

"I don't think so," Kerney said.

"Why not? Any sharp PI can put in a good system. The way I heard it, Mrs. Terrell had the big bucks, and was sleeping around. Proof of infidelity could be worth a lot of money to an aggrieved husband."

"You know nothing about any court-ordered, official surveillance at the Terrell residence?" Kerney said.

"That's what I've been telling you, Kerney. Look, if a court order had been requested by us and not the State Department, I'd know about it. But then I still couldn't tell you anyway. You know the routine; both the application and order would have been sealed by a federal judge."

Powers adjusted his necktie. "Since we're talking about people being watched, here's some advice: Stay out of this. Agent Perry doesn't like you. I don't know what that's about. But if you're smart, don't give him an excuse to play hardball."

"Charlie can be obnoxious," Kerney said.

Powers shrugged. "There are over twenty-two thousand special agents in the Bureau, Chief, and there is no charm-school requirement for academy applicants."

Kerney walked down the post office steps. Powers had deliberately warned him that he was being watched. That made Frank's other assertions seem highly questionable.

While his wife skied the mountain, Randall Stewart kept an eye on his two young sons, Lance and Jeremy, as they practiced on the kiddie slope. The boys, ages six and eight, had improved their technique this season, but they were at least a year away from being able to ski the more difficult intermediate runs.

Stewart's interrogation by the FBI agent had put him into a total panic, and the only thing he could think to do was leave town for a while. Springing the idea of an impromptu skiing trip on his wife hadn't been easy. Lori liked everything planned and orderly. Keeping up a cheery front, Stewart had prevailed with Lori by pointing out that her business was slow this time of year, both children were doing extremely well in school, and it was time to be a little more spontaneous about family fun before the boys were grown and gone.

He booked a suite in a lodge in Red River, high in the Sangre de Cristo Mountains near Taos, packed up Lori's Volvo, and drove the family out of Santa Fe as soon as he possibly could.

As Lance, his youngest, took a spill and got up laughing, Stewart tried to contain his worry about the threats the FBI agent had made. To have his affair with Phyllis exposed would most likely mean the end of his marriage, and to be branded a suspected traitor would surely destroy his career. He had no doubt that the threats would be carried out if he ever mentioned anything at all about the envelope.

Still stunned by the memory of his interrogation, he shook his head in an attempt to wipe it out of his mind. He looked up just as Lori came down the mountain, and fixed a smile on his face when she approached.

"There's eleven inches of new powder on top of the mountain," she said, eyes dancing, waving at the boys. "It's wonderful."

"Aren't you glad I talked you into this?" Randall asked.

"Very," Lori said, brushing his cheek with her lips. "It's your turn on the slopes. But you'd better get up there before the storm closes in. I'll take the boys back to the lodge and get something whipped up for lunch."

"I'll be back in an hour," Randall said, reaching for his skis. "It's dinner out tonight, just you and me. I've made reservations and the lodge has found us a sitter."

"This is a lot of fun," Lori said.

"That's what I wanted to hear," Randall said. He kissed his pretty wife, wondering why he'd been so stupid about Phyllis Terrell. He watched her gather up the boys, and ski them off to the lodge, a short distance away.

Randall turned his attention to the mountain. A good, hard run was just what he needed. Work up a sweat. He got in the lift line and a woman joined him on the chair.

"Have you skied Red River before?" she asked.

Randall nodded and looked at the woman. Rather ordinary in appearance, he guessed her to be about his age. "Several times."

"Some people who just came down the mountain said the Cat Skinner run is excellent. Have you done that?"

"It's rated difficult," Randall said, nodding. "Are you a good skier?"

"I am. But I've never skied here before and I'd rather follow someone down who knows the terrain. Would that be an imposition?"

"Not at all," Randall replied.

The woman flashed a big smile. "Super."

They got off the lift. Randall waited while the woman adjusted her bindings. People flowed around them and skied off.

"New equipment," she explained apologetically as she buttoned up.

"Cat Skinner is to the left," Randall said.

"Lead on," the woman said. "Get me pointed in the right direction and I'll beat you to the bottom."

Randall smiled at the prospect of some friendly competition. "We'll see about that."

A third of the way down, Randall Stewart picked up good speed. He caught some air on a small bump and the woman stayed right with him.

The woman took a quick look back. No one was behind her. She ran Stewart off the powder and into a tree. The glancing impact sent him careening, spinning wildly on his backside, his left ski twisted awkwardly under his body. He slid to a stop and tried to get his leg untangled, but the pain was too intense.

The woman reached him as he lay in the snow under some trees out of sight of the run.

"Jesus, why the fuck did you run into me?" Stewart asked, panting from the pain.

The woman took a handgun from inside her parka, bent over, slammed it full force against Stewart's forehead, and heard his skull bone shatter.

That should do it, Agent Applewhite thought, as she watched Stewart's breathing slow and finally stop.

The snow fell harder now as the cloud dipped over the mountain. Soon their ski tracks would be completely covered.

She turned away from the body and continued her run down the mountain, feeling a rush of adrenaline as she cut through the fresh powder.

Chapter **8**

Detective Bobby Sloan returned to headquarters, took possession of an empty office assigned to the crime prevention unit, and spent the rest of the morning and part of the early afternoon going through the paperwork in Father Mitchell's briefcase, viewing some of the videocassettes found in the locker at the college, and sampling excerpts of what looked to be at least ten hours of audiotapes Mitchell had also stashed in his briefcase.

In a general way the video- and audiotapes Sloan previewed explained a good deal about Mitchell's research. The priest had been probing into intelligence matters. But it was hard to see what his focus was. Mitchell had conducted interviews about the U.S. Army School of the Americas, the Drug Enforcement Agency, the National Security Agency, the U.S. Army Intelligence and Security Command—Sloan now knew what INSCOM stood for—and a host of other agencies that included the departments of state, treasury, and defense.

A number of interviews touched on a government institution he'd never heard of before, a Joint Military Intelligence College that offered undergraduate and graduate spy-craft degrees to carefully selected military and civilian intelligence personnel.

It was all eye-opening, informative stuff about the scope of government intelligence operations. But it was also all over the map, and Sloan couldn't get a handle on what the priest had been trying to accomplish. However, he was willing to bet the farm that Mitchell's murder was directly tied to his research. That at least gave Sloan a start on figuring out the motive for the killing.

Mitchell had kept copies of some important personal and professional documents in the briefcase. His army retirement papers showed that his last posting had been at the School of Americas, at Fort Benning, Georgia. There was a letter from the secretary of the army to Mitchell's mother, expressing condolences regarding the death of the priest's brother, another letter from a U.S. embassy official that reported the colonel had been attacked and killed by bandits, and a copy of the resignation letter Father Mitchell had submitted to the college where he'd been teaching. The priest had quit his job a month after his brother's death.

Sloan pawed through an envelope stuffed with credit-card, hotel, and airplane-ticket receipts. Mitchell had been doing some whirlwind traveling during the last three months, taking short trips to places like San Antonio and Tucson, and many longer jaunts to Washington, D.C., and Georgia.

Sloan arranged everything by date to get a clear picture of Mitchell's schedule, then totaled up the charges, which ran over five thousand dollars. Bobby wondered how the priest had been able to pay for such travel on a retired major's pension.

Sloan fanned through a pocket notebook filled with the names and addresses of people Mitchell had kept track of. He'd known a hell of a lot of folks scattered all across the country. Some addresses correlated with the places Mitchell had recently visited, some names had stars or checkmarks next to them, and some entries had been crossed out.

Bobby put the notebook aside and went through two correspondence files from the briefcase. One held six years' worth of letters Mitchell had written to the secretary of the army requesting more specific information about the death of his brother under the Freedom of Information Act. Each request had been turned down. All Mitchell had received for his efforts was an official army criminal-investigation report that basically repeated the facts contained in the letter from the embassy.

The second file contained letters to the Armed Forces Records Center in St. Louis demanding the release of his brother's military service records. Those requests also had been rejected. There was, however, a recent letter from a former officer who'd served with Mitchell's brother when he had been deputy commandant at the U.S. Army School of the Americas. The correspondent wrote that he had no information that would be helpful to the priest but wished him good luck with his research.

From his time in the service Sloan knew that immediate family members of deceased veterans were, by law, entitled to those records. What was the army hiding about the brother's death?

Mitchell had kept his checkbook in a briefcase sleeve. Sloan scanned through the entries. Two five-thousand-dollar deposits had been made the past three months. His retirement pay went into the account automatically. From the looks of the checks Mitchell wrote, he lived frugally and was a heavy supporter of a group that politically opposed the continued operation of the School of the Americas.

Sloan filled out evidence inventory sheets and then got on the Internet and started surfing for supplemental information that might help him fill in some of the blanks. When he was done, he checked the clock. Day shift was over, and he hadn't even started writing up his supplemental report.

Bobby decided to talk to the chief first. He dialed Kerney's extension and the chief picked up immediately. Sloan started talking about Mitchell's briefcase filled with intelligence goodies. Kerney cut him off and told him to meet him in the staff parking lot with the evidence in five minutes.

Sloan toted everything out the back door. The chief was waiting in his unit with the motor running and the passenger door open. He got in, wondering where in the hell they were going and why. Kerney's jaw was tightly set and his mouth formed a thin, compressed line. Sloan decided it was probably better not to ask.

Kerney took Sloan to the downtown library, where they settled into the second-floor audiovisual room. Bobby gave him a quick review of the Mitchell evidence.

"Also, Brother Jerome told me that an envelope mailed to Father Mitchell was missing from his office," Sloan said, "so we've got a connection between the homicide and the burglary."

Kerney gazed out the window that overlooked Washington Avenue and the bank building across the way. "Don't you think it's odd that we have two homicides involving national security?" Kerney asked.

"According to what I heard, the feds took that issue off the table in the Terrell case," Sloan said.

Kerney turned away from the window. "Two things you told me put it back on the table. During his military career Ambassador Terrell served as commandant of the School of the Americas and later was the commanding general of army intelligence."

"That's interesting," Sloan said. "Do you think Mitchell was trying to get something on Terrell?"

Kerney sat in a straight-back chair and shook his head. "I don't know. Mitchell's brother was at the School of the Americas long after Terrell's retirement. But he was killed while serving as a military attaché in Venezuela. That raises two additional points. Embassy attaché assignments are heavily geared to intelligence gathering. And Terrell is a member of a trade mission to South America."

"You're racking up a whole lot of coincidences here, Chief."

"Give me your thoughts on Mitchell's research."

"It's a real slumgullion. At first I thought Mitchell was concentrating his investigation on the murder of his brother in South

America, six years ago. That seemed to be what got him started. He left his teaching position right after his brother's death and wrote dozens of letters to the army trying to get more information about it. The army stonewalled him."

Sloan took a sip of coffee from the jumbo-size takeout container the chief had bought him on the way to the library. It was cold and bitter tasting. "But when you watch the videos you'll see that they jump from one subject to another, so I don't know where Mitchell was going."

"We can start with the fact that Mitchell didn't buy the story of his brother's death," Kerney said.

"Okay, at the very least a cover-up took place," Bobby said. "Maybe the priest's brother wasn't whacked by banditos who simply wanted his cash and his car. But based on what I saw on the videotapes I watched, that theme isn't even touched on. There's an interview that concentrates on vague accusations that the army has been burying a sizable amount of money for the last five years in DEA aid to Colombia. There's a Q and A with a U.S. Treasury official about drug money being laundered through banks in Panama. In another tape a retired army major is talking about the time he spent at the Fort Benning School of the Americas with the priest's brother that doesn't reveal diddly."

"Let's watch the tapes," Kerney said.

Some of the videos were brief, and none ran over twenty minutes. An ex–Canadian intelligence officer talked about the National Security Agency sending cryptologists to Brazil for an unknown purpose. A former DEA agent revealed that the Joint Military Intelligence College had developed a field-intelligence and drug interdiction curriculum for the Ecuadoran army. A professor of economics explained "dollarization," an effort to persuade Latin American countries to join Panama and Ecuador in adopting U.S. currency as their official legal tender.

A treasury official detailed information about a financial crimes advisory on Panamanian drug-laundering schemes. An expert on international banking summarized the ways in which large sums of money were electronically transferred between foreign and domestic financial institutions.

Kerney quickly ran through the tapes Sloan had previewed and then clicked off the VCR with the remote.

"What do you think, Chief?" Bobby asked.

"I've been thinking about geography," Kerney said. "Panama, Ecuador, Venezuela, and Brazil. If I'm not mistaken, all of those countries border Colombia. Some political analysts are saying that Colombia could be our next Vietnam. Half of the country is controlled by rebels, including a lot of the coca-growing regions. Maybe the government is getting all their ducks lined up before they send in the troops. That kind of planning can't be done openly. It would raise too much of a stink here at home."

"A secret trade mission might be the way to go," Sloan said.

"I'd say a major clandestine military and civilian intelligence operation has been launched," Kerney said. "A trade mission could well be part of that strategy."

"We always seem to come back around to the ambassador," Sloan said. His butt felt numb. He shifted in his chair to ease the discomfort.

"It does seem that way," Kerney said. He straightened the leg with the blown-out knee and rubbed the sore tendons.

Sloan yawned. "This stuff about banking, money laundering, and international finance may have something to do with cutting off the drug money flowing in and out of Colombia."

"Maybe so," Kerney said. "Without money the *jefes* couldn't fund their private armies and pay off the rebel forces they do business with."

"So what did Father Mitchell learn that the government didn't want him to know?"

"That's what we've got to find out," Kerney said. "Have you dug up any more background about him?"

"A couple of things. Like his brother, Mitchell pulled a tour of duty at Fort Benning. In fact, that was his last post before he retired. He could have probably stayed on active duty if he'd wanted to. I cruised the Internet and learned that army chaplains are in real short supply. He made some trips back to Benning recently, but I haven't found any documentation by Mitchell about it yet. Maybe something will surface on the audiotapes.

"Mitchell ran up travel expenses of over five thousand dollars in the last three months. You don't have that kind of money to throw around on a retired major's pay, especially if you're sending half your pension to a group called the School of the Americas Vigil Committee. I think somebody helped Mitchell out financially. He made two recent deposits totaling ten thousand dollars."

"Follow the money, Bobby," Kerney said.

"First thing in the morning."

"What's this School of the Americas Vigil Committee all about?"

Sloan swallowed hard and pinched his throat to cut off the bile. "It's run by a peace and human rights advocacy group. They want the school shut down and refer to it as 'the school of assassins.' They say it violates U.S. foreign policy, doesn't promote democracy, and infringes on human rights. If that's true, I can see their point."

"Let's wrap it up," Kerney said, eyeing Sloan's tired face. "I want you to make a complete copy of everything we've got—the papers, letters, videos, and audiotapes—everything. Do it first thing tomorrow and get it to me. Nothing goes into evidence until I say so."

"You've got it, Chief."

"Tell no one in the department about this," Kerney added.

Sloan nodded.

Kerney helped Sloan pack up. They carried everything downstairs, where library staff were roaming around announcing closing time.

"Remember when this building was city hall?" Sloan asked.

Kerney nodded. "City hall, the jail, and a fire station combined."

"Doesn't seem that long ago," Sloan said.

"Stop it, Bobby. You're making me feel old. Let me buy you a late dinner."

Sloan rubbed his gut. "No, thanks, Chief. I've had this gas thing in my gut all day."

Kerney drove through the quiet plaza. The stores were closed, only a few people were out, and traffic consisted of one car turning onto Palace Avenue. Crystal snowflakes drifted slowly past the streetlamps, glistened briefly in the soft light, and then melted away on wet sidewalks. At night downtown Santa Fe still felt like a small town.

After a quick run down Cerrillos Road he dropped Sloan at headquarters and headed home. He couldn't shake the notion that Charlie Perry and Agent Applewhite might be staying on in Santa Fe to monitor the Mitchell homicide investigation. What else was there for them to tidy up? If that proved to be the case, Kerney didn't know how he'd react. He decided he would have to play it by ear and watch his back as much as possible.

Charlie Perry waited until the lights went out in the second-floor room of the public library before stopping the tape recorder. Applewhite pulled out her earphone and shut down the video camera.

"That's it," Perry said.

"We only got half of it," Applewhite said.

In the darkness Perry gave Applewhite a nasty look. After tailing Kerney and the detective to the library and spotting them with binoculars in a second-floor room, he'd hustled to find a way to gain fast entry to the bank office building across the way. Fortunately, the Internal Revenue Service housed criminal-investigation agents in the building, so he'd been able to get in after cooling his heels waiting for the man with the keys.

Perry had called Applewhite as soon as he had a fix on Kerney's location. She'd breezed in well after Charlie had the sensitive long-range directional recording equipment up and running. Where, she'd been all day and what she'd been doing, Perry didn't want to know.

"This cop may not be as dumb as you make him out to be," Applewhite said.

"Anybody can connect the dots," Perry replied. "Even Kerney."

"You sound agitated, Charlie," Applewhite said as she lowered the blinds and turned on the lights. Her look reminded Charlie of his second-grade teacher just before she unleashed a scolding.

Perry gave her the finger.

"Calm down, Charlie," Applewhite said, dismissing the gesture. "All I'm saying is that, based on what we heard, Kerney's deductions are reasonable. But he doesn't have anywhere near the information he needs to figure out what's going on. The last remaining link in the paper trail between Phyllis Terrell and Father Mitchell has been secured."

"You should have been the one to do the job at Brother Jerome's office," Charlie said. "No, I take that back, you would have pistol-whipped him."

Applewhite smiled sarcastically and shook her head. "Let's wrap it up for the night, shall we?"

"What about the evidence Detective Sloan has in his possession?" Perry asked.

"I'll take care of that," Applewhite replied.

"How?"

Applewhite crossed her heart and smiled. "I promise there will be no pistol whipping, Charlie," she said, although the idea obviously held some appeal.

Bobby Sloan didn't get home until late. After Kerney dropped him at headquarters, he'd decided to get everything duplicated while the building was quiet. That way he didn't have to worry about when he could get to use the copy machine or the other equipment he needed. Since nothing had yet been entered into evidence, he stowed the copies at the office and carried the originals home.

He stepped out of the shower, toweled off, and slipped into his threadbare terry-cloth robe. It had holes in the armpits and a stain of red wine down the front that had never completely washed out. But Bobby wasn't about to give it up, no matter how much his wife, Lucy, complained about it.

When Sloan got home late he always left the living room lights off and used the small bathroom at the far end of the house so he wouldn't disturb Lucy. He ran the towel over his balding head, brushed his teeth, turned off the light, saw a thin glow seeping under the bathroom door, and silently cursed. He'd woken Lucy up anyway.

He padded down the hall to the living room, ready to apologize, only to find Lucy sitting on the couch in her nightie staring at Special Agent Applewhite with wide, startled eyes.

Applewhite's coat was pulled back behind her holster to expose her semiautomatic. Her FBI credentials dangled from a cord around her neck.

"What in the hell do you think you're doing here?" Bobby asked.

"Official business," Applewhite said, extending the piece of paper in her hand. "I have an order from a federal judge requiring you to turn over all evidence pertaining to the murder of Father Joseph Mitchell."

Sloan tore the document out of Applewhite's grip, his eyes never leaving her face. "Citing what legal authority?" he asked.

"Read the order, Detective," Applewhite responded, "and then give me what I came for."

Sloan read the paperwork. Sections of federal laws Bobby had never heard of were cited. It had national security written all over it. The name of the federal judge and the signature looked valid.

"The order has a no-knock provision," Applewhite said. "But your wife was kind enough to let me in."

"Get screwed," Sloan said. "First I'm going to call my chief."

"Go ahead, Detective," Applewhite said, looking around the room while Sloan dialed Kerney's number. The couch, a recliner model facing a large-screen television, had a center console designed to hold remote controls and beer cans. The wall held cheap, poorly matted prints in do-it-yourself frames. A particularly gaudy image showed a bright pink pony grazing in a blue pasture against a sunflower-yellow sky.

"Nice place you've got here," Applewhite said to Sloan's dumpy, chubby-faced wife.

"Fuck you," Lucy replied sweetly.

The phone brought Kerney out of a deep sleep. He listened to what Sloan had to say and told him to resist Applewhite's attempt to take possession of the evidence until he could speak directly with the judge who'd signed the order. After confirming by phone that the order was valid, he called Bobby back, told him to comply, and hung up fuming.

He sat in the small living room of his South Capitol cottage, stared at the pencil drawing of Hermit's Peak that Sara had given him as a surprise gift just before they were married, and fought down the impulse to roust Charlie Perry out of his hotel bed and bounce him off the wall a few times. That wouldn't accomplish anything.

In a way Perry and Applewhite had done him a favor. Kerney no longer had any doubt that the two homicides were connected. But that certainty failed to cheer him. He was into quicksand up to his neck, confronting an incredibly sophisticated intelligence apparatus with unlimited resources that could easily squash him.

The red light on his answering machine blinked at him. He'd forgotten to check for messages when he got home. He pushed the play button. Sara had called wanting to know why he hadn't phoned her as promised.

Kerney stared at the telephone. Calling her back would only make him miss her more than he already did. In truth, the relationship felt like a long distance love affair, not a marriage. When they were together, everything was perfect. But he wanted more than just a weekend or two with her every month.

He went into the bedroom, thinking that it would be best to keep Sara in the dark about his current entanglement with the FBI, especially since he now knew for certain he was under surveillance. Applewhite's appearance at Bobby Sloan's house had made that abundantly clear. Was it directed at him alone, or were other members of his investigative staff getting the same treatment?

He looked around the cramped bedroom. What in the hell was he doing still living here when he could easily afford so much more? And what in the hell was he doing running a police department in need of a major overhaul when he could be settled on a beautiful piece of land living the good life of a gentleman rancher with the freedom to spend more time with Sara? A baby was coming. He should feel happy. Instead, he felt crabby.

He turned out the light, got into bed, and fell asleep, still grouchy.

An early riser, Kerney woke before dawn. His grumpiness lingered as he set up the coffeepot and tromped outside to get the morning newspaper. Through the bare branches of the trees the sky was a quilt of puffy low gray clouds except on the eastern horizon, which slowly flushed vermilion before quickly turning gold and fading away.

He passed by his landlord's house, which faced the quiet street, found the newspaper on the snow-covered walkway, pulled it out of the protective plastic sleeve, and scanned the front page. There was nothing in the headlines that he absolutely needed to know about.

Never a fan of the daily local press—so much of what got reported was yesterday's canned news from other sources—Kerney subscribed anyway, figuring that as chief he needed to stay current on what did filter into it about community issues.

Inside, he sat at the small table in the galley kitchen, drank the one cup of coffee that his shot-up gut could tolerate in the morning, and quickly roamed through the paper. A wire-service report from Red River caught his attention. Randall Stewart, a Santa Fe stockbroker on a skiing vacation with his family, had been reported missing. Search-and-rescue, along with the state police, had been called out, but a heavy snowstorm had blanketed the mountains and stalled overnight efforts to find him.

To have Santiago Terjo go missing was one thing. But to lose a second possible informant in the Phyllis Terrell homicide seemed highly improbable.

He called Glenn Bollinger, the Red River town marshal, who'd served under Kerney back in the days when he'd been chief of detectives. Bollinger told him that although Stewart had yet to be found, the storm had broken and a search team had just started moving up the mountain.

After asking Bollinger to check carefully for foul play, Kerney left a voice message for Helen Muiz at the office to cancel all his appointments. The phone rang when he hung up.

"You've been busy this morning," Sara said. "I've been trying to get through to you for the last ten minutes."

"The joys of the job," Kerney said. "Everybody wants to talk to the police chief. I'm sorry I didn't call you back last night."

"You're forgiven. Are we still on for the weekend?"

"I think so."

"That's not a firm answer, Kerney."

"I'll free up some time for you."

Sara laughed. "That's very considerate. Do you know what love is, Kerney?"

"Tell me."

"The inability to keep your hands off your sweetie pie. Gotta run. Another class is about to start."

"I miss you."

"Rest up for the weekend," Sara said.

Sara disconnected and Kerney took off for Red River.

*   *   *

The curving snow-packed road that followed the Rio Grande River north to Taos made for slow going. Greeted by a clear blue sky, Kerney topped out on the high plateau south of Taos where white-capped mountains dominated to the east and to the west the river cut a deep gorge in the high plains. Snow had rolled down the foothills, cloaked the rangeland, bathed the forest, and drifted against the brown adobe buildings lining the narrow main street that cut through the old part of Taos.

Kerney kept his radio tuned to the state police frequency and monitored the search-and-rescue team's progress. At Questa, a small village economically hammered by the closing of a molybdenum mine, he made the turn for the last ten-mile stretch to Red River just as the report on the state police band came in that Stewart's body had been found. He keyed the microphone, identified himself, and asked the somewhat startled state police officer to leave the body untouched and keep the area clear. Glenn Bollinger cut in at the end of Kerney's transmission and said he had the scene secured.

The walls of the narrow valley pinched together as Kerney ran a silent code three, pushing his unit to the limit on the icy pavement. He passed a mountainous slag pile that had polluted the nearby river for years while mine operators kept insisting that the government's environmental studies were flawed.

The hills closed in around him, hiding the mountains. Wooded slopes buried in fresh powder lined the small river that gave the town its name and hid the watercourse from view. He drove into the village and the valley widened to reveal a towering subalpine peak with gleaming ski runs glaring white under a full sun. The state highway cut through the town, spoiling the spaghetti-Western motif of the buildings that had sprung up as the local merchants discovered there was more gold to be mined from the pockets of Texas tourists than from the veins of ore left in the mountains.

Kerney pulled into the ski-area parking lot, where he spotted Glenn Bollinger standing at the bottom of the kiddie run. Bollinger waved to him in a hurry-up motion when he got out of the car. Kerney didn't know what had Bollinger so excited, but he did know that the full-size sedan following him from Santa Fe had turned back at the Questa intersection. He put a small evidence kit he'd taken from the glovebox in his coat and crossed the parking lot.

Bundled up against the cold, Glenn Bollinger watched Kerney move carefully across the icy parking lot, favoring his bum leg. He thought back to the time Kerney had been shot by a drug dealer in a Santa Fe barrio. Bollinger had been in the neighborhood doing a burglary follow-up when the officer-down call came in on the radio. He'd arrived at the scene within minutes, to find Officer Terry Yazzi kneeling over an unconscious Kerney, trying to stem the blood flow from a stomach wound that looked fatal. A bullet had also shattered Kerney's knee.

Yards away lay the lifeless body of the drug dealer, with two center-mass shots in the chest. Critically wounded, Kerney had put the asshole down before going into shock and passing out.

Nobody in the department expected Kerney to recover, let alone resurrect his career, yet somehow he did both. Bollinger found it all totally amazing.

Kerney looked good, Bollinger decided, as he came closer. A little older perhaps, but still fit. His cold-weather gear consisted of blue jeans, a felt cowboy hat, and pair of sturdy hiking boots that showed beneath a rancher's-style three-quarter-length winter coat. *He's still doing the cowboy thing*, Bollinger thought to himself. Of course, he'd been born to it.

"Damn, I'm glad you called me," Bollinger said with a smile as Kerney drew near. "If you hadn't, Stewart's death would've been written off as accidental. Instead I've got myself a homicide. First one since I've been here."

"How was he murdered?" Kerney asked, shaking Bollinger's hand.

"Blunt trauma to the head, made to look like he slammed into a tree at full speed," Bollinger replied. "His leg hit the tree, all right; you can see little bits of bark in the gash and the blood around the wound, along with pine needles on his clothing below his waist. But the head wound shows only bruising and a deep laceration, with no foreign matter imbedded in the flesh. The new snow kept everything nice, clean, and frozen. There was nothing at the scene that pointed to a collision between Stewart's head and the tree."

Bollinger grinned. "To the search-and-rescue guys it looked like just another dumb skier who went too fast down a mountain, lost control, and wiped out. The medical examiner thought so too."

"Who's your ME?" Kerney asked.

"We've got several. The guy who took the call is a former Taos County deputy sheriff. You know that department's reputation. Need I say more?"

"Any other physical evidence?"

"Nope. About a foot and a half of new snow fell starting yesterday morning, and the runs were groomed at four this morning before the search-and-rescue team started out. We found no tracks or footprints. I've got the ski run closed and the crime scene cordoned off."

"Was anyone skiing with Stewart?" Kerney asked.

"His wife said he went up the mountain alone."

"Has she been told?"

"Yeah, but only that her husband is dead, not that he was murdered."

"Where is she?"

"At my girlfriend's place with her two boys."

"You've got a girlfriend, Glenn?"

Bollinger grinned again. "Had to, Kerney. The winters up here are just too cold and the nights are too long. I hear you got married."

"Had to," Kerney replied with his own grin. "The woman was just too irresistible."

Bollinger gestured at the ski lift. "Want to take a ride to the top? The view is real pretty."

Kerney eyed the mountain. It looked extremely cold and un-inviting. He had been raised on a ranch in the desert basin of the Tularosa, and while he found winter scenes aesthetically pleasing, he didn't like to do anything more than look at them from a distance.

"Just don't make me ski down that mountain," he said.

Bollinger chuckled. "We'll get you down safe and sound. But if you come up on your days off, I'll give you some lessons and have you skiing in a couple of hours."

"Not on that slope or on this knee," Kerney replied, tapping his right leg.

"That leg won't keep you from mastering the kiddie run, Kerney."

"Thanks, but I'll pass."

"Care to tell me what made you suspicious about Stewart's disappearance?"

"It's probably better if you don't know," Kerney said.

Bollinger's entire contingent of three officers controlled the crime scene, which consisted of keeping a well-equipped group of searchers far away from the body at the edge of the ski run. Standing in a tight circle, the men were jawing over the homicide with a state police officer and the medical examiner, and sipping coffee out of insulated, covered mugs.

Kerney got introduced around and then trudged with Bollinger through the snow to the yellow tape surrounding Stewart's body. There were footprints all around the corpse and the body had been moved from its original position. Except where the snow had been carefully cleaned away from his forehead, Stewart's face resembled a stark white frozen plaster cast. The leg wound had been revealed in a similar fashion.

Glenn told him the scene had been photographed, including a number of close-up shots of the wounds, and the snow he'd removed to expose the wounds had been saved in evidence vials for further analysis.

With Bollinger following, Kerney stepped over the crime-scene tape, knelt next to the body, and studied Stewart's face. The hard freeze and new snow had kept swelling around the wound to a minimum. The bleeding out of one ear looked like a long solidified dark crystal droplet. The forehead laceration showed a slightly angled horizontal groove and one circular imprint in the skin. The pattern injury was unusual.

Kerney looked up at Bollinger.

"I noticed that too," Glenn said.

"What do you think?" Kerney asked.

Bollinger unholstered his semiautomatic sidearm. "Thumped hard with one of these is my guess."

"Mine too," Kerney said. "I want the body taken to Santa Fe for an autopsy and a forensic work-up. But don't transport right away." He handed Bollinger the small evidence kit. "Have your search-and-rescue people thaw him out enough so the ME can take hair, blood, and skin samples for me."

"We'll put him in a toasty ambulance and warm him up," Bollinger said. He holstered his weapon and looked quizzically at Kerney. "Should I even bother asking what you're hoping to learn?"

"Probably not," Kerney said. The knee tortured him as he stood up. "You did a good job here, Glenn. Can you hold off on telling the news media or anyone else who might be interested that Stewart was murdered?"

Bollinger shrugged. "If I'm asked, I'll say we're waiting on the autopsy report. How much time do you need?"

"Eight hours will do. More if you can swing it."

"I'll do what I can," Bollinger replied, glancing back at the group that watched impatiently from a distance. "All of those guys owe me at least one favor. That doesn't mean that the news won't leak out. This is a small town."

"Just try to keep the leak from spreading to Santa Fe too fast," Kerney said.

Chapter 9

In his office at the state police headquarters, Andy Baca took a call from Melody Jordan, a senior crime-scene technician. She curtly asked him to visit her in the lab right away and hung up before he could ask any questions. Andy put the phone down and the button on his very private phone line blinked off.

Only his wife, his secretary, Kevin Kerney, the governor's chief of staff, and a few high-ranking commanders in the department had access to the number. Melody Jordan wasn't one of them.

Andy dialed Melody's extension, dropped the handset in the cradle after twelve unanswered rings, and checked the time. He had ten minutes before a scheduled meeting. The state police lab did most of the forensic testing for local police departments, including the Santa Fe cop shop. Only Kevin Kerney would've been able to get Melody to pull such a stunt. He went to the laboratory to find out what Kerney wanted.

Through a window in the lab he saw Kerney and Melody Jordan standing in front of a stainless-steel table in the small clean room, a sterile environment designed to ensure no contaminants adversely affected DNA testing results. He watched as they filled out evidence labels, attached them to fluid vials and evidence bags, and sealed everything in a Plexiglas box.

They stepped out of the clean room and removed their white lab coats and plastic gloves. Melody Jordan gave Andy a disconcerted look. Kerney had a gleam in his eye.

Ignoring Kerney, Andy smiled reassuringly at Melody. "You called?" he asked blithely.

Melody blushed in embarrassment.

Kerney intervened. "Blame Melody's phone call on me, Andy."

"I already had that figured out. Why are you here taking up Ms. Jordan's valuable time?"

"She ran a few tests for me," Kerney said. "I thought you'd be interested in the results."

"You have my undivided attention."

"I've analyzed the hair, skin, and blood samples taken from Scott Gatlin with the remaining physical evidence we have from the Terrell case," Melody said. "Phyllis Terrell did have sex with Scott Gatlin prior to her death."

Andy shot Kerney a quizzical look. "So the FBI let you confirm their findings. What's the big deal?"

"That's not quite how it happened," Kerney said.

"How did it happen?"

Kerney turned to Melody. "Will you give me a few minutes alone with Chief Baca?"

Melody nodded and left the room.

"Well?" Andy said.

"Charlie Perry faked the DNA findings. The night Phyllis Terrell died her bed partner was a neighbor named Randall Stewart, not Scott Gatlin. The whole FBI investigation is a scam—their evidence, Gatlin's confession, and his suicide."

"Do you have Stewart in custody?" Andy inquired.

"That's not possible," Kerney answered. "He was murdered."

Andy raised an eyebrow. "When?"

"Sometime yesterday up in Red River. It was made to look like a skiing accident."

"Suspects?"

Kerney shrugged. "I'd like to think it was Charlie Perry. But he's not the professional-killer type. My best guess is that it's someone who is operating under the color of law."

Although he didn't want to believe it, Andy had no reason to doubt Kerney. "Does Perry know you've blown a hole in his case?"

"He will in about four hours when the news of Stewart's murder is made public."

"Jesus, what have you fallen into?" Andy asked.

"Quicksand," Kerney said.

"What are you going to do?"

"I want to move the bar up a notch. Let me use your criminal intelligence people to wire Perry and Applewhite's hotel rooms for sound and tap their telephones."

"Have you got a court order?" Andy asked.

"Do you know a judge who'd give me one?" Kerney replied. "I'd be laughed out of chambers. At worst it's my word against the FBI. At best it's pure speculation."

"You're asking me for something I'm not willing to do."

"Would you be willing to change your mind if I told you that I have reason to believe Father Mitchell's murder is directly tied to the Terrell case?"

"What reasons?"

"Start with the fact that yesterday Bobby Sloan found a stack of videotapes and a briefcaseful of information Mitchell had assembled that points to a major government espionage operation in South America. Add to that Applewhite's arrival at Bobby's house after midnight armed with a federal court order requiring that all the evidence be immediately turned over to the Bureau."

"You better give me the whole story."

"Not in your office," Kerney replied.

Andy reached for a phone. "Let me cancel a meeting and we'll find a nice, private place in the building to talk."

Andy took him to the armory, a room with thick, reinforced-concrete walls and a steel door, where tactical weapons and ammunition were stored.

"Start at the beginning," Andy said, closing the door.

Kerney ran it down.

Andy said nothing until Kerney finished. "The connection between Terrell and Mitchell is a stretch, Kevin," he said. "The MOs are completely different."

"All four murders, if you include the Gatlin suicide, are different," Kerney countered. "Which is exactly the way a professional killer would operate."

"You're assuming one killer, possibly a government agent, did them all?"

"I think it's highly probable."

"This is risky business, Kevin."

"I know it."

"I don't think you do. You've got a new wife, a child on the way, and a career to think about."

"I'd be very happy if none of this had happened, Andy. But it has. Would you let it slide?"

"Not completely," Andy said. "I'd want some answers, but I wouldn't risk my neck to get them."

Kerney thought about Sara, his impending fatherhood, and all he had to look forward to. "I don't plan on going off half cocked. I want information, not confrontation. Will you help?"

"You want electronic surveillance on Perry and Applewhite?"

"That could get us some of the answers I need."

"And ruin our careers," Andy said. "Okay, you've got it."

"Thanks."

"Don't thank me," Andy replied. "I'm already regretting my decision."

The police radio squawked Kerney's call sign. Larry Otero wanted to talk to him, Helen Muiz had paperwork needing his signature, Detective Sloan wanted a few minutes of his time, dispatch had three messages to pass on from Cloudy Herrera's pushy lawyer.

He didn't respond and drove out of town along the two-lane state road that passed by the state penitentiary and the new county jail. He kept his eye on the rearview mirror as he passed the jail and didn't turn around until he was certain he wasn't being tailed.

He had to assume that his office, house, and car were bugged, tapped, wired, and videotaped; that Andy was also under some sort of electronic surveillance; and that vehicle-tracking devices had been planted on department vehicles to keep tabs on the where-abouts of key personnel.

Doing a sweep or a grid-search for wiretaps and bugs at police headquarters wouldn't catch everything, not with the new remote technology that made long-distance eavesdropping easy. Ripping out bugs and inspecting vehicles for tracking sensors wouldn't be smart anyway. You could never be sure if you found everything and it would only serve to alert the listeners that their surveillance had been compromised.

He parked and went inside the county jail. It was a safe place to put his plan into motion. Cops went in and out of jails all the time, so his presence at the facility shouldn't raise suspicions.

He introduced himself to the receptionist, showed his shield, and asked to use an empty office. In a small space used by shift supervisors he dictated everything he knew and all his conjectures about the Terrell-Mitchell homicides into a microtape recorder. When he finished he wrote out a message to Helen Muiz that read:

Hand-carry this confidential message to Lt. Sal Molina and Detective Robert Sloan. Do not speak to anyone about this message or make a copy of it. Destroy this message immediately after the officers have read it.
TO: Lt. Molina, Det. Sloan
Assemble all remaining Terrell-Mitchell case documents and meet me at the county jail ASAP. Do not travel together or use departmental vehicles. Do not reveal your destination or engage in any radio or tele-

phone communication about this assignment after you receive this message.

He signed the message and faxed it, hoping that the two officers didn't show up looking at him like he was a paranoid nutcase.

Kerney's early-morning phone call to the Red River marshal, and his voice message to Helen Muiz canceling all his scheduled appointments, had forced Elaine Applewhite out of a warm bed in her hotel room and into her car. She'd followed him all the way to Questa before turning back. She didn't give a damn if the fatal accident got turned into a homicide. It had been a good hit that wouldn't come back to bite her. None of them ever had.

What bothered her was Kerney. He was acting a bit too clever. What put him on to Randall Stewart in the first place? What made him think that Stewart was a target?

Applewhite knew the ambassador wouldn't be happy when she called him in Washington with the report of Kerney's snooping. He expected everything to go smoothly, thought that all field contingency problems were caused by sloppy procedures, and stomped hard on operatives when pissed off.

Maybe there wouldn't be a need to raise the old boy's blood pressure. Applewhite decided to wait and see what shook out from Kerney's little jaunt up north. She had lots of time before a call had to be made; Terrell wasn't scheduled to return to South America until tomorrow morning.

She'd watched for Kerney's return from the outskirts of Santa Fe, monitoring the Taos district state-police-band frequency through a computer satellite link that fed directly into her laptop. The last transmission from the officer at the scene came in when Stewart's body had been loaded on the meat wagon for transport. He'd coded his report as an accidental death and resumed patrol.

That had made Applewhite smile.

When Kerney passed by, she'd switched the laptop to a vehicle-

tracking program that would record the travel and location of his
vehicle in a fifty-mile radius. Then she went back to the hotel for a
late lunch, feeling much more positive about the phone call she
needed to make to Ambassador Terrell.

Maybe fuss-bucket Charlie Perry, whom Applewhite longed to
whack just for the fun of it, had been right about Kerney being an
over-the-hill lightweight cop who occasionally got lucky.

Kerney hoped that Molina and Sloan would buy into his
scheme. While he waited for their arrival, he faxed a request to
Andy Baca that would put the plan into play, if his officers agreed,
and got a good-to-go response back. Bobby Sloan arrived first, carrying a cardboard box. He dumped it on the table in the meeting
room Kerney had taken over and gave him a wily smile.

"What's all that?" Kerney asked.

"Applewhite didn't get everything, Chief. I stayed late at the office last night and copied all the Mitchell documents and tapes."

"Did anybody see you do it?"

Sloan shook his head. "Nope. I've got more news, Chief. Phyllis
Terrell made two five-thousand-dollar cash withdrawals on the
same days that Mitchell entered identical deposits in his checkbook."

Kerney smiled. The link between Terrell and Mitchell was now
real. "What will it be, Bobby? A commendation or a promotion?"

"I'll pass on the promotion, Chief. I've already got the job I
want. But a commendation for my personnel file would be nice."

"Consider it done," Kerney said.

"Thanks." Sloan popped an antacid pill. "I figure we're meeting
at the jail because some naughty FBI agents have been listening in
on our private conversations."

"You're not wrong. They haven't been playing nice. It's our turn
to bend a few rules. Are you game?"

"You bet, if I'm allowed to do great bodily harm to Applewhite.
She freaked my wife out last night."

"That's not a good idea."

"I can dream, can't I?" Sloan said with a grin.

Sal Molina arrived. Kerney asked Sloan to bring the lieutenant up to speed on the Mitchell case. Bobby summarized the important events and what had been learned from the new evidence.

Molina sat silent and stone faced. "I should have known about this, Detective," he said when Bobby stopped talking.

Irritated by Molina's officious response, Kerney fiddled with a loose paper clip before reacting. "Detective Sloan came to me because you were out in the field, Lieutenant. I asked him not to talk to anyone about the developments in the Mitchell case without my permission."

"You don't think I can be trusted?" Molina asked.

"You wouldn't be here if I thought that. It's almost a sure bet that we're under electronic surveillance. On top of that I acquired conclusive proof today that the FBI lied big time about Scott Gatlin."

Kerney spelled out the facts surrounding Randall Stewart's murder and the DNA test results. Bobby Sloan sat wide eyed in his chair, rubbing a hand over his stomach. Molina let out a low uncharacteristic whistle.

Kerney continued. "In about an hour Charlie Perry will know that we know Randall Stewart's death was a homicide. He'll assume, quite rightly, that the Terrell murder cover-up has been blown. We've been under surveillance since day one. As of now I'm returning the favor to the fullest extent possible. There are phone taps, video cameras, and microphones planted in Perry's and Applewhite's hotel rooms."

"You got a court order for that?" Molina asked disbelievingly.

"No." Kerney leaned forward in his chair, concentrating his attention on Molina. "You were right to bust my balls about shutting down the investigation, Sal. But I'd been warned off by Perry and I didn't want to telegraph my intentions to keep digging into the case—not with the Feds listening. I thought I could do enough hunting out of season on my own to get a handle on what is really going on, but I can't. I need help."

Molina thought about his career and his short-timer's calendar. He thought about doing time in the slammer if the feds decided to hand him *his* balls on a silver platter. There would be no trips in the camper, no fishing excursions to Idaho.

"Okay, what do you need from us?" Sal asked, his mouth dry.

"I want to put tails on Perry and Applewhite," Kerney said. "We need to track their movements. Surveillance only. No intervention regardless of what goes down. We photograph or videotape anything that's out of the ordinary."

"For how long, Chief?" Bobby Sloan asked.

"Forty-eight hours."

"Who else gets assigned?" Molina asked.

"Just the two of you," Kerney replied.

"Impossible," Molina said. "Perry and Applewhite know us."

"If you agree to this, I've registered both of you for a class at the law-enforcement academy starting tomorrow. Two vehicles seized by the state police and outfitted for undercover narcotic work will be waiting for you there. Each is fully equipped. The sheriff's department will handle all your radio traffic, utilizing the tri-county drug task force channel. I'm betting the feds aren't going to be expecting us to look outside the department for help."

"Speaking of that," Sloan said, "who set up the electronic surveillance? It wasn't any of our people, that's for sure."

"Chief Baca," Kerney answered. "His criminal intelligence people will monitor and stay in touch with you through the sheriff's dispatch. This will be a straight forty-eight-hour assignment. You'll sleep in the cars, eat in the cars. No breaks, no relief."

"This scheme could bring a lot of good cops down," Molina said.

"Which is why I'm asking for your help, not ordering."

"Jesus, Sal, let's do it," Bobby said, who like Kerney had pulled a tour in Nam. "This country isn't a fucking police state. At least, not yet."

The consequences scared Molina, but he had to decide. Either he took the risk or he bailed out on his chief. He shored himself up. "Okay. Forty-eight hours."

"I'm apprehensive too, Lieutenant," Kerney said, reading Molina's expression.

Breath whooshed out of Molina. "Yeah."

Charlie Perry raged while Applewhite sat at the hotel-room desk punching up the vehicle tracking records for Kerney and the other key investigative personnel in his department on her laptop.

The lead detectives assigned to the homicides were off duty and at home, and Kerney, after making a stop at the state police headquarters, was parked at the county jail, where he'd been for a very long time.

"I thought Kerney had canceled all his appointments for the day," Applewhite said. "Why did he go to state police headquarters and then the county jail?"

"Are you even fucking listening to me?" Perry snapped.

"Yes, the Red River marshal is treating Stewart's death as a homicide," Applewhite said blithely. She wished she could garrote the son of a bitch. "I heard you."

Perry put both hands on the table and stuck his face in Applewhite's. "Who sanctioned the hit?"

"That's a pretty cheeky question to be asking me, Charlie," Applewhite said, closing the laptop cover. "Neither of us knows the who, what, or the why of the matter."

"Look, if I have to cover your ass, I want to know now."

"All you have to do right now is throw your weight around a little, Charlie. Scoop up Stewart's body and make sure only a trusted forensic pathologist does the autopsy."

"What trustworthy doctor do you have in mind?"

Applewhite wrote out a name and number and waved the slip of paper under Charlie's nose. "Call this number in Albuquerque. The man who answers the phone will be a doctor who holds a Q clearance. Get the body to him."

Perry snatched the paper. "What about Kerney? He's got to know by now that we've been feeding him pure bullshit."

"But can he prove anything?" Applewhite said. "I doubt it. If it becomes necessary, Chief Kerney will be dealt with."

"How?"

Applewhite knew it wouldn't be her call to make, but she loved thinking about the possibilities if a sanction removal was authorized. The anticipation of it made her smile.

"Firmly but gently, Charlie," she said, getting to her feet. She steered Perry out the door, returned to the desk, and dialed a Washington number.

With the phone cradled against his ear, Hamilton Lowell Terrell made notes while listening to Applewhite's report. She finished speaking and he lapsed into a long silence.

"Your instructions, sir?" Applewhite finally asked, unable to repress her apprehension. If she was due for a butt-chewing, she wanted it over and done with.

Terrell let the silence grind deeper into Applewhite, then said, "This isn't the containment we had in mind."

"I'm aware of that, sir."

"I've heard nothing about your plans to help our third friend reach his destination."

"I've got the itinerary finalized, Ambassador."

"Make sure his trip is uneventful," Terrell said, consulting his notes. "Are you quite sure that the local police chief has nothing more than suppositions to go on?"

"At this point, yes. But that could change."

"Do you have reason to believe it *will* change?"

"He's much more resourceful than I was led to believe."

"Did the materials he reviewed give him an advantage?"

"Not really, but they did provide a connection we were hoping to avoid."

"If we manage the situation correctly from here on out, that shouldn't be a problem. Since truth, in this instance, is heavily mingled with falsehood, I doubt he'll be able to probe too deeply."

"Take no action?" Applewhite inquired.

"Let me see what I can learn about him that might be useful for future planning, if the situation warrants."

"And Agent Perry?"

"I know you wish to be rid of him, and you have my sympathy. But ask yourself this question: Where would you like the burden of guilt to fall if all does not go well?"

"I understand, sir."

"Henceforth, there are to be no more contingencies," Terrell said. "Do I make myself clear?"

"Perfectly, sir."

Terrell disconnected and dialed a DOD number.

The phone rang once and a voice said, "Yes, Ambassador."

"Santa Fe, New Mexico, Police Chief Kevin Kerney. Best-case scenario for sanctioned removal. All particulars to me, eyes only, by twenty-three hundred hours."

"Under DOD regulations pertaining to the National Security Act, I am required to inform you that contemplated sanctioned removals require concurrence from the national security advisor, CIA, and the commanding general of the Defense Intelligence Agency."

"Particulars to me by twenty-three hundred," Terrell repeated.

"Aye-aye, sir."

Kerney left the county jail and did some shopping. He stopped at a discount chain store, bought cellular phones, and paid the activation fees. At a video store he bought a stack of used movies. He topped off his shopping spree at an electronics superstore, where he purchased a small TV with a built-in VCR, a tape recorder, two privacy earphones, and a radio wave frequency detector.

He drove home, dressed to go running, and slipped a night vision scope in the pocket of his lightweight pullover parka. Outside he did a few stretching exercises and took off down the driveway past his landlord's house. Once he turned the corner of the block, he pulled up, and walked down the utility easement that ran behind his cottage. He climbed a lot wall and used an electric meter box as a stepping-stone to get to the roof of an old garage. He flattened out in a prone position and scanned with the scope looking for any evidence of a surveillance video camera. He spotted it at the base of a TV satellite dish mounted on the porch roof of a neighboring house, angled to get a clear view of the front of his cottage. He looked around for more and found none.

He wondered if the uplink to the watchers and listeners was local or remote. He scrambled down, completed a circle around the block, and stopped in front of the house with the TV dish. No lights were on inside. He gauged the distance between the top of the porch railing and the roof line. If he stood tiptoe on the railing he could probably disable the camera. But why tell the watchers that he knew he was being watched?

At the cottage Kerney punched the playback on his answering machine, and carted in the Mitchell evidence he'd sneaked onto the back patio before parking in the driveway. He caught snatches of messages left by Sara, each one sounding a little more terse, as he brought in his new TV/VCR and the other purchases. He dumped it all in the bedroom, stuck a movie in the living-room VCR, turned up the volume, and closed the bedroom door.

John Wayne kicked butt chasing Indians while Kerney hunted bugs in his bedroom and bath. On his first visual sweep he found three, one in a lamp, one in a wall outlet, and one in the bedroom telephone. He swept again, taking apart everything he could think of, searching every surface—bed frame, mattress, dresser, pictures, walls, ceiling. He found a third inside a doorknob, a fourth behind the toilet tank, and a fifth on the underside of a floor heating duct. Except for the bathroom device he left everything else in place.

Using a handheld scanner Kerney made a grid-by-grid pass of the walls, floors, and ceiling in the bathroom, bedroom, and closet, and didn't find any more bugs. With what he'd bought, he could work in the bedroom without raising the suspicions of his listeners.

He carried everything he needed into the bedroom and closed the door. Just before he plugged in the earphones and started listening to the audiotapes, the living room TV blared the notes of a bugler sounding a cavalry charge.

Unlike *real* cities with *real* morgues and coroners, the Santa Fe local-yokels stashed their stiffs at the regional hospital. That made scooping up the body, as Applewhite had so inelegantly put it, a relatively easy chore for Charlie Perry. He followed the rent-an-ambulance to an HMO facility in Albuquerque near the air force base, within shouting distance of the VA hospital. Two white-coats and an armed uniformed security guard waited at the back door.

The white-coats transferred the corpse to the gurney and the guard led the way into the building. Perry tagged behind. The inside didn't look anything like an HMO clinic. There were laboratories, research suites, and communications rooms, offices identified by numbers only, contamination vaults and refrigerated storage lockers posted with radioactive warning signs, a video surveillance room, and finally a *real* morgue.

The white-coats dumped the body on a stainless-steel autopsy table and left. The guard remained in the room. Perry smiled at the guard. He got a tight nod back.

CIA, thought Charlie. Maybe something to do with the vast nuclear weapons stockpile stored in the mountains on the air force base. He thought human radiation exposure, epidemiology testing for rare forms of cancer, forensic pathology studies to determine unusual causes of death, psych testing to assess mental functioning.

Charlie decided it was smart to put the facility right next door to the base and close to the VA hospital so all the civilian and military worker bees could be easily examined, probed, and tested, to study the effects of exposure to plutonium, uranium, anthrax bacilli, Ebola, or whatever else the government was playing around with.

A man in a lab coat walked in. He flipped off the sheet covering the cadaver and did a visual head-to-toe inspection. Maybe on the early side of forty, he wore a Naval Academy class ring.

"Cause of death appears to be blunt trauma to the head, with some very interesting lacerations," the man said. "Someone drew blood, did a mouth swab, and took a skin sample. What's that all about?"

Perry froze. That son of a bitch Kerney had all he needed to wash the Terrell homicide cover-up down the tubes. He didn't know whether to lie or tell the truth. He knew Applewhite wasn't FBI. But was she CIA? Military intelligence? State Department counterintelligence? He had every reason to believe she'd killed four, possibly five people. It was time to start covering his ass.

"Who took the samples?" the doctor asked.

"I had those done," Perry lied.

The doctor nodded. "Want me to open him up?"

"If you think it's necessary."

"What do you need?"

"The local police are calling it a homicide," Perry replied.

"I doubt they're wrong. What do you want done?"

"It needs to become an accidental death," Perry said.

"Who gets the autopsy report?"

"The Red River town marshal."

Sal Molina's undercover vehicle was a minivan equipped with a radio, a pinpoint shielded privacy light, cell phone, .35mm camera, night-vision binoculars, video camera, and an array of weapons held in a rack above his head. While it looked like an anonymous soccer-mom car, a souped-up eight-cylinder engine powered the vehicle and a new suspension gave it a surefooted feel on the road. The van could top out at 140 mph and manage a high-speed emergency U-turn without flipping over.

It had been used by a local real estate agent to transport crack cocaine to wealthy clients who divided their time between Santa Fe in the summer and trendy, upscale Colorado skiing destinations in the winter.

Sal had tailed Charlie Perry and the ambulance to Albuquerque. Watching Perry play body snatcher demolished the last of his doubts about Chief Kerney's plan. He took snapshots, scribbled surveillance field notes, and followed Perry back to Santa Fe, expecting to spend the remainder of the night parked outside of Charlie's hotel. Instead, he waited and watched as Perry parked at the back of the federal courthouse two blocks from the plaza and went inside.

The FBI offices were next door in the post office building. What was Perry doing at the courthouse? Unless he had a late-night meeting with a judge or a federal prosecutor from the U.S. attorney's office in from Albuquerque, it made no sense. Other than Charlie's unit there were no cars in the spaces reserved for judges and staff. But behind the post office there were five nice, shiny new Ford sedans that screamed FBI.

Only one full-time resident agent, Frank Powers, worked out of Santa Fe. Why the late-night caucus?

Sal reached for the Santa Fe telephone book, found a number, and dialed up a retired sheriff's captain who worked as a federal-court security officer. Six years ago Molina had busted the man's youngest son for drug dealing, turned him into a snitch, and let him walk. After the kid cleaned up his act, Molina had cut him loose.

A sleepy voice answered on the second ring.

"Jake."

"Yeah."

"It's Sal Molina. Who's holding a late-night convention at the courthouse?"

"Man, I don't know what you're talking about. The courthouse is locked up at night."

"Wrong answer, Jake. I just watched an FBI agent go in the back door." Sal heard Jake catch his breath.

"I don't know nothing about that," Jake said.

"I hear Joey's doing okay. Married. Kid on the way. Got a good job as an auto mechanic with the highway department."

"Jesus, don't do this to me, Sal." The words came out pinched.

"That's not a trade someone learns in the slammer," Sal said evenly.

"Okay, okay, I owe you. There's an off-limits suite of rooms in the basement. People come and go. I don't know what they do down there."

"I need more than that, Jake."

"This has to stay off the record," Jake said. "I'm not supposed to talk about it."

"You've got my word."

"You gotta pass through a retina- and palm-print-scan foyer that's behind a keypad access door on the first floor, just off the back entrance. That's all I know."

"You said you see those people come and go, Jake. Who do you think they are?"

"Some are FBI suits and Beltway types, but most of the current crew look like computer geeks to me."

"Is the basement in constant use?" Sal asked. "Staffed regularly?"

"The last group to use it was the Secret Service. They were here when the vice president came to Santa Fe."

"When did the computer geeks set up shop?"

"About two months before the FBI task force came to town on the Terrell homicide."

Sal decided not to push it any further. "Thanks, Jake. Give my best to Joey."

After sampling the Mitchell audiotapes to get the meat of each interview, Kerney worked up a set of questions he would use in the morning. He planned to call some of the people Mitchell had interviewed. He figured it would be safe to use each of the new cell phones three or four times before the feds got on to it.

He stared at Mitchell's list of names and numbers. How did the priest make contact with these people? There was no phone in his room at the brothers' residence hall, and the two phones in the common areas where the brothers congregated weren't suitable for private conversations.

Kerney went into the bathroom, turned on the shower, and used one of the cell phones to call the residence hall. Brother Jerome answered.

Kerney identified himself and jumped right to the point. "Did Father Mitchell have access to a campus telephone?"

"None was assigned to him, but he did use my office telephone when he needed to make a call. He used a calling card when he was in the field that was billed to my number. He was very prompt about paying the college for the charges."

"Do you have a record of his calls?" Kerney asked.

"Of course. Every personal and long-distance call charged to the college must be logged on a special form. Each month we get a printout of all charges incurred from each office telephone. Every faculty and staff member is honor bound to identify nonbusiness calls and reimburse the college."

"Does that include local calls?" Kerney asked.

"I have my department faculty and staff log all calls, regardless of whether they're local or long distance. That policy applied to Father Mitchell."

"I need copies of those records, Brother Jerome. Can you have them ready for me in fifteen minutes?"

"Certainly. Come to my office."

Kerney got to the college in a hurry and gathered up the copies, thanked Brother Jerome, and left. Back at home he stuck a Steve McQueen movie in the VCR to entertain his unknown listeners, and started in on the log sheets. Each showed date, time, and number-called information. Using Mitchell's notes, Kerney matched a good two dozen names to numbers. In the morning he'd work all of Mitchell's most recent calls, starting with area residents.

Kerney switched his attention to the computer printouts and

broke into a smile. Over the last three months Mitchell had made eight—no, ten—phone calls to Phyllis Terrell in Santa Fe and Virginia. The connection was getting stronger and the proof more convincing.

Chapter **10**

Fred Browning was on a natural high. The new job in Silicon Valley had turned into a very sweet deal. A company vice president had met him at the San Francisco Airport and chatted him up on the drive to the corporate headquarters. He offered Fred a big bump in salary, the rent-free use of a town house for the first six months, and a stipend to pay all relocation expenses.

With Tim Ingram's promise of a job that would get him back to Albuquerque in a year, Fred jumped at the offer. Before catching an evening flight back to Albuquerque, he spent the day signing pre-employment paperwork, touring the facility, and meeting with members of his new security staff. During the Phoenix layover he called Tim Ingram and gave him the news.

Tim proposed they should celebrate by heading down to the lake a day early instead of waiting until Saturday. Fred thought that was a fine idea. He downed a couple of self-congratulatory whiskeys in the airport bar, had another one on the short hop to Albuquerque, and rolled up the jetway with a bit of a buzz. Tim greeted him inside the terminal.

Fred grinned at his friend. "Is it Friday already?" he asked.

"No," Tim said, grinning back. "But knowing you, I figured you would have already started celebrating. I bet you're a point or two over the blood alcohol legal limit."

"Maybe just barely."

"Come on, I'll give you a ride home."

"What about my car?" Fred asked.

"Leave it here. You can pick it up on Sunday when we get back from the lake."

Fred shrugged. "Why not? Let me buy you a drink."

"Not necessary," Tim said. "I've got a flask in my glovebox."

"That'll do."

Browning took two hits from the drug-laced flask and passed out on the short drive to the air force base. Ingram checked his carotid artery and found a strong pulse. As an intelligence operative Ingram had carried out a number of disagreeable assignments. But delivering a man to be killed, especially one he'd worked hard to keep alive and who wasn't a clear security threat, made Ingram feel like a sadist. At least he wouldn't have to watch Fred Browning get wasted.

He flashed his headlights as he approached the guard gate, and the air policeman waved him through. On the tarmac a car and a helicopter waited. Ingram rolled to a stop. Applewhite opened the passenger door, gave him a cold look, and jammed a syringe into Browning's neck.

Ingram wanted to shoot her, stomp her, slug her. Instead he counted seconds. Browning convulsed and died in less than a minute. He got out of the car, sucked in some fresh, cold air, and watched the body get loaded into the helicopter.

Smiling, her eyes dancing, Applewhite came around the front of the car.

"You're a stone-cold bitch," Ingram said.

Applewhite laughed at her old West Point classmate. "I didn't want to leave you out of the loop, Tim."

"You like killing people, don't you, Elaine?"

"This Bureau detail has made you soft," Applewhite said darkly.

Ingram watched the chopper take off. In two hours Browning's body would be fed into a high-temperature furnace at a primate research laboratory on a southern New Mexico air force base.

"Ashes to ashes," Applewhite said.

Ingram turned away, drove to his quarters, swallowed a quick double shot of single mash, and stared at his reflection in the bathroom mirror. It didn't matter that the hit had been sanctioned by the chain of command, an innocent man was dead. That made it capital murder. In a just world he would be arrested, charged, convicted, and sentenced for the crime.

None of this should have happened. Not to Browning, Terjo, or Stewart.

He turned out the light, wondering what had become of the fresh-faced, idealistic kid from Iowa who'd wanted to be a career officer, a war-fighter, a kick-ass, gung-ho soldier? Could he ever put on the uniform again?

Bobby Sloan's undercover four-by-four Chevy Blazer came with all the customary surveillance goodies, plus the added bonus of a laptop computer linked to federal crime information computers and state motor vehicle data banks. After checking out the vehicle Bobby had clipped a wallet-size photograph of his wife to the visor, just like in his regular unit. Lucy had never been a babe in the Hollywood sense of the word, but she was his babe. The photo reminded Bobby that his first priority on the job was to survive and go home to Lucy when work was done.

Tailing Applewhite to Albuquerque had been a breeze, but he'd been forced to break off contact when she entered Kirtland Air Force Base at a guard checkpoint station. Bobby waited away from the gate and down the street to avoid raising suspicion. Over the years Sloan had trained dozens of new detectives in undercover and surveillance techniques. He'd always hammered away at the mantra to observe, record, take nothing for granted, and get the details. Bobby practiced what he preached.

Only a few cars entered the base while Bobby waited. He used his time spotting license plates through binoculars, running MVD record checks on the laptop, and writing down the information. It was a boring task, but it kept him focused. His interest jumped when a car approached the gate, flashed its headlights, and got waved through without stopping. Somebody important was in a hurry.

Sloan ran the plate, got the name of the registered owner, and searched motor vehicle files for driver's license information. The likely driver of the car was a Timothy Ingram. Sloan saved the information, which came with a color photograph of the subject, on a floppy disk.

After spending all night poring over the Mitchell evidence, Kerney allowed himself two hours of rack time and fell asleep immediately. The alarm jarred him awake. He cleaned up, spooned down a bland-tasting bowl of instant oatmeal, and played back Sara's telephone messages.

Message 1: *"You sounded edgy the last time we spoke. Call me. I'm worried about you."*
Message 2: *"Are you busy? Should I cancel the weekend trip? Call me."*
Message 3: *"Nobody at your office knows where you are. I can't spend all day trying to track you down. Dammit, Kerney, where are you? I'm flying in. Meet me at the airport if you can."*

Kerney winced. Sara was justifiably pissed at being ignored.

He'd put Molina and Sloan deep undercover. That meant no contact with their families or the department, no disclosure of the assignment, and no communication that could compromise the operation. Stupidly, he'd been operating with the same mind-set, which was exactly the wrong thing to do. He needed to act like everything was normal.

Kerney checked the clock. Because of the difference in time

zones it was an hour later at Fort Leavenworth. If Sara was true to form, she would be out on her morning run before heading off to classes. He called and left a message. The week had been hellishly busy, he couldn't wait to see her, nothing was wrong, and he was sorry he hadn't called sooner. He'd pick her up at the airport.

He went to the bathroom, ran the shower, and called Reynaldo Valencia, a professor of Latin American studies at the university in Albuquerque. Mitchell had phoned the professor a number of times from Brother Jerome's office. He woke Valencia up and explained his reasons for calling. Valencia agreed to meet with him immediately.

His house phone rang before he could leave. He picked up and Helen Muiz asked him if he was ever planning to come into the office again.

"What's up?" Kerney asked.

"Mr. Demora, the city manager, is eager to see you."

"About?"

"He wouldn't say. But he left three messages last night after six P.M."

"You're at the office early."

"Someone has to hold things together in your absence."

"I have a deputy chief now, Helen."

"Yes, and thank goodness he's here to assist me. You also have other tasks waiting that need your attention."

"Can they hold?"

"I suppose so." Helen sighed.

"Call Demora and ask him if this afternoon would be convenient."

"And where will you be until then?"

Kerney thought fast. "I have a doctor's appointment in Albuquerque."

"Is something wrong?"

"Just the knee acting up again."

"You should get it looked at," Helen said sympathetically.

"You've been limping rather badly lately. I'll put you down on sick leave for the morning."

Even though he had no visible tail, Kerney ditched his unit in front of his orthopedist's office in Albuquerque and called a cab to pick him up at the back of the building. Reynaldo Valencia lived near the university on a street named for one of the early presidents. The house was a fifties post-war, Santa Fe–style single-story residence sheltered from the street by mature shrubs and large trees.

Valencia was a tall man with graying hair that matched the color of his neatly trimmed mustache. He greeted Kerney with a serious, questioning expression and guided him to a family room that proclaimed an enjoyment of books and learning. Shelves crammed with books filled walls from floor to ceiling, magazines, journals, and newspapers filled tabletops, and thick dictionaries and atlases rested on pedestal stands.

"I don't know if I can help you," Valencia said. He gestured at a comfortable chair and took a seat in a rocker. He spoke perfect English with a slight Spanish accent.

Kerney sat down. "I'm sure you'd like to see Father Mitchell's killer brought to justice."

"Very much so. But my experience has made me rather distrustful of police officers."

"I'm sorry to hear that," Kerney said. "Have you had some bad experiences with the police?"

"Indeed, I have. For example, it was the police who inadvertently introduced me to Father Mitchell," Valencia said. "We met in jail, after having been arrested during a peaceful, nonviolent demonstration at the entrance to Fort Benning. The police roughed us up, handcuffed us, put us in paddy wagons, and locked us in a cell for hours. They had no cause to do it."

"That doesn't sound pleasant," Kerney said. "Unfortunately, not all police officers are competent or well led. Would a belated apology from an officer who had nothing to do with taking you to jail make it better?"

"You're joking," Valencia said

"Only partially," Kerney replied. "I don't appreciate cops who make the rest of us look bad. It destroys the public's trust and makes the job more difficult."

"Why should I assume that you're really any different? How can I be sure of your motives?"

"Perhaps if we talk for a while, you'll be able to form an opinion or make a judgment about those questions," Kerney said.

Valencia studied Kerney for a few seconds. "That's fair enough. But if I think you've come here to investigate my political beliefs and actions, or those of my friends and associates, I will cut you off."

"That's more than reasonable," Kerney said. "I take it you came to know Father Mitchell fairly well after your time together in jail."

"Yes, we were both active in the School of the Americas Vigil Committee."

"From what I've learned, he seemed intent on discovering the specifics about his brother's death."

Valencia took a pipe from a side table and toyed with it. "It was constantly on his mind. He spent a year in Venezuela and Colombia searching for answers."

"What did he uncover?" Kerney asked.

Valencia filled his pipe. "He believed that his brother had been put in charge of establishing a secret training facility for assassins who were to be sent into Colombia to murder members of the drug cartels."

"Funded and operated by our government?"

Valencia nodded. "Using the same ruse that failed so miserably in Vietnam, military advisors."

"Father Mitchell was convinced of this?"

"Yes. His brother was an experienced intelligence officer who specialized in training field operatives."

"Did he have proof?" Kerney asked.

Valencia lit his pipe and the scent of tobacco filled the room. "He was never able to corroborate his theory. Most of the information came to him as rumor or supposition."

"What did he learn about his brother's death?"

"Supposedly, the murder was arranged by drug lords who learned of the colonel's mission from a bribed Colombian army officer. As I understand it, Colombian police were to be trained in Venezuela by the U.S. Army, then sent home to infiltrate the cartels and kill the *jefes* and their associates. At the time a commonly held belief among American intelligence agencies was that the cartels were nothing but a large-scale version of common street dealers. In fact, the cartels had a superior intelligence-gathering apparatus."

"Did the mission go forward after the colonel's death?"

"Yes, but not quite the way it was supposed to," Valencia said. "Our government unwittingly placed in the hands of the cartels a cadre of qualified assassins who were used against the supporters of the American-backed drug interdiction program."

"The *jefes* infiltrated the project?"

"No, they simply identified the recruits, waited until they were trained, and bought the services of most of them. Jump ahead in time. The police assassins who refused to serve the *jefes* are murdered one by one. Car bombs kill ranking federal prosecutors. Politicians running on anticartel platforms disappear. The federal official in charge of drug interdiction, a man of impeccable reputation, is killed by a sniper's bullet. Journalists sympathetic to the anticartel movement are found burned to death in tragic automobile accidents. Judges are kidnapped, held for ransom, and then shot. Are these the acts of untrained, unsophisticated street thugs?"

"I doubt it," Kerney said. "But weren't some arrests made?"

"Of course. Teenagers mostly, with no knowledge of the inner workings of either the cartels or the hit squads."

"So, you believed Father Mitchell," Kerney said.

Valencia tamped out the tobacco in his pipe and laid it aside. "I was born and raised in Colombia, Chief Kerney. I know how the rich, the powerful, and the privileged are treated because of the resources they possess. I've seen firsthand how money can purchase special favors. Even though Father Joseph had not one shred of proof to back up his contentions, I believed him."

"It seems as though Father Mitchell was trying to uncover much more than just the truth about his brother's murder."

"He was an expert in modern U.S. military history with an emphasis in Latin American affairs," Valencia said. "He had strong fears that something more was at hand."

"Such as?"

"The people of Colombia are poor, the government is corrupt, and the elite rule. Rebels and bandits roam the countryside, where the army refuses to go. The country is only partially under the control of the government. Cartels earn billions of dollars from the illicit American drug economy. Growers are now raising opium to get a share of the North American heroin market. Counterfeiting of American currency is rampant. The United States has overthrown governments, supported dictators, and started wars in South America for fewer reasons than that."

"Can you be more specific about Father Joseph's concerns?"

"He thought that a number of federal agencies were participating in a clandestine plan to eliminate the drug cartels, install a new government in Bogota, and support a full-scale ground war against the rebels."

"Did he ever mention a secret American trade mission to South America?" Kerney asked.

Valencia looked quizzical. "No, and I've heard nothing about it from any other sources. Does one exist?"

"I've been told that one does."

"Interesting," Valencia said.

"How so?" Kerney asked.

"If Washington's goal is to overthrow the Colombian government and make war on the cartels and the rebels, it would be wise to have a compact with countries bordering Colombia that supported U.S. intervention."

"Would such a compact be possible?"

"Criminals give bribes to achieve their goals, governments call it foreign aid. And all of South America is in desperate need of economic assistance."

"Do you know a woman named Phyllis Terrell?" Kerney asked.

Valencia reached for his pipe. "The ambassador's wife who was murdered in Santa Fe? I never met her."

"Did Father Mitchell know her?"

"I don't know if he did or not. Last fall he gave a talk about the growing threat of military intervention in South America at a peace forum in Santa Fe. He called me to talk about it a few days later. He said a woman had come to the meeting specifically to meet him, and that she might have some highly sensitive information that would be helpful to his research. He never mentioned a name. But he sounded very excited about it."

"Do you know of any earlier attempts on Father Mitchell's life?"

Valencia stood up. "We never talked of such matters, although I'm sure he knew he took some risks. There must be a dozen government agencies that would find his research bothersome. You must excuse me. I have a class at the university within the hour."

"Yes, of course," Kerney said, getting to his feet. "Did Father Mitchell stay in touch with you only by telephone?"

"Most of our communication was by e-mail."

"Do you have his e-mail address?"

Valencia nodded and reached for an address book from a bookcase shelf. "I have little faith in computers. They crash far too often, so I always write e-mail addresses down. Joe had two: one for general use and another for more private communication."

Valencia read off the information.

"Did you have copies of Father Mitchell's e-mail letters?" Kerney asked. "Or perhaps keep them stored in your computer?"

Valencia shook his head and smiled. "Copies, no, and I make it a practice to have very little about my private or personal life in the computer. I trust them even less than I trust most police officers."

"Thank you for your openness, Professor."

"You strike me as a sincere, fair-minded man, Chief Kerney. I wish you well in your investigation. Father Joseph deserves justice."

One of Mitchell's Internet service providers was an Albuquerque-based company with corporate offices in a business park adjacent to the Interstate. With walls of glass facing the outside world, the building presented what passed for a sleek, modern look. To Kerney it seemed nothing more than a five-story rectangular box, plopped down next to another equally unattractive box, with nice landscaping designed to hide its pedestrian dullness.

A directory inside the lobby next to the elevators listed the various company suites. Kerney found his way to the ISP's offices, where a young woman smiled genially as he approached the reception desk. She wore a bright yellow lapel pin that read ASK ME ABOUT SWAMI. On the wall behind the desk a poster proclaimed SWAMI: THE NEXT GENERATION OF INTERNET TOOLS. A swirling, modernistic, multicolored turban served as the logo.

He showed the woman his shield and asked to speak with the person in charge of the subscriber database. A young man no more than twenty-five answered the receptionist's call and introduced himself as Wallace Brooks. He guided Kerney into an office cluttered with computers and thick black notebook binders.

Kerney asked for Joseph Mitchell's e-mail records.

"Do you have a court order?" Brooks replied.

"Can't we dispense with the details?" Kerney asked.

Brooks smiled and shook his head. "That's not possible, especially now. We're retooling, our subscriber list is frozen, and we can't release any information."

"Why is that?"

"Our current customer base is being used to test the SWAMI software. With the trade secrets involved I can't possibly give you access to anything without a court order. Even then, our attorney would probably challenge it immediately."

"What can you tell me about SWAMI?" Kerney asked.

The young man's eyes lit up. "SWAMI stands for System-Wide Application for Managing Information. It's a breakthrough tool for Web content management that's going to revolutionize how people use the Internet. And it's scalable, which means it can accommodate everyone from home computer users all the way up to major corporations."

"How does it work?"

"Right now the World Wide Web is a monster. There are millions of sites with astronomical amounts of data and information getting added at an exponential rate. SWAMI allows users to filter and organize the stream of information. And it's a server add-on software package, so users won't have to worry about upgrading to new versions."

"Sounds like a good investment," Kerney said. "Tell me about your corporate structure."

"We're a subsidiary of an investment corporation. The technology we've developed is based on research done at the national science laboratories right here in New Mexico."

"Isn't this a risky time for a new start-up?" Kerney asked

"We're not worried about the dot com or the technology stock shake-out. Everybody is going to use SWAMI."

"Who supplied the venture capital?"

"We're wholly owned by APT Performa, a subsidiary of Trade Source."

"Does Trade Source own the rights to SWAMI?"

"Clarence Thayer, the CEO of APT Performa, owns the rights to SWAMI."

"When does SWAMI hit the marketplace?"

"In three months, max. We believe the trade name is going to be as well known as Intel and Microsoft."

"What are the royalty arrangements?"

"A fee will be passed on to consumers by the server companies. But we're talking about tens of millions of users worldwide paying a small monthly add-on charge."

"I hope you have some stock options," Kerney said.

Brooks smiled gleefully and said yes.

Kerney left, questioning silently if SWAMI's software tricks might be used for intelligence gathering. The FBI already had Carnivore, an Internet wiretap system, in service. Wasn't that enough? Or did the feds want something that had a more global reach?

He followed the connection that ran from Phyllis Terrell to Father Mitchell, and on to the ambassador and Clarence Thayer. Could the murders have had anything to do with SWAMI?

At the top of La Bajada Hill, Santa Fe spread out below him and the mountains filled the horizon. Kerney barely noticed the soft sheen of mare's tail clouds nestled in the foothills. He keyed his microphone, spoke to the detective sergeant on duty, and asked for a court order to access Father Mitchell's e-mail accounts.

He gave the sergeant enough information to start the paperwork process, tossed the microphone on the passenger seat, called Sara on his department cell phone, and left a message for her not to come to Santa Fe for the weekend. He was going to be busy after all.

Outside Applewhite's hotel Bobby Sloan ate a gooey jelly doughnut and sipped lukewarm coffee from a vacuum jug, hoping the sugar and caffeine would keep him going. He hadn't eaten a real meal since lunch yesterday and he knew better than to load up on food if he wanted to stay awake. While he didn't like going hungry, the upside was his stomach gas had eased off considerably. Maybe it was time to think about changing his diet.

Applewhite didn't move until ten in the morning. But when she did, she left in a hurry. Sloan tailed her to the Rodeo Road Business Park, where she parked and went inside a building marked by a sign on the front lawn that read, APT PERFORMA.

Five minutes later Charlie Perry arrived to join the party, followed by Lieutenant Molina, who parked at an adjacent building. He spotted Molina with his binoculars, and Sal pointed in sequence at the row of cars in front of the APT Performa building and made a camera clicking motion with his finger. Bobby got busy taking photographs and running plates.

He finished up as a car eased into an empty slot. The plate registered in his mind as he snapped the shutter: it was the same vehicle that had breezed through the guard checkpoint at the air base without stopping. He got three good shots of the driver's face before the man entered the building.

Sloan accessed the floppy disk with the driver's license photo and MVD record he'd saved last night. The driver was Timothy Ingram and he had a Kirtland Air Force Base address.

For whatever it was worth, another player in the game had been identified.

Tim Ingram tried without success to get interested in the shapely legs of the young woman who led him down the office corridor. Instead, the image of Applewhite sticking the syringe into Fred Browning's neck replayed through his mind, as it had since he'd awakened.

At a conference room Ingram gave the woman a weak smile, pushed through the door, and found Applewhite, Charlie Perry, and Clarence Thayer huddled at the far end of a large oval table. Thayer made a "join us" gesture and Ingram took a seat next to Perry. Applewhite looked at him briefly, expressionless.

Ingram concentrated his attention on Thayer, noting the expensive black wool turtleneck under a perfectly tailored gray sport coat. He'd last seen Thayer in army fatigues with colonel's eagles on the collar when both had been tasked to the SWAMI project. Officially, Thayer had "retired" to start APT Performa and Ingram had "resigned" from the service to go FBI. In truth both remained serving officers, as did Applewhite.

That left Charlie Perry the only true civilian in the room and therefore the one most likely to be slam-dunked should the need arise.

"Good, you're here, Tim," Thayer said in his Back Bay accent.

"Soon as I could make it, sir," Ingram said, thinking that Thayer could easily pass for a Kennedy with his lanky athletic frame, good looks, and patrician style.

"This is your show, Charlie," Thayer said, smiling graciously at the special agent. "Bring us up to speed."

Nervously, almost turned away from Thayer, Perry laid out what he knew. Kerney had factual knowledge he was being watched; factual knowledge that Phyllis Terrell's murder had been cleansed; factual knowledge of Mitchell's probe into SWAMI; factual knowledge of the existence of the SWAMI project. Additionally, he had made a hard evidence connection between Father Mitchell and Phyllis Terrell.

"Are there any other holes that need plugging?" Thayer asked.

"One of the Santa Fe detectives made a copy of the Mitchell evidence Agent Applewhite seized under a court order," Perry said. "It's in Kerney's possession."

Thayer swung his attention to Applewhite. "Does that cause a problem?"

"Not for SWAMI, sir," Applewhite replied. "Although it could bring public attention to sensitive matters of an historical nature."

"Which is not our immediate concern," Thayer said. "Anything else, Charlie?"

"Arrangements have been made to have the official autopsy report show that Randall Stewart's death was accidental. Kerney knows better. When the report comes out, he could decide to challenge the findings. The report won't be released until Monday. Stewart's body will be held until then."

"That gives us enough time to set the problem aside for now," Thayer said. "By Monday we'll have closure."

"Also," Perry said, "Kerney is moving for a court order to get Mitchell's e-mail correspondence."

"The files have been sanitized, so let him have what's left. Is he acting alone or mobilizing his department's resources?"

"As far as we can tell, except for some minor paperwork assistance, he's doing this solo," Charlie replied. "The primary investigators, a detective and a lieutenant, are attending a law-enforcement training seminar."

"Very good," Thayer said, smiling in Ingram's direction. "I'm tasking Agents Applewhite and Perry on a special assignment and I need you to temporarily fill in. Monitor the situation and handle any cleanup items. You'll have full operational control."

"Yes, sir."

Thayer nodded and opened a slim folder. "We shut everything down in forty-eight hours. Here's the preferred scenario if our difficulty with Chief Kerney cannot be resolved in a less extreme manner. A few years ago Chief Kerney earned the displeasure of a Mexican drug lord named Enrique DeLeon. In fact, he did it more than once, but I won't go into details. To retaliate DeLeon approached a high-ranking Mexican army intelligence officer who happens to have his hand in the drug cartels' pockets while drawing a nice retainer from the CIA. DeLeon asked the officer to make available two highly trained Cuban assets for the express purpose of removing the source of his annoyance."

Thayer turned a page. "Unfortunately, both men were killed in a plane crash while machine-gunning a squad of Mexican federal police who were protecting a drug shipment, so the officer has been unable to fulfill DeLeon's request."

Thayer patted the folder and looked at Applewhite. "Señor DeLeon continues to express an interest in Kerney's demise, which has been well documented by several DEA agents in Juárez as well as a highly reliable Interpol informant. DeLeon is in Juárez expecting to meet with you and Agent Perry this afternoon in the hope that you might be willing to take the contract.

"He knows you're Americans, believes that you're former CIA field operatives, and that you're now freelancing in the States. He has no reason not to trust the officer who supplied him with the information, although you both will be carefully scrutinized. You're expected to leave enough of a trail so the Mexican authorities can document the visit. DEA, of course, will confirm the Mexican report. Your true identities will not be revealed. Make your arrangements with DeLeon and then come back to Santa Fe."

"Is all this necessary?" Charlie asked.

"In terms of establishing plausibility, yes," Thayer replied. "In terms of taking definitive action, I hope not. But that will depend on what Chief Kerney does or doesn't do over the short term."

Ingram knew that Thayer was placating Perry. Thayer wouldn't be talking about a removal sanction if the hit hadn't already been approved. Applewhite must be creaming in her pants. Ingram kept his expression neutral, but inside his stomach turned over.

"Maybe I should talk to Kerney again," Perry said.

"I think we're at a point where it's best to let Chief Kerney's actions speak to us," Thayer replied.

"I don't like this," Perry said.

Thayer nodded in agreement. "None of us do, Agent Perry. But we keep our disagreements within the family, so to speak, which you apparently forgot last night when you made unauthorized contact with your superior and asked to be removed from your assignment. That request has been denied."

Charlie's jaw dropped.

Ingram remembered a commercial that used to run on television when he was a kid. Charlie, the talking tuna fish, would swim around in the ocean trying to get caught by the world's best tuna company. But Charlie wasn't good enough to get hooked, processed, vacuum-packed, and served up in a white bread sandwich.

Sorry, Charlie, you poor son of a bitch, Tim thought grimly.

Chapter 11

olina pointed at the car containing Perry and Applewhite, tapped his finger on his chest to signal he'd take the tail, and followed the two agents down Rodeo Road. Bobby Sloan stayed put. Clarence Thayer and Timothy Ingram walked out the front door of APT Performa, Thayer talking earnestly, his hand on Ingram's elbow.

Sloan cracked his window, pointed a high-powered directional mike at the two men, and cranked up the volume. A gust of cold air wiped out everything but wind noise in his headphones. Whatever Thayer had said to Ingram made him stop in his tracks. The wind died down.

Thayer said, "The order comes direct from CG INSCOM, Major. You're to backstop Applewhite and handle any contingencies."

"Yes, sir."

Thayer said more, his words lost in another blast of air through Sloan's headphones.

Sloan knew CG meant commanding general. He knew IN-SCOM stood for the U.S. Army Intelligence and Security Command. That meant Ingram was no Salvation Army major.

He followed Ingram to Charlie Perry's hotel. Ingram went in and came out quickly, carrying luggage. He slammed it into the trunk of his car and wheeled out of the parking lot, driving fast. The man acted like a very unhappy camper.

Sloan put the Blazer in gear and scooted into traffic four cars back. Ingram led him to the airport. Lieutenant Molina came out of the terminal as Ingram toted luggage inside a nearby flight school building. Bobby flashed his lights at Molina. Sal walked over and got in the Blazer.

"Well, here we are, LT," Sloan said. "What's up on your end?"

"Applewhite and Perry are airborne in a private plane," Molina said. "No flight plan was filed. I got an ID on the plane. It's leased to APT Performa."

Sloan watched as Ingram come out of the flight-school building and hurried across the tarmac to a waiting helicopter. The chopper revved up and took off. Bobby read off the numbers, "N-O-four-three-zero Oscar Whiskey."

Molina used the laptop to connect with the FAA aircraft-identification Web site. "Have you got a make on your guy?"

"His name is Timothy Ingram. Albuquerque address out of Kirtland Air Force Base. But I think he's probably military. Thayer addressed him as 'major.' "

"I'll ID the chopper, you check for a flight plan," Molina said.

"Be right back," Sloan said, exiting the vehicle. He went into the terminal, flashed his shield at the video camera above the entrance to the tower, got buzzed through, and asked for a flight plan for the chopper. *Nada.* Coming out the door Sloan saw Lieutenant Molina talking on a pay phone.

Molina hung up as Sloan approached.

"The chopper didn't file a flight plan," Sloan said.

"It's registered to a Department of Energy subcontractor," Molina said. "Touch Link Satellite Systems. Ingram is the director of security. Guess where they're located."

"On an air force base in a galaxy not too far away?" Sloan replied, straight faced.

Tired as he was, Molina laughed. "Kirtland."

Sloan glanced around the parking lot. "We're here with two un-attended vehicles, Lieutenant. Let's slap some tracking devices on them."

"Get the slim jim," Molina said.

They jimmied open the cars, planted homing devices that tied into the Global Positioning System, and put bumper beeper vehicle-tracking devices on the undercarriages.

Sloan filched Ingram's car registration and proof of insurance from the glovebox, and smashed the rear license-plate lights. He kicked the glass fragments under the vehicle.

"What's that for?" Molina asked.

"Just in case we want to stop him for a traffic violation."

They talked about tagging Perry's unit at the APT Performa of-fices and decided not to do it. The vehicle was parked too close to the entrance under direct video surveillance.

In his unit Sloan keyed up the radio and asked one of Andy Baca's agents for a beacon check. Molina handed the slim jim to Sloan through the open Blazer window while they waited for a re-sponse.

"You're up and running," the agent said.

"Ten four," Sloan said. He keyed off and looked at Molina. "What's next?"

"We've got some downtime," Molina said. "Let's try to get a meeting with the chief."

Helen Muiz insulated Kerney while he cleared off his desk. He waded through the important stuff, first concentrating on the affi-davit for the court order to access Mitchell's Internet account. He passed the information on to criminal investigations and spent twenty minutes in a phone conversation with Cloudy Herrera's lawyer. He listened to threats of legal action, demands to restore Herrera to patrol duty, a thinly veiled accusation of racism, and a final pitch to resolve the problem before it became "politicized."

Kerney resisted a desire to laugh, told the lawyer he would think about it, and hung up.

Helen brought papers so Kerney could prep for a meeting with Larry Otero. Larry had hired a new secretary and put the five-year strategic planning process back on track. He needed sign-off approval to implement new department standards on child sexual abuse investigations and wanted Kerney to review the final field training reports on six new academy graduates due to start independent patrol.

Kerney signed off on routine matters, reviewed management information reports from the various units, and put nonurgent items in a pending file. He called Helen into his office and gave her documents to be routed.

She put a note on his desk. Molina and Sloan had made back channel contact through the sheriff's department. They wanted an ASAP meeting with Kerney and were standing by at the law-enforcement academy.

"I'll meet with them as soon as possible," Kerney said, wondering why they'd broken off surveillance. "Did Chief Otero consult with you on his choice of a new secretary?" he asked.

"Yes, indeed. She'll fit in very nicely, I think," Helen replied. "You have a meeting with Mr. Demora at city hall in an hour."

"Push it back for me, will you?"

Helen flashed a disapproving look. "I'll see what I can do. Are you ready for Chief Otero?"

"Send him in."

Larry Otero came in stiff and formal. Kerney forced himself not to clock-watch as they worked their way through the agenda, wondering what was eating his number two.

They finished up and Kerney commended Otero's good work. He got a curt nod and a frosty look. "Let's take a walk," he said.

He led Otero out of the administrative suite to a basement room, closed the door, and asked Larry what was bothering him.

"I've got people questioning me about this special training you sent Molina and Sloan to," Otero said.

"Questioning you about what?"

"The training supervisor knows nothing about this academy class. He says it's not on the schedule. The union rep wants to know why other officers weren't offered a chance to sign up for it, and the two detectives forced to pull doubles and work the weekend on short notice aren't happy campers. What's going on, Chief?"

"I've put you in an awkward situation," Kerney said.

"Big time, Chief."

"I won't do that again."

Kerney explained what Molina and Sloan were really doing. Otero's look of skepticism faded when Kerney laid out the facts of the faked evidence in the Terrell murder case, the hard evidence of a tie-in between Father Mitchell and Phyllis Terrell, and the listening devices he'd found at his quarters.

"If I get the boot because of this, you're going to have to run the department," he added.

"Not likely. Demora will have me back in technical services within a week. What can I do to help?"

"For now, just keep covering for me," Kerney said, "and make whatever decisions you need to. Act like it's business as usual. I'll call if I need you to do more."

They separated on the first floor. Otero went to his office thinking it might be wise not to get too attached to the three stars on his collar.

In the years since Kerney's graduation from the law-enforcement academy, the facility had been transformed from a spartan, barracks-style operation into a modern campus with comfortable classrooms, up-to-date equipment, and a strong training curriculum.

After learning why Sloan and Molina had dropped their surveillance, Kerney asked for a briefing.

Andy Baca walked in just as things got started. "Don't let me stop you," he said, sliding into a seat.

Kerney nodded and made notes while Sal Molina talked. Molina sketched the recent events at APT Performa, the airport, the appearance of Timothy Ingram on the scene, and the little they knew about him.

"Ingram may be military," Molina said, passing over the verbatim transcript of the snatches of conversation between Thayer and Ingram that Sloan had picked up outside of APT Performa. "But he's carried on the books as the security chief for Touch Link Satellite Systems, headquartered at Kirtland. The company has a big government contract to do remote nuclear weapons disarmament monitoring."

"More hush-hush stuff," Kerney said. He wrote down INGRAM.

Molina nodded. "But what it has to do with us is anybody's guess. We put vehicle-tracking devices on the cars at the airport parking lot."

Kerney wrote down "APT PERFORMA," "TOUCH LINK," and "KIRTLAND AFB," in capital letters, and looked up from his notepad. "What else?"

Bobby Sloan pushed photographs toward Kerney.

"Ingram?" Kerney asked.

Sloan nodded.

"Back up and give me a surveillance chronology," Kerney said.

Molina started with Perry's body-snatcher trip to the Albuquerque HMO, followed by his return to Santa Fe and visit to the federal courthouse.

Kerney scribbled "HMO" and drew a line to "KIRTLAND." "What's at the courthouse?" Kerney asked.

"That's unknown for certain, Chief. I checked with an informant who says there's a secure basement room that's off limits to all courthouse personnel. It was used by the Secret Service when the vice president came to town, and a bunch of computer geeks have been going in and out for the last couple of months."

Kerney wrote down "SECRET ROOM, COMMAND CENTER, LISTENING POST," and put a question mark at the end. He thought about how convenient it would be to have a listening post within a few steps of the resident FBI agent's office.

"Stop there for a minute," he said. "Is there any way to confirm this information?"

"Not likely, Chief," Molina said. "The guy's a federal employee, bound by a signed oath to keep the government's secrets."

"Let's move on."

Sloan picked up the ball. He detailed Applewhite's trip to Kirtland and Ingram's first appearance on the scene.

Kerney wrote down "INGRAM, RENDEZVOUS, WHY?" and circled it. "Andy, you're up next."

"After you," Andy replied.

Kerney went over some of the basics: the phone logs that showed Mitchell and Terrell had personal contact with each other, the possibility that Phyllis Terrell may have passed information to Mitchell, and the strong likelihood that Mitchell had been delving into the possible existence of a U.S. intelligence plot to destroy the drug cartels and bring down the Colombian government.

"If Phyllis Terrell was passing on information," Kerney said, "it mostly likely came from her husband."

"That would explain a lot," Molina said. "But we still don't know what the information was."

"I'm betting it had something to do with the trade mission along with all the interviews Mitchell conducted. He was trying to determine the extent of the operation, learn what was on-line and what was in the pipeline."

"That would be enough to have Mitchell and Terrell whacked," Sloan said. "But we still don't have anything that ties the ambassador to the murders."

"In a roundabout way we might," Kerney said. "My meeting with Professor Valencia led me to one of Mitchell's Internet providers. It's part of a conglomerate owned by Trade Source, APT Performa's parent company. Up until the time Terrell was given a new appointment as an ambassador without portfolio, he sat on the Trade Source board of directors, but his ties to the company are still strong, and he has a relationship with Clarence Thayer, the APT Performa CEO."

"You think these corporations are involved in government espionage?"

"Perhaps not directly," Kerney answered. "But these are high-tech companies developing cutting-edge computer tools. They could be supplying part of what's needed to implement the next phase of the intelligence operation."

"I can take Terrell's involvement a step closer than that," Andy said. "Applewhite called Ambassador Terrell to report on your trip to Red River, and gave him reassurance that everything was under control. She later met with Charlie Perry, learned that you'd cracked the murder cover-up, and made a second call to Terrell, revising her report. Unfortunately, his phone is encrypted, so we've only got Applewhite's side of the conversations from the remote room bugs."

Andy passed transcript copies around. "If you read between the lines, I'd say that Kerney and possibly Charlie Perry are next in line for the disappearing magic trick."

"So far, that trick has only been used with Santiago Terjo," Kerney said.

"Wrong," Andy replied, glancing at Molina and Sloan. "To bring you up to speed, I made contact with Fred Browning, a retired state police captain who now works as security chief for a computer chip manufacturer in Albuquerque. I asked Fred if he could quietly use his contacts to verify Agent Applewhite's identity and credentials. He reported that she was who she appeared to be. Browning may have been fed bad information."

"What makes you say that?" Kerney asked.

"Fred has gone missing, according to his daughter. She called the Albuquerque PD this morning and reported that her father had flown out to California on a quick one-day trip for a job interview. He promised to call her when he got home last night to tell her how it went. He got off the plane in Albuquerque, didn't go home, never called, and hasn't been seen since. His car is still in the airport parking lot. APD is checking the passenger list and flight crew to see if anyone knows anything. So far, zilch."

Andy poked the paper. "Fred is the state chapter president of a national professional security society. I borrowed a copy of the chapter membership roster from one of my agents who recently joined. Timothy Ingram is also a member."

"What time did Browning's plane land?" Sloan asked, flipping through his field notes.

Andy read off the time.

"Give Browning five minutes to clear the terminal, a couple more for Ingram to drive to the air base, and that's when I saw him pass by."

"Did you see a passenger?" Kerney asked.

Sloan shook his head. "Too dark."

"Look at the transcript of the Applewhite-Perry conversation," Andy said. "Aside from the fact that Applewhite is clearly in command, note Perry's demand to know who sanctioned the hit on Randall Stewart and what was going to happen to Chief Kerney. Applewhite feeds him pure bullshit about both questions."

Andy flipped more pages. "Jump over to the second Applewhite-Terrell phone transcript. Terrell asks or says something. Applewhite replies that 'the itinerary is finalized.' Another statement from Terrell. Applewhite replies that someone is more resourceful than originally thought, and that a regrettable but not damaging connection has been made. Applewhite listens and then asks, 'Take no action?' followed by the phrase 'And Agent Perry?' "

Andy looked hard at his old friend and placed his palm on the papers. "This is all about you becoming a target, Kevin. Are you sure you want to keep pushing this?"

"For now, it's just talk, Andy," Kerney said, thinking that the last thing he wanted, with a baby on the way, was to put himself at risk. "Let's keep watching and listening before we overreact."

Kerney smiled reassuringly at Andy, who shook his head in response.

"Moving on," Kerney said. "Clarence Terrell may be supplying the intelligence community with a new toy. Let me tell you about SWAMI."

Charlie Perry's in-flight reading consisted of a briefing document on Enrique DeLeon. Drugs were his bread and butter, but DeLeon dabbled in the theft of historical artifacts and fine art. Kerney had spoiled two of DeLeon's heists: a cache of mint-condition nineteenth century military equipment discovered in a secret Apache cave at White Sands Missile Range in southern New Mexico, and millions of dollars in twentieth-century art taken from the New Mexico governor's suite. DeLeon's attempt to have Kerney whacked had failed, but he'd succeeded in eliminating a number of competitors, and was now *jefe número uno* in northern Mexico.

Applewhite and Perry disembarked at the El Paso Airport. A special operative from the El Paso Drug Interdiction Intelligence Center logged their arrival and handed the information off to an army criminal investigator. Perry drove Applewhite across the bridge into Juárez. A U.S. Customs agent pulled the videotape of the crossing, made a copy, and sent it by courier to an intelligence officer at nearby Fort Bliss. On a dirty, gaudy, crowded Juárez street a DEA undercover agent wheeled his taxi three cars back behind Perry's car and reported the start of his surveillance to a special army intelligence drug-interdiction unit at Fort Huachuca, Arizona.

With Applewhite at his side Perry rang the doorbell at an opulent house on a tree-lined street close to the Juárez mayor's mansion. The DEA taxi driver broke off contact and ended his surveillance as a CIA deep-cover agent snapped front-step photos of Perry and Applewhite from a slow-moving car passing by. The undeveloped film would be flown to Headquarters, Air Intelligence Agency, at Kelly Air Force Base in Texas.

A stocky, balding Mexican Army general wearing civilian clothes and a wire opened the front door. The feed went to an up-stairs room, where a U.S. State Department counterintelligence operative manned a remote receiver. Wordlessly, the general ushered the two agents into a mahogany-paneled library and closed the door.

"Señor DeLeon has asked me to cover the preliminaries for him," the general said.

"What preliminaries?" Charlie Perry asked, casting a glance at Applewhite, who merely shrugged. "No DeLeon, no meeting." He turned on his heel to leave.

"Let's hear the general out," Applewhite said.

Perry swung around, gave Applewhite a harsh look, and nodded abruptly.

The general continued. "Señor DeLeon wishes me to inform you that you will be paid five hundred thousand dollars for the elimination of Kevin Kerney, half today and half upon completion of your assignment."

"Where's DeLeon?" Perry snapped.

"The task must be done in such a way as not to draw attention to Señor DeLeon. While he has full confidence in your discretion and abilities, if at the end of your assignment he believes otherwise, he will not release the balance due you."

"Forget it," Perry said.

"This isn't going to work, General," Applewhite said, "unless we include DeLeon in on the proceedings."

"If you agree to these terms, the ground rules for meeting with DeLeon are as follows: You will be searched by my aide for weapons and listening devices. He will then drive you to a place outside the city. There you will finalize your agreement with Señor DeLeon in person and receive your first payment."

"Why all the hoops?" Perry asked.

"Señor DeLeon is a cautious man who wishes to make sure that I am thoroughly embedded in the transaction. Since you are unknown to him personally, and he is accepting you on the basis of my recommendation, my complicity in the operation is required."

"Let's get on with it," Perry said.

Applewhite sat up front with the general's aide. They rolled south past the Juárez Airport, through a couple of ugly shanty towns, and into the desert—a vast, dusty, windblown expanse that made Charlie yearn for the Beltway, traffic congestion, and mobs of people.

On a dirt road they pulled up next to a black Lincoln limo. A driver got out and opened the rear door. The general's aide got out and stood at attention. DeLeon emerged from the backseat. Perry half expected the young officer to salute. The *jefe's* brown curly hair stayed put in the wind. The lips below his narrow nose carried a smirk that widened as Applewhite stepped out of the car.

"I want particulars of how you plan to proceed," DeLeon said to Perry, dismissing Applewhite with a look.

Applewhite shot him in the face, wheeled, pumped two quick rounds into the driver, and delivered a coup de grace to the back of DeLeon's head.

"Jesus fucking Christ," Perry said.

The aide stepped to the Lincoln, fetched a suitcase, and took the semiautomatic from Applewhite's outstretched hand.

"We must leave now," the young officer said.

"Jesus fucking Christ," Perry moaned.

"Get in the car, Charlie," Applewhite said, leading Perry to the aide's vehicle, "and I'll bring you up to speed."

She got in the backseat with him. Perry leaned his head back and closed his eyes, his heart thumping in his chest. The car made a U-turn and accelerated.

"Here's the way it plays," Applewhite said. "By midnight some very factual reports from a variety of reliable intelligence sources will be sanitized, assembled, and analyzed at the Department of Defense. Those reports will prove beyond a doubt that you and you alone entered into a contract with DeLeon to assassinate Kevin Kerney, and that you murdered DeLeon to ensure his silence after accepting a quarter-million-dollar advance to do the job, which by the way will be deposited shortly in an offshore account you recently opened. Should you ever decide to purge your guts to the Bureau about what really happened, both the general and his aide will be called upon to give statements corroborating what I've just told you. I guarantee that should you decide to try to disprove these accusations, you'll spend the rest of your life in a federal prison."

"Why kill DeLeon?" Perry asked, his eyes still shut.

"Because the opportunity might not have presented itself again, and it makes some important people on both sides of the border very happy."

"Kerney's next, isn't he? No matter what he does or doesn't know."

Applewhite patted Charlie's knee. It made him recoil and open his eyes.

"Don't concern yourself about that."

"When do you ice me?"

"Not to worry, Charlie. You get to go back to the Beltway after all. There's a nice desk job waiting for you at the J. Edgar Hoover Building. Your new bosses are looking forward to working with you."

Charlie didn't believe her. "You're a lying bitch."

Applewhite jammed a thumb into a pressure point on Perry's neck and his chin hit his chest. She punched a syringe through Perry's trousers into his thigh and emptied the contents. The fast-acting drug would keep him knocked out for hours.

The aide handed her the semiautomatic. She put on plastic gloves, ejected the magazine, emptied the clip, cleaned everything with a rag, and pressed Charlie's fingers against the cold metal surfaces, including the unspent rounds. She bagged the evidence and tossed it on the front seat next to the briefcase that held DeLeon's quarter-million-dollar up-front payment.

The car swung through a military gate at the Juárez Airport and drove into a Mexican Air Force hangar, where the general waited. Two uniformed soldiers pulled Perry from the car, carried him to a small fixed-wing airplane, and pushed his rag-doll body inside.

The aide got out and handed the briefcase to his general. The general hefted it to gauge the weight of its contents and smiled at Applewhite.

Applewhite stared him down until the smile vanished. She handed the aide a slip of paper. "These are the clearance codes the pilot will need to enter restricted airspace and land at White Sands Missile Range."

In an hour Perry would be back in the States under guard in a safe location at a high-security testing facility.

The aide nodded and stepped off to the ready room to find the pilot.

"You are not happy with the success of your mission, señora?" the general asked, oozing false charm.

"I've got a message for you from Langley," Applewhite said. "The quarter million dollars in that briefcase better be the last drug money you ever take. If you sell your services to the *jefe* who steps in to take DeLeon's place the CIA will kill you, your family, and your aged mother. Where's my car and driver?"

The general's eyes turned pinpoint murderous. "Behind the hangar."

From a pay phone at the El Paso Airport, Ingram booked a room at a bed-and-breakfast in Charlie Perry's name. He used the credit card number from Perry's Santa Fe hotel bill to guarantee the reservation and said he was sending his luggage over by taxi because he had meetings that would keep him from checking in until very late.

The woman said they locked the front door at seven. She gave him a room number and told him she'd leave a guest key under a chair cushion on the front porch.

Outside the terminal Ingram hailed a cab, paid the driver in advance to deliver the bags to the B & B, added a nice tip, and went looking for the bar. He had hours to kill before he needed to get to the B & B, make the room look slept in, pick up Charlie's luggage, and leave a cash payment for the room on the dresser.

He ordered a single malt. The bar TV showed a taped Hawaiian triathlon. The drink came and Ingram raised the glass in a mock toast to Charlie Perry. Deluded by feelings of self-importance, blinded by a faith that the Bureau could do no wrong, eager to think he'd been tapped for a fast-track promotion assignment, Charlie was without a doubt the perfect patsy.

What a fall Perry was about to take. Tim slugged down the whiskey and thought he'd been spending too much time drinking over the past six months.

City Manager Demora, the rah-rah proponent of open-door management, made Kerney sit outside his closed office door and wait well past normal office hours. Kerney used the time to review the discussion notes he'd taken after briefing Andy, Detective Sloan, and Lieutenant Molina about SWAMI.

Question: What covert information-gathering need would SWAMI serve? From what Kerney had read about Carnivore, the FBI Internet wiretap system, its capacity was limited to gathering on-line messages. Did Swami duplicate or go beyond Carnivore's capacity to acquire information?

Question: Was the government using Trade Venture, APT Performa, and Touch Link as corporate shields? If so, why was it important for SWAMI not to be a bona-fide intelligence tool?

Question: What did money have to do with it? The Mitchell-Terrell murders occurred after the priest had started looking into the trade mission's economic agenda, drug-money laundering, and financial crimes.

Question: What, if any, was Ambassador Terrell's role in SWAMI?

* * *

Kerney put his notes away. Bobby Sloan believed SWAMI might well be the mother of all computer-based covert technological snooping devices. It was what computer geeks called a packet sniffer, which sounded innocuous, but the implications gave Kerney the shivers. If Sloan was right, they were truly on the verge of a big-brother world. Had Carnivore opened the door on a digital world where private information about citizens would be routinely collected, whether they were suspects in a crime or not?

Kerney looked up. An unsmiling Demora stood in his open doorway. Kerney stepped inside and sat down. A new plaque pronouncing Demora a valued member of another civic organization had been added to the wall. Face time came cheap in Santa Fe.

Demora eased into his desk chair and quickly read Kerney out, using all the politically correct buzzwords and catchphrases of the enabling, empowering administrator. But it boiled down to this: He wanted his chief to be available when he called; he wanted his chief full-time at police headquarters running the department; he wanted closure on the Herrera reassignment, which meant Kerney was to meet with Officer Herrera's lawyer ASAP; he wanted weekly updates on Larry Otero's performance as deputy chief; he wanted to be kept fully informed, not blindsided by phone calls from unnamed sources complaining about things.

Kerney kept his cool by busily scribbling notes. He stopped and said, "How have you been blindsided, Bill?"

Demora pursed his lips, sat up straight in his chair, and adjusted the drape of his sport coat. "I'll give you an example: I've been told you're playing favorites, that you personally selected two senior officers for a special training seminar at the law-enforcement academy without going through the proper departmental channels. That kind of behavior doesn't engender confidence in your management style."

"I see. Anything else?"

Demora rocked back in his chair and forced a smile. "Actually, there is. Over the past several days persistent comments have been made to me about your continuing probe into the successfully concluded FBI investigation of Mrs. Terrell's murder. It seems to me your time could be much better spent ensuring that your detectives bring Father Mitchell's murderer to justice. If I were you, that would be my first priority."

Kerney felt screwed. If the rumor mill had fed Demora information about his end run around the Bureau, that meant his finesse moves had surely failed. He was more vulnerable than he'd realized.

"Who's telling you this?" he asked.

Demora put his hands up to block the question. "That's not the issue. I told you when you came on board as chief that I make myself available to any and every city employee as well as all the members of this community. My policy works because employees understand that they can speak freely without fear of reprisal, and citizens know their grievances and concerns will receive a fair and quick hearing."

"Tell me, are those voices of concern from inside or outside the department?" Kerney asked, trying to keep sarcasm out of his voice.

"Don't turn this into a witch hunt, Chief Kerney."

"That's not my style."

"Very well. To this point the concerns are internal." Demora's expression softened. "We're both in the early stages of sorting out our working relationship, Chief. All I'm suggesting here is that we don't let small matters turn into big problems. Both of us need to stay alert and keep each other fully in the loop. Open, free-flowing communication is the key to good management."

Tired of Demora's control-freak bullshit, Kerney stood up. "I agree with you wholeheartedly, Bill. I'll get everything back on track."

Demora flashed an approving smile. "That's what I wanted to hear."

Lights were on in Kerney's bedroom and the only vehicle outside the cottage was his truck. He slid out of his unit at the front of the driveway, pulled his handgun, and used the shadows to approach the cottage. He went low under the living room window, flattened himself against the wall, and turned the knob to the front door. It was unlocked.

He quietly pushed the door open, listened, and caught the sound of movement in the bedroom. He eased his way inside, weapon in the ready position, let his eyes adjust to the darkness, and did a visual sweep of the living room. Clear. He took a quick glance into the galley kitchen. Clear.

He backed into the kitchen, where he had a direct line of sight down the hallway leading to the closed bedroom door. He heard a hinge squeak on the bedroom closet door, followed by a thud as something hit the carpeted floor.

The door opened and light washed down the hallway. Kerney said, "Freeze. Don't move, or I'll blow you away."

Sara stood backlit in the doorway. "For God's sake, it's me, Kerney." She hit the hall light switch in time to see Kerney holstering his handgun.

"What are you doing here?"

"It's nice to see you too," Sara snapped.

"Didn't you get my message? I asked you not to come this weekend."

"That's exactly why I'm here. What is going on with you?"

"I'm sorry." Kerney walked to Sara and took her hands. "I am glad you're here."

She pulled away and gave Kerney a blistering look. "I don't believe you. Answer my question. Except for a short conversation and some confusing phone messages, I haven't heard from you all week."

"I've been busy, that's all."

"You've never been too busy not to call before. Are we going down the tubes, Kerney? Does the prospect of fatherhood have you scared?"

Kerney shook his head. "That's not it at all."

"Then talk to me."

"Let's go out, get something to eat, and talk over dinner."

"I'm not hungry. Talk to me now, Kerney. What's going on with you?"

"Sara, it's work. Just the job. It's not you, there isn't anything strange going on in my head, and it's not us. Believe me."

"I don't need reassurances, I need conversation. Something's wrong and I want to know what it is."

Kerney put a finger to his lips and pulled Sara into the bedroom. He showed her the telephone tap and the bug in the floor vent.

"Can we talk about it over dinner?" he asked again. "I haven't eaten all day."

Sara's distressed expression lightened. Her green eyes scanned Kerney's face. "If we must," she said. "But you'd better really talk to me, Kerney, otherwise I'm getting a hotel room for the night."

They ordered a light meal at a restaurant favored by locals. Gray-headed couples danced to bland renditions of soft-rock tunes played by a trio of old men wedged together on a small platform near the entrance. Muted televisions above the long bar entertained a row of blue-collar workers drinking their way deep into a Friday night. Area politicos sat at the back of the tiny dance floor, talking loudly, and waving to any constituents they knew by sight. Civil servants and their families out for a Friday-night dinner filled circular dining tables adjacent to the bar and ordered up the specials of the day.

Sara listened as Kerney described the chain of events starting with the Terrell murder. He gave her the facts and his carefully thought-out suppositions about the case, and listed the reasons why he believed that military intelligence was heavily involved.

Sara's head swam. She knew Kerney to be an exceptional investigator and not one to exaggerate. But she didn't like what she was hearing. Everything she knew about the regulations that governed army intelligence activities argued against his hypothesis.

On the one hand, she knew nothing about SWAMI or a secret training base in Colombia. On the other hand, she'd heard about Carnivore through her own contacts and a few brief news stories, and she knew about the controversy surrounding the School of the Americas. She also knew about how army intelligence kept an eye on its own, especially soldiers and civilians in sensitive, highly classified positions.

She bit back a desire to challenge Kerney's suppositions and let him finish up. He looked at her expectantly, waiting for a response.

"Interesting," Sara said.

"That's it?"

"For now."

"You're usually not so noncommittal."

Sara toyed with her academy class ring. "I have to think, Kerney. You've thrown a lot at me in a very short time."

"Do you think I'm overreacting?"

"I don't know."

"I've caught you off-guard."

Sara replied with a weak smile. After a hellish week at the Command and General Staff College, made worse by draining bouts of morning sickness, she'd come to Santa Fe concerned and worried about Kerney. Now that she knew more, it meant the timing was wrong to talk to him about the strong maternal feelings that were shifting her focus away from the army and making her yearn for a real home life.

They had yet to resolve the issue of whether or not Kerney would join her at her next permanent duty station or remain in New Mexico. She doubted he'd willingly transform himself into a full-time military dependent. So in theory, she'd be married and a mother. But in practice she'd be raising a child as a single parent, with occasional visits from a distant, part-time husband. The prospect held little appeal.

Her next assignment after school would most likely be a fast-track staff position at the command level that would require twelve-hour days and seven-day weeks.

She'd known women officers who'd left husbands and children behind for three-year assignments. And women who, for the sake of their children, had branch-transferred to jobs that cut short their advancement and froze them at their current rank until retirement. Women like Sara, who'd been promoted ahead of schedule only to resign from active duty because their family life was suffering.

She reached out and took Kerney's hand. "Let me think about it some more."

They drove home in silence. Kerney was tense, on guard, his eyes searching the rearview mirror. She believed he was being watched, followed, and spied on, that he'd been threatened with consequences if he didn't back off on the investigation. Over dinner he'd sidestepped her question about the risks he was taking with assurances that everything was under control. That, she didn't believe.

She decided she needed do more than just think about what Kerney had told her. "I want to review your case material," she said.

"You're not part of this. It's not your problem."

"I'm not asking for permission, Kerney."

Kerney shot her a sidelong glance. A stern expression greeted him. "Fine. You can look at it when we get home."

"I'm not staying with you tonight."

Kerney slowed the truck and gave Sara a long look. "Why not?"

"Because I want to draw my own conclusions."

"You don't believe me?"

"Did I say that?" Sara asked in an icy tone.

"Take whatever you want, Colonel."

"Don't be sarcastic, Kerney."

Kerney pulled up at the cottage. "Are we fighting?"

Sara jumped out of the truck. "Yes, but for now it's just a skirmish."

Chapter 12

Sara booked a four-hundred-dollar suite at a downtown hotel, called for a cab, and hung up.

"I can give you a ride," Kerney said.

"Weren't we supposed to spend the weekend looking at some property?"

"We were."

"What's it going to take to get you to move out of here into something decent?"

"Enough free time to do it," Kerney said.

"You've got about six months," Sara said, patting her still-flat stomach. "This baby isn't going to wait any longer than that."

"We won't be living here when the baby comes."

"Where will we be, I wonder." She made a dismissive gesture. "Never mind."

Kerney followed her into the bedroom. "Is that what you wanted to talk about?"

"Not now." Sara's gaze skimmed across the clutter of paper, files, and tapes, her eyes frost-green. "We'd be up all night and I'm too tired for a marathon."

"Should I come to the hotel in the morning?" Kerney asked as he sorted through case notes and materials, passing pertinent items to Sara.

"Call me first," Sara said.

He gave her field notes, progress reports, document inserts, lists of names, lists of informants, and duplicates of Bobby Sloan's investigative reports. "Perhaps we could meet at the hotel restaurant for breakfast," he said.

"I don't have much of an appetite in the morning, these days," Sara said. "Just call, okay?"

He gave her Sloan's summaries of the videotape contents, his own chronological event log, crime-scene photographs, and transcripts of recorded conversations. "Okay."

He pointed at the audio- and videotapes. Sara shook her head and zipped everything into her travel bag.

The taxi driver sounded his horn.

"Let me send the cab away," Kerney said. He passed her one of the new cell phones and a new number to use to get in touch. "I'll take you to the hotel."

Sara grabbed her coat and stuck the cell phone in a pocket. "I don't want you to. I'll see you tomorrow."

Kerney watched her walk out the door, wondering what they were really at odds about. He decided it was a bit of everything: the investigation, the baby, the marriage, the army, the cheerless cottage he lived in, their busted weekend plans.

Sara confirmed his observation when he heard the taxi door slam shut.

Two blocks from the Santa Fe Plaza, in the basement of the federal courthouse, Tim Ingram, just back from El Paso, reviewed transcripts of police radio transmissions and phone calls made to and from the Santa Fe Police Department. Nothing appeared to be out of the ordinary.

Once a bomb shelter during the early days of the cold war, the basement had been converted to a sophisticated listening post that targeted suspected foreign agents working at the Los Alamos National Laboratory, thirty-five miles away. Within recent years a British Army major on detached duty at the lab and a visiting Israeli physicist had been uncovered trying to stick their hands into Uncle Sam's cookie jar of nuclear weapon secrets.

Four operators sat at consoles in the sealed room. Two worked the SWAMI data that flowed into computers from phone lines, cell phones, and wireless Internet devices. Much like the NSA computers, SWAMI automatically scanned for millions of key words and phrases and immediately downloaded any that were programmed for intercept. The current operating program was case specific to the Terrell-Mitchell containment operation.

A woman manned a Carnivore unit that tapped into the Santa Fe Police Department's on-line computers and retrieved electronic communications. The fourth technician monitored vehicle-tracking devices planted on key police department units, watched real-time video of the front of Kerney's house, and taped audio transmissions from external remote listening stations and the fixed bugs at the police department, Kerney's residence, and the state police chief's office.

Every person on duty was a member of a team of military intelligence specialists who'd been handpicked as watchers, listeners, and monitors.

When SWAMI launched in three months as a private corporate enterprise, every illicit, suspicious, or fraudulent electronic or wire-transfer monetary transaction flowing out of Colombia would be tracked and either seized or frozen.

Because SWAMI could burrow into the data banks of financial institutions around the world, it would violate international laws, compacts, and trade agreements, and intrude on the sovereignty of nations.

Revolutionary in design and concept, SWAMI would also capture sensitive economic and financial data from foreign governments and multinational corporations. That capacity virtually

guaranteed long-term continued American domination of technological intelligence gathering.

Ingram watched the videotape of Sara Brannon's arrival at
Kerney's house, caught on camera by a transmitter placed on a
neighboring house. He watched Kerney's cautious approach and
entry. He listened to the tape recordings of their conversations,
including their after-dinner exchange in Kerney's truck that had
been picked up by a mobile unit trailing a kilometer behind the
vehicle.

Tim shook his head at the thought of Sara Brannon's involvement in the case. With her army credentials and contacts, she just
might be able to break through the Trade Source and APT Performa corporate shields. While that wouldn't get her to the
SWAMI secrets, it was unacceptable nonetheless.

Ingram knew Brannon personally. A recent blurb in the West
Point alumni magazine had reported she'd been the first in their
class to make lieutenant colonel and earn the highly coveted Distinguished Service Medal for exceptionally meritorious service
while serving in Korea.

Elaine Cornell, aka Special Agent Applewhite, was a member of
the same graduating class. He wondered how Applewhite would
react to the news of Brannon's arrival.

He went to a SWAMI console, where one of the operators had
locked into Sara's Internet server. The screen rolled data in from
Sara's laptop. Information about Cornell from the West Point Association of Graduates Web site scrolled across the screen. It confirmed her cover as a resigned officer now serving as a special agent
with the FBI. The next name Sara entered was his own.

Ingram clamped his mouth shut. How in the hell had she got
onto him? He was supposed to be embedded deep enough to be
under anyone's radar. Who had made him, and how?

He had to report the breach.

Tim ran over the current body count in his mind. Too many had
died in an operation that was supposed to be bloodless. Kevin Ker-

ney and Charlie Perry would soon join them. Would the brass be willing to neutralize Sara Brannon, too, one of their own?

Under the guise of national security it had been done to others before, quietly and away from public scrutiny. There were any number of ways to wind up accidentally dead in the military: training-exercise disasters, chopper crashes, getting washed off the deck of a ship in choppy seas.

He wanted to call Sara, a woman he liked and respected, and tell her to get her butt on a plane back to Fort Leavenworth right away. But that wasn't possible. He watched as names he didn't recognize got entered into government Web-site search engines from Sara's laptop.

"Who the hell are those people?" he asked the operator.

"One moment, sir," the operator said, switching his attention to a computer keyboard. "I'll add them in as SWAMI key words."

He typed in the names and SWAMI answered back. "People who attended Mrs. Terrell's funeral," the operator said.

Ingram pulled up a chair. "Let's see where else she goes."

It was after midnight when Kerney knocked on Sara's hotel-room door. She opened up wearing shorts and a sleeveless tank top. She had a ballpoint pen clenched in her teeth.

Kerney resisted an impulse to take her in his arms. He leaned forward to kiss her on the cheek. She pulled back.

"You called?" he asked.

"Do you really want to hear my take on this?"

"I do."

Sara walked barefooted to the large writing desk in the nicely furnished sitting room, and picked up a notepad. "First, Trade Source and APT Performa are legitimate companies with solid performance records as military subcontractors, and as far as I can tell SWAMI isn't being treated like some big secret government project. Instead, it's being touted as a private-sector technological breakthrough."

"I'm aware of that," Kerney said. "But private outfits have been fronts for intelligence agencies before. The CIA used both private companies and nonprofit aid agencies to run covert operations in Vietnam."

"True, and more recently they've done the same in Latin America. But that's the CIA. I've never heard of the military going outside their sphere of authority."

"Would it be possible?"

Sara moved to the couch and sat. "Possible, but not likely."

Kerney took the easy chair. "We have Thayer on tape referring to Ingram as 'major' and telling him the commanding general of INSCOM—army intelligence—had ordered something done."

"It could simply be a matter of Thayer using military etiquette. I did some Internet surfing. Ingram and Cornell—that's Applewhite's real name—are West Point graduates. In fact, they were members of my class. I was able to easily identify them from the photographs you gave me. According to their alumni biographies they resigned their commissions as captains. But Ingram may be serving in the reserves as a major. I haven't checked that out yet."

"How well did you know them?" Kerney asked.

"Not well. They were in the middle of the class academically and both were hard-core jocks. Ingram seemed nice enough, Cornell was the competitive type who hated to lose."

"What were their service branches?"

"Both were in military intelligence before resigning and joining the FBI."

"That doesn't ring any bells for you?"

"Not in and of itself," Sara said. "On the federal level it's not difficult to transition between law enforcement and intelligence work. Stay with me, Kerney. As I mentioned, APT Performa is an army subcontractor. It could be that Thayer was talking about a procurement fulfillment order for INSCOM."

"Placed by the commanding general?"

"It's common practice to reference the highest authority for a procurement. Especially one that has priority."

"That's a stretch, Sara, and you know it."

"It's within the bounds of possibility."

"I think you're seeing things the way you want to see them."

Sara gave him a withering glance. "Let me finish, before you accuse me of shortsightedness. If Ingram and Applewhite are military intelligence, they could have a legitimate assignment that's connected to APT Performa's contract with INSCOM."

"Like meddling in a civilian criminal investigation and posing as FBI?"

"You've heard of undercover work, haven't you?" Sara snapped. She tossed the notepad on the cushion. "But since you brought it up, let's deal with it. You were told right at the top of the investigation that national security was involved and your role was to offer support. That's not meddling, to my way of thinking."

"The feds didn't play it that straight with me."

Sara sighed in frustration. "Because, if it's a national security matter, you don't have a need to know."

"What about Terrell's murder, Mitchell's murder, Stewart's murder? The disappearance of Terjo and Browning? I have a need to know about all of that."

"Do you have even one remotely credible homicide suspect?"

"No, but that doesn't address the fact that Charlie Perry and Applewhite took Terjo into custody and lied to me about it."

Sara shook her head. "That's a guess you've made. Which means you're down to one missing person, Browning."

"That's right, I'm guessing. But I'm not guessing that Perry faked the lab results that turned Scott Gatlin into a murderer."

"Gatlin may well have been the murderer in spite of the faked physical evidence," Sara said. "Granted, Randall Stewart had sex with Phyllis Terrell the night she was killed, and that does cast suspicion in his direction. But it proves neither Stewart's guilt nor Gatlin's innocence."

"Stop giving me the party line, Sara," Kerney said. "I can get that from Charlie Perry or Agent Applewhite."

"You're acting like a blockhead, Kerney. If you came here expecting a knee-jerk endorsement of your theories, you might as well go back to that dump you're renting. Do you want to talk this out or not?"

Kerney composed himself. "What else have you learned?"

"Here's where it does get interesting. Clarence Thayer is a retired army finance corps colonel. That could easily explain why he addressed Ingram by his rank. He was on the promotion list for his first star when he left the service. Lifers don't normally do that, so I called a friend who took a Harvard MBA and served under Thayer. He said Thayer was recruited to head up APT Performa, offered four times his salary, and jumped at the opportunity."

"That just makes my case about APT Performa stronger," Kerney said.

"Lifers are part of a good-old-boy club, Kerney. There are thousands of retired field-grade and general officers working in defense-related industries. They recruit one another for plum civilian jobs. It's a common practice."

Sara peeked at her notes. "What did grab my attention were some of the people who put in an appearance at Phyllis Terrell's funeral. The special assistant to the undersecretary for international affairs is a former lieutenant colonel. He's a graduate of the Defense Language Institute in Monterey, fluent in Spanish, and served in DOD as a strategic intelligence analyst."

Sara flipped a notepad page. "The treasurer of Trade Source is an ex–navy captain who served as deputy director of DOD financial services. At that level he was privy to information about all clandestine operations throughout all service branches."

Her finger ran down the page. "Treasury sent the financial crimes enforcement director who was once an air attaché at the U.S. embassy in Panama. Those postings normally carry intelligence-gathering responsibilities. And the Justice Department sent an ex–Marine JAG attorney who was on staff at the National Security Agency and who holds an adjunct faculty appointment at the Joint Military Intelligence College."

"Are you still thinking it's just a good-old-boy club and I'm having paranoid delusions?"

Sara put the notebook aside and curled her feet up on the couch. "Not at all. These are policy-level intelligence specialists who advise important decision-makers. I think you've cornered an angry mountain lion that's about to bite your head off."

"How do we crack it?"

"Are you really that naive? Missions like this have been blessed by the White House, cabinet secretaries, the Senate Select Committee on Intelligence, and every cooperating spy-craft shop, including the military."

"I can't walk away from this, Sara. People have been murdered, possibly by agents of the government. That can't be tolerated in a free society."

Sara's eyes stayed on Kerney's face. "It violates what I believe in also, dammit. But you can't solve every homicide. Nobody can, nobody does. That only happens in the movies, or in bad pulp fiction. This time the stakes are off the chart."

"So, I'm out of my league. Is that what you're saying?"

"Put your ego away, Kerney. I want a life for us and our baby. Maybe I'm being selfish, but that's what's important to me right now."

"That matters to me just as much," Kerney said.

"Then act like it. I called Andy after I checked in. He thinks you've taken it as far as you can go. You're over the line."

"Maybe so, but it seems to be working. I've made some people very nervous."

"Congratulations," Sara said. "I can use that as part of my eulogy for you, and I'll tell your child what a hero you were. Can't you ever just back off?"

"All I'm doing is listening and watching, Sara. There's not much risk to that."

"People get killed all the time because of what they know," Sara said.

"I'll be careful not to let that happen."

Sara swung off the couch, turned on her heel, went to the window, and stood with her back to Kerney. She thought about his hard-nosed bullheadedness, and the image of Jim Meehan's face floated through her mind. Meehan would have raped and killed her in the ruins of an old Mexican hacienda, if Kerney hadn't crossed the line, beaten a drug dealer's henchman almost senseless, and shown up in time to stop the action.

"You're a stubborn man, Kerney," she said.

"I know that."

Sara turned, squared her shoulders, and put on a determined look. "Okay, there's work to be done. From what I've read, there are two big gaps in your investigation: no follow-up with Randall Stewart's widow, and no contact with Proctor Straley or his daughter."

"That's right," Kerney said, unwilling to say anything that sounded like an excuse.

"What else has been left hanging?"

"There's a remote surveillance video camera on a utility pole across from the Terrell residence. The FBI had denied any knowledge of it. I have an idea where the tapes might be, but I'm not certain. If I can pinpoint the location of the tapes, I might be able to ID the killer."

"Okay, that's three things that need doing," Sara said on her way into the bedroom. She came out with a blanket and a pillow and tossed them on the couch. "In the morning we talk to Mrs. Stewart, pay a visit to Proctor Straley, and locate the videotapes."

"We?" Kerney said.

"That's what I said. Someone has to keep an eye on you. You get the bed, Kerney. I'll sleep on the couch."

"That's not the best way for us to spend a night together in a four-hundred-dollar hotel suite."

Sara pointed at the open bedroom door. "Go. I've got a little more digging I want to do and I need to use the laptop."

Kerney got to his feet. Sara stepped up and gave him a quick kiss. "I'll be sick in the morning. It's not a pretty sight."

"You're not well?"

"Morning sickness, Kerney, that's all."

"You didn't tell me."

"I figured you'd find out about it firsthand this weekend. Go to bed, you look exhausted."

Sara ushered Kerney into the bedroom, gave him another kiss, closed the door, and started surfing the Internet looking for Proctor Straley.

When Applewhite arrived at the Santa Fe Airport without Charlie Perry, Sal Molina stayed put while Bobby Sloan tailed her. Later in the night Ingram showed and Molina followed him to the federal courthouse. He parked next to the pink-colored stone Scottish Rite Temple, where he had a clear view of the back entrance, and waited.

The temple confused tourists who thought it had to be either a church or a museum. Although it was a Santa Fe landmark, Molina knew very little about it. A guild or some sort of Freemason society owned it, and supposedly an old dead guy was buried beneath the front steps.

Time dragged for Molina. To keep awake he drummed his fingers on the steering wheel, hummed songs to himself, and kept the window open to let cold air circulate through the minivan. Ingram finally emerged. But instead of going to his vehicle he walked toward the plaza.

Molina put his hand on the door latch and hesitated. There wasn't a person other than Ingram on the sidewalk and traffic was nonexistent.

Ingram turned the corner. Molina hurried on foot to the end of the block and slowed his pace when he saw Ingram making his way down the sidewalk. He stayed well back. Ingram led him into the historic La Fonda Hotel, which touted itself as the inn at the end of the Old Santa Fe Trail.

Ingram peeled off into the bar adjacent to the reception area. Molina kept moving, counting one bartender, a waitress, and three customers as he passed by. He walked down a corridor, through the entrance to the parking garage, and took up a position outside the hotel that gave him a view of the two main entrances.

The wind was biting cold and the temperature way below freezing. That suited Molina; he wasn't sleepy anymore.

Tim Ingram sat at the end of the bar, slugged down a single malt, and ordered up another. The television was off, the bar almost empty, and the silence deafening. It was too damn quiet and genteel. He needed a raucous dive that would force him to stop thinking.

He rubbed his head and twisted his trunk in an attempt to loosen up the muscles in his back. He'd failed to call in a report on Sara Brannon, hadn't put her hotel room under electronic surveillance, and hadn't told anyone that his cover had been partially penetrated.

That still needed to be done. But not until he could think of an untraceable, safe way to warn off Lieutenant Colonel Brannon. She deserved that much consideration.

He decided on a plan, asked the bartender for a phone book, and paged through it until he found what he wanted.

Ingram left the La Fonda Hotel. Molina paralleled him from one street over to the courthouse. He got to the minivan just in time to see Ingram's vehicle with the broken license-plate lights cruising away from downtown toward St. Francis Drive. He hauled ass through a red light to keep Ingram in range.

Traffic lights showed green down the quiet thoroughfare that led to the Interstate, and Molina grouchily wondered if Ingram was heading back to Albuquerque. He didn't relish the prospect of making the drive.

Ingram turned off on St. Michael's Drive and stopped at a twenty-four-hour-a-day franchise copy service and print shop.

Molina took some blank property receipt forms off his clipboard, went inside, ran them through a self-serve copier, and watched Ingram fill out a form and hand it to the clerk. The clerk fed it into a fax machine and rang up the charges. Ingram paid the clerk, shredded the paper, and walked out.

Molina waited until Ingram left the parking lot. The vehicle-tracking monitor and Global Positioning System would give him a fix on his travel direction.

He went to the clerk and flashed his shield. "Did you see who that fax was sent to?" he asked.

"We're not supposed to look," the kid said, wide eyed.

"Did you look?"

The kid, no more than eighteen, shook his head. "No."

"Can you call the fax number up on the machine?"

"I guess so."

"Well, do it," Molina said.

The kid came back with the number. Molina dropped a five-dollar bill on the counter, went to the minivan, and got a fix on Ingram's direction from the state police agent manning the tracking devices. He was heading back downtown.

Molina cross-checked the phone number in the city directory. It didn't show, but the next number down listed a downtown hotel.

Molina hung a turn onto the street, called the hotel night clerk, and identified himself. "You just received a fax. Who was it for?"

"Colonel Sara Brannon. It's being delivered now."

Lights ran red up and down St. Francis Drive. Molina busted through them and picked up Ingram passing by the last downtown turnoff. He slowed and watched Ingram pull into the parking lot of Applewhite's hotel on the north side of town.

He found Sloan staked out in the Blazer, eased the minivan up next to him, and opened his window.

"I was just gonna give you a call, LT," Sloan said.

"Do you know a Colonel Sara Brannon?" Molina asked.

"Isn't the chief married to an army officer? I think that's her name. What's up?"

Molina dialed Kerney's home phone. It rang unanswered. "Ingram just faxed her a message at a downtown hotel. I'm going there now. If he moves, switch off and follow him. I'll come back and baby-sit Applewhite."

"Ten-four. Why would the chief's wife be staying at a hotel?"

"Maybe they checked in together."

"Must be nice," Sloan said. "I can't even afford to buy my wife dinner at one of those places."

Applewhite opened her door. Wrapped in a hotel robe, she stared up at Ingram from under heavy eyebrows. Indentations from a pillow ran across her cheek. Her sleepy face showed no signs of softness. She looked damn ugly without any makeup.

Ingram sucked breath mints. He told Applewhite about Sara Brannon's arrival on the scene, where she was, and her subsequent activities.

"Not good," Applewhite said. "How did you get made?"

"I have no idea."

"Do you have listeners in place at the hotel?"

"They're setting up now. Give it thirty minutes."

"Why is it taking so long?"

"Everybody was tasked. I had to free up some people."

"Did you bring hard copies?"

Ingram dropped a file on the dresser. "This is what she's done so far. It's all Internet surfing. I think we should go at this cautiously."

"What do you have in mind?"

"Find a way to have Brannon's weekend cut short. Let's get her back to Leavenworth and take her out of the picture."

"I'll run the idea by the ambassador," Applewhite said. "Did you know that bitch made light colonel?"

A spiteful, jealous expression on Elaine's face almost made Ingram flinch.

"Yeah, I know," he said, stepping to the door. He couldn't resist pushing Applewhite's buttons. "And she was decorated with the Distinguished Service Medal. I heard they wanted to give her the Silver Star, but that would have meant admitting that she'd been in a hostile action with North Korean troops. Isn't that something?"

"She's an ass-kissing bitch," Applewhite said. "That's what got her the DSM and the promotion."

Sara fell asleep on the couch. She woke up to a knock, saw that a piece of paper had been slipped under the door, and looked through the peephole, expecting to see a bellhop waiting for a tip. Instead, she saw a man holding up an SFPD shield. Kerney wandered out of the bedroom groggy eyed and in his underwear as she picked up the piece of paper and unlatched the door.

Molina held up his clipboard with an attached piece of paper that read: YOUR ROOM IS BUGGED. MEET ME IN THE LOBBY.

Sara nodded, closed the door, and glanced at the paper. It was a handwritten fax message to her that read:

G
O
B
A
C
K
T
O
Y
O
U
R

P
O
S
T

A five-digit number followed the message. They dressed and hurried to meet Molina.

"Who wants you to go back to your post?" Kerney asked as they walked down the corridor to the elevators. "And why?"

"I don't know," Sara replied in a troubled voice.

The elevator doors slid open on the ground floor to reveal Molina pacing impatiently. The night manager behind the guest check-in counter looked on with unabashed interest.

"How did you locate us?" Kerney asked Molina.

"Ingram faxed your wife a message," Sal said, holding up an office key. "I've got a place where we can talk. What did the message say, Chief?"

Sara answered. "Basically, it said get out of town."

Molina took them into the general manager's office and slipped a minicassette into his pocket tape recorder. "This was just picked up from Agent Applewhite's room," he said. "I recorded it off my handheld radio, so the sound quality isn't great, but you can still make it out."

Sara and Kerney listened to the tape of Ingram's conversation with Applewhite. Molina glanced over Ingram's fax message. When the tape ended Sal asked, "What do the numbers in the fax message mean?"

"Each West Point graduate is assigned what's known as a Cullen number," Sara said. "It's named for the general who began chronicling biographies of every graduate in 1850. The numbers are assigned alphabetically and in sequence starting from the first graduate through the most recent class. Everyone has a unique number. I'm betting this one is Tim's. He wanted to make sure I'd know who sent the message."

"So that you'd take it seriously," Kerney added. "He also gave Applewhite a suggestion on how to ease you out of the picture."

"Exactly. Something nasty is in the works and Ingram isn't happy about it. He risked a lot to warn me."

"How did he get onto you so fast?"

"I think I know," Molina said. He looked totally sleep deprived. "Perry never showed at the airport, so Sloan took Applewhite. I waited until Ingram arrived and followed him. He went directly to the federal courthouse, where he stayed for a good three hours."

"Did you keep a surveillance log?" Sara asked.

"I can give you exact times," Molina said, consulting his notepad. He read off a chronology of Ingram's movements in hours and minutes.

"He tapped into my laptop," Sara said.

"Either through Carnivore or SWAMI," Kerney said, swinging his attention to Molina. "This is the second trip someone's made to the federal courthouse."

"Yeah, Perry last night," Molina said with a weary smile. "But it feels like it happened a week ago."

"That's where the tapes are," Kerney said. "How reliable is your informant?"

"Jake? He's a retired sheriff's captain."

"Perfect. That makes him a rock-solid source. See what more you can squeeze out of him. Get specific information about what's inside that room. Concentrate on communication equipment, radio and television monitors, computers—any kind of hardware that's used for electronic surveillance."

Molina took notes. "He might not budge."

"Find a way to push him."

"Anything else?"

"Get background information on his law-enforcement career. I'll need to be able to show that he has expert knowledge of undercover operations and equipment."

"Are you going for a search warrant?"

"You bet I am. That room may hold exactly what's needed to break this investigation wide open. Where's Sloan?"

"Following Ingram back to Albuquerque."

"Someone has to keep an eye on Applewhite while you're busy with Jake. Have Deputy Chief Otero backstop you. He's filled in on the operation. If Charlie Perry makes an appearance, Larry covers him."

"How long do you want us to go with this, Chief?"

Kerney looked at his watch. It was four in the morning. "We pull the plug in twelve hours, as originally planned. Can you hang in there?"

"Ten-four, Chief. Where will you be in case we need to make contact?"

"Sara and I will be paying some early visits to a couple of people. I'll keep in touch with you by cell phone."

Chapter **13**

Sara's early-morning cranky stomach slowed them down. She drank a special herbal tea she'd brought along and waved off Kerney's suggestion to proceed without her. His attempts to comfort her were likewise rebuffed.

She dressed while Kerney booked the hotel suite for the remainder of the weekend. She emerged from the bedroom looking shaky and pale. Kerney wondered how she could do a five-mile run every weekday morning before her classes at Fort Leavenworth.

On the streets school buses collected small groups of waiting students at intersections, slowing up impatient drivers who zipped around the buses as soon as the red warning lights stopped flashing.

They waited behind a bus and Sara said, "Before Lieutenant Molina showed up, I did some Internet surfing on Trade Source. Proctor Straley was one of the original investors. He netted fifty million dollars after the company went public, and still holds a sizable block of shares."

The school bus moved. Kerney let cars go around before passing. "That tangles the web a bit," he said. "What if the information Phyllis Terrell passed on to Father Mitchell came from her father and not the ambassador?"

"I've given that some thought," Sara said. "If Straley is involved in the cover-up, Ingram will have warned him by now about our interest in his Trade Source connection."

"If Straley's guarded when meet with him, or not the grieving father, that could us tell he's been alerted."

"Not necessarily," Sara said. "Straley's a heavyweight corporate player. He's dealt with hostile take-overs, angry shareholders, and a Justice Department antitrust probe. I bet he knows how to hold a good poker hand."

On the valley road to the Stewart residence an SUV filled with school-aged teenagers sped by. Sara looked at the hillside houses and the sweet mountain views. Cloudlike wisps of snow floated off higher peaks. Soft morning light sparkled against the tree cover.

"Nice neighborhood," she said. "Why don't we rent something up here until we build?"

"Are you serious?"

"Don't be such a penny-pincher, Kerney. Spend some of those riches you've inherited."

Kerney rolled to a stop in Stewart's driveway.

"Let me girl-talk with Mrs. Stewart," Sara said.

"Are you feeling up to it?"

Sara ate a saltine cracker, gave Kerney a winsome smile, swung her legs out of the truck, and said, "I'm fine."

Kerney hung back and let Sara take the lead. The older woman who let them into the foyer spoke in hushed tones. Her daughter couldn't possibly be disturbed, the family was in mourning, the children would become even more upset than they already were.

Sara countered with a sympathetic smile and reassurances. She understood completely, the visit would be brief, there was new information to be shared.

The woman left to consult with her daughter. She came back and took them down a long hallway past a kitchen where an older man was preparing breakfast for two silent young boys sitting at a long country-style table. They climbed stairs to a second-floor master suite where Mrs. Stewart sat on a couch in a sitting room clutching a pillow around her stomach. A long velour skirt covered her legs. Her hair, parted in the middle, fell loosely across her shoulders. She had a sharp nose that didn't detract from her wholesome good looks, and eyes that seemed slightly tranquilized. An untouched cup of coffee sat within arm's reach on an end table.

"Lori, are you sure you want to talk now?" the older woman asked.

"It's all right, Mother."

"Do you want me to stay with you?"

"No, you go on."

The woman left and Sara sat on the far end of the couch. Kerney moved to a horizontal window that framed the valley panorama below and perched silently on a low ranch-style bench.

Sara turned to face Lori. "Thank you for seeing us. I know this must be hard."

"What do you want to tell me?"

"We have evidence that strongly suggests your husband was with Phyllis Terrell the night she was killed," Sara said.

Lori Stewart studied Sara unflinchingly. "What bearing does that have on Randall's death?"

"You're not surprised?"

"From what I've read, her killer was identified by the FBI," Mrs. Stewart replied. "Randall may have been many things, but he was not a murderer."

"Many things?" Sara echoed.

"I'd rather not go into it."

"I can understand how you might want to keep family matters private," Sara said.

"My parents adored Randall," Lori said. "Now that he's gone I see no need for them to feel otherwise."

"He was with Phyllis the night she was murdered."

"I'd rather not comment."

"I know how difficult it can be to talk about personal matters with strangers," Sara said. "If you wish, for the sake of your parents and your children, what you tell us doesn't have to be made public."

Lori reached for her coffee with a shaky hand. She clasped the cup with both hands, took a sip, and said, "You can promise me that?"

"Yes," Sara said. "Please tell me about Phyllis and Randall."

"I never wanted Randall dead. I only wanted him out of my life. I knew he was sleeping with Phyllis. It wasn't the first time he'd been unfaithful."

"Tell me how you knew."

Lori Stewart put the coffee cup down. "It started six months after Phyllis moved in. We'd met her socially at neighborhood gatherings, and I could see that Randall was drawn to her. She started calling and asking if she could borrow him to help her with her computer. He liked to think he was something of an expert. Soon after that it became obvious what was happening."

"How so?" Sara asked.

"He changed his jogging schedule. Said he thought it would be better to go running later at night, especially during the warm weather. He'd be gone much too long."

"Did you confront him with your suspicions?" Sara asked.

Lori Stewart shook her head. "No. I talked to an attorney about divorcing him. He said I'd be much better off to wait until after our tenth anniversary to do it. The court takes a more favorable view of equitable settlements if the marriage has had longevity."

"Was that your plan?"

"Yes, I was going to file for divorce in six months."

"And Randall didn't know about it?" Sara asked.

"No one did. It would've been hard enough to face my parents and the boys when the time came. As far as Randall was concerned, he was happily married with a nearby honeypot to dip into."

"On the night Phyllis Terrell was murdered, did you know he was with her?"

"Yes. He said he had to stay up late to do some work. I went to bed. After he thought I was sleeping, he left the house. I saw him cut across the arroyo to the Terrell property. I stayed awake until he came back. He was gone for an hour."

"What time was that?"

"He left at a quarter to eleven and got back shortly before midnight. The next day, when I learned that Phyllis had been murdered, I thought about telling the police. But I was certain in my mind that he couldn't have killed Phyllis. No one who has done something terrible like that can fall asleep so easily."

"Could he have left the house again after you went to sleep?"

"I would've known it. Randall always wakes me up when he gets out of bed. I'm a very light sleeper."

"Thank you," Sara said.

Kerney stood up. "What size shoe did your husband wear?"

Lori Stewart gave Kerney a bewildered look. "A size nine. He had very narrow feet. Why do you ask?"

"Just curious," he said, stepping to the door. The shoe print found at the Terrell residence was a size larger. "That's all for now. We won't take any more of your time."

Traffic backed up along the feeder road to the Interstate. Soccer moms cut across lanes, hurrying to get kids to school before the tardy bell rang. Big-rig truckers pulled off on the shoulder of the road at a twenty-four-hour stop-and-rob near the southbound on-ramp for coffee refills.

"If you're going to become an alley cat, Kerney, tell me now," Sara said.

Kerney laughed. "I bet Lori Stewart, on advice of counsel, kept a diary of her husband's late-night visits to Phyllis Terrell."

"What a good idea," Sara said brightly. "I'll have to remember that. I almost choked when she said she didn't want her husband dead."

"At least she managed to keep the dollar signs from flashing in her eyes."

"Tidy-looking lives can be so messy," Sara said.

"Let's not do that," Kerney said.

"Do what?"

Kerney shrugged. "Fake it with each other."

Sara patted Kerney's cheek. "Not a chance."

"You don't think it's possible?"

"Ask me in ten years."

Kerney accelerated south down the Interstate. It was a good four-hour drive to Ramah, where Proctor Straley lived. None of the vehicles behind him looked suspicious. He kept his eye on the rearview mirror anyway.

Sal Molina went to Jake's home, only to be told by his wife that he was up on the mesa for the weekend at the family's ranch feeding cattle. She gave him directions and Molina drove the all-wheel-drive minivan up the unpaved rocky country road, skidding over frozen mud bogs, digging through deep snow-covered slushy ruts, until he reached the old abandoned farming settlement of Ojo de la Vaca. Roofless church and schoolhouse walls still stood along the dirt road and a few dilapidated cabins peppered the valley. Molina drove down a dirt track to a cabin where smoke rose from the chimney and a hay trailer hitched to a pickup truck was parked outside.

An unsmiling Jake waited for him on the front step. Bits of hay clung to his faded sweatshirt and dusted his curly salt-and-pepper hair.

"What are you doing here?" Jake asked.

"You've got cows, Jake?" Molina said. "I didn't know that."

"Yeah, I've got cows. What do you want?"

Molina looked across the narrow valley to a pine forest that filled a ridgeline. "It's pretty out here. Old family place?"

"My great-grandfather settled it. Get to the point, Molina."

"You know what I want."

Jake shook his head. "You got your favor for helping my son, so I'm off the hook with you, Molina."

"Don't put me in a position that could cost you your job, Jake," Sal replied. "You've gotta need the money it brings in. Look, up to now, you're a nameless confidential informant. Let's keep it that way."

"Don't threaten me."

"Come on, Jake. You were a cop for twenty-five years. How many times did you have to give somebody a little push?"

"Enough. But I never ratted off a snitch."

"Neither have I, and I don't want to. I've only got a couple of questions. Did you ever get a look inside the basement room?"

"What if I did?"

"I don't care about the people in the room. I'm just interested in the equipment and machines you might have seen, stuff you would have easily recognized."

"Are you going for a search warrant?"

"If we do, there will be no names in the affidavit and we'll ask for a sealed order."

"Good luck," Jake said.

"Help me out here, Jake. I've got dead bodies piled up and the feds lying through their teeth to me."

"The way I hear it, the damn case is solved."

"You heard about the murdered priest? It's part of the same investigation."

"You gotta be kidding me," Jake said.

"I'm not. Cut me a break, Jake. I promise you won't be involved. What's in the room?"

"I only went in once to do a search when a bomb threat was called in. That was seven, maybe eight months ago. Mostly it's filled with communication gear and computers."

"Any surveillance equipment?" Molina asked.

"Some of that too."

"Like what?"

"Wand microphones, wiretap units, miniature video cameras, room bugs."

"Keep going," Molina said, writing everything down.

*   *   *

Blindfolded, cuffed, and shackled, Charlie Perry felt hands lift him off the bed into a standing position. His body felt rubbery, alien, feeble. The heavy dose of muscle relaxants made his knees buckle, his arms flap at his sides. His mind was giddy, untroubled, his thoughts scatterbrained. He could sense the presence of a goofy smile on his face. He giggled and wondered what type of psychotropic drug they'd used on him.

Two pairs of hands removed his cuffs and shackles and stripped off his clothes. The blindfold stayed in place throughout. He shivered as the cold metal cuffs and shackles were tightened down and locked around his wrists and ankles. Guided to a chair, he sat and waited. A hand rubbed warm lather with the scent of cheap shaving cream across his face. A razor scraped across his chin. He felt the blade nick his Adam's apple. A hand grabbed his wrist and straightened his arm. He felt the prick of a needle in a vein.

The cuffs and shackles came off again. He was lifted to his feet and dressed. Everything fit perfectly. Keys and a wallet went into his trouser pockets, socks and shoes went on his feet, tape was pressed over his mouth, an empty shoulder holster was strapped on.

Restrained again, walked to the bed and laid out, Charlie wondered why the hands didn't just kill him and put him in a coffin. He tried to keep track of time, but lost count as a wave of memories flooded his mind. He was back salmon fishing in Alaska with his father, then walking a Jamaican beach with his first girlfriend after college. He couldn't remember her name.

The sound of chopper blades intruded. He was pulled to his feet and marched outside. The cold air had a parched, dusty smell, his feet crunched on hard-packed sand, the wind whistled relentlessly.

Bundled into the helicopter, Charlie knew he was leaving the desert. But he didn't care. He was still trying to remember the name of the girl on the beach.

*   *   *

Outside Albuquerque, Kerney and Sara headed west up Nine Mile Hill. Soon the old trestle bridge that straddled the Rio Puerco on a dead-end stretch of old Route 66 came into view. Fifty miles to the south Ladron Peak, a hideout for thieves and rustlers in the territorial days, broke the horizon.

They sped through hill country that dipped and rose to reveal the ancient Laguna Indian Pueblo, where low adobe homes clustered around a humble white church.

Kerney eased off the Interstate at Grants. Established as a coaling station for the railroad, the town had thrived on logging and mining operations for a time, but now survived on the payroll from a state prison and the money travelers left behind as they stopped for meals, gas, or a night's lodging.

The icy state road to Ramah forced Kerney to slow down. For a while Sara imagined herself simply on a pleasant weekend outing. The porous black lava beds of the malpais mesmerized her. Stark and vast, it had a harsh, unrelenting beauty.

The badlands drew Sara's thoughts to Kerney. Could he ever be drawn away from a place of such breathtaking horizons, immense spaces, limitless skies, sweeping mountains? Probably not. Much like her father and brother, who ranched in Montana, Kerney's connection to the land was inbred and strong. In her heart that affinity made him even more endearing.

She rubbed her hand on his leg.

"What's that for?" he asked.

"Nothing," Sara said.

The weather closed in, bringing wind-driven snow. Past the badlands they moved through frosted mountain woodlands that gradually gave way to fallow pastures and glimpses of red rock mesas. The storm lifted outside of Ramah, swirling away to reveal a cold blue sky.

They passed El Moro National Monument, a massive sandstone butte with Indian ruins on the top and inscriptions carved into the soft rock at the bottom by early Spanish and Anglo explorers. Beyond El Moro giant monolithic figures, carved out of the sandstone by wind and rain, stood like sentinels overlooking a broad valley. They climbed a gentle rise, dropped into a shallow basin, and entered the Mormon settlement of Ramah, a charming village of stone and wood-frame houses with pitched tin roofs, fenced yards, and massive cottonwood trees. The fresh snow made everything look picture-postcard perfect.

Kerney stopped at a restaurant and got directions to Proctor Straley's ranch. He cut fresh tracks on a snow-covered dirt road that wandered past some ancient cliff dwellings, narrowed down to a fence-lined track, and then opened onto miles of rangeland. The road led to one solitary round-top mesa where a cluster of buildings stood.

As they drew closer, Sara studied the buildings. The original ranch house had a hand-chiseled stone exterior, an enclosed front porch, and dormer windows. Some distance away on a small rise stood a flat-roof, modern Santa Fe–style adobe home. Beyond it, a little higher still, an estate-size residence with separate guest cottages, a swimming pool and cabana, and a detached six-car garage surrounded by perfectly landscaped grounds sprawled at the foot of the mesa.

"My, my," Sara said as Kerney braked to a stop, "what a nice place Proctor Straley has here."

"Where's the barn?" Kerney asked. "The shipping pens? Equipment sheds? Not to mention the cattle."

"Gentlemen ranchers prefer to have such things out of sight," Sara answered in a highbrow tone. "After all, it's a question of ambience."

Kerney laughed. "You mean they don't want to get cow shit on their boots."

"Exactly," Sara said, climbing out of the truck. "Let's go see what kind of feed supplement Proctor Straley favors for his herd."

Kerney laughed again. It felt good.

*   *   *

A housekeeper took them through a great room with an arched wood ceiling offset by pale white smooth plaster walls. Recessed lighting accentuated oversized western paintings by modern cowboy artists. Deep green sofas and chairs were arranged to create quiet conversation areas. Large slabs of polished marble on pedestal bases served as tables, and expensive Navajo rugs littered the hardwood floor.

Proctor Straley waited for them in front of a floor-to-ceiling stone fireplace in a study room. A row of windows gave a view of the open range and forested ridge beyond. Under his feet on the flagstone floor was an early Navajo chief's blanket with strong alternating black and red horizontal stripes broken by a series of zigzag diamond motifs.

Heavyset with a ruddy complexion and closely clipped gray hair, Straley carried his seventy-plus years well. He had the eyes of a man who knew how to watch and listen.

Kerney flashed his shield and introduced Sara as Lieutenant Brannon. Straley moved behind an oval mahogany desk, motioned at two low-back leather chairs, and waited for Kerney and Sara to settle in.

"Did you get a call that we were coming?" Kerney asked.

"No," Straley replied.

"Then I'm sorry if we've inconvenienced you," Kerney said with a smile. "My secretary was supposed to call."

"She didn't," Straley said. "Why are you here?"

"We'd like to ask you a few questions."

"What are they?"

"Were you aware of your daughter's affair with Scott Gatlin?" Kerney asked.

"Yes, but what's the point?" Straley asked.

"We're not convinced your daughter was murdered by Gatlin," Kerney said. "Does that possibility interest you?"

Intense curiosity flickered in Straley's eyes. "I hired Scott Gatlin, brought him to this ranch, treated him like a member of the family, trusted him. If he killed my daughter, I bear part of the burden. How do you think that makes a father feel?"

"Terrible," Sara said softly. "How did you learn of her affair with Gatlin?"

"Phyllis never hid who she was or what she did from me, although there were times I wished she had. It took me many years to accept that she was a woman with strong appetites who didn't care what other people thought of her."

"It must have been difficult to raise such a daughter," Sara said.

Straley smiled wanly. "We were always clashing. She could be as tough minded as any man I've known. While her mother was alive, she protected Phyllis from my censure. I was very disapproving of the way she lived. We had what you might call an uneasy truce over the past ten years."

"But you kept a relationship with her," Sara said.

Straley nodded. "Absolutely. I did love her and I miss her deeply. She could light up a room with her exuberance. She had a special charisma that drew people to her, especially men."

"What do you know about her relationships with men?" Sara asked.

"She would only talk about them if I asked, and for a long time I avoided the subject. She had what she called her one-lover-at-a-time rule. As far as I know she never deviated from it, no matter if the affair lasted a week or a year. Occasionally a lover would filter back into her life, but most were permanently banished. I think, in her own way, she was looking for the perfect mate to match her."

"You know this as fact?" Sara asked.

Straley nodded. "After years of arguing she forced the issue with me. We spent an entire night staying up and talking right here in this room over a bottle of Scotch. She wanted me to understand why she lived as she did."

"What did you learn?" Sara asked.

"That she saw no reason not to find pleasure with men. That few could match her as equals. That she had no desire to be possessed or owned. She firmly believed she could live by her own rules."

"Was she faithful to the ambassador?" Kerney inquired.

"Until the point of their separation, I'd say yes."

"What caused the break?" Sara asked.

"She never said, but it came suddenly. I assume Hamilton tried to dominate or control her, which was something that wouldn't do with Phyllis. After all, he had spent many years in the military as a high-ranking officer and was used to being in command. Starting out, I think Phyllis may have been drawn to the qualities of leadership she saw in Hamilton. Perhaps she felt she'd found that perfect match."

Sara asked questions about the ambassador's personal qualities. Straley sketched Terrell as confident, mature, responsible, and even tempered. He noted that Terrell had been aware of Phyllis's reputation, appeared unconcerned about it, and seemed very much in love with her.

It wasn't a portrait of the bullying, self-serving officer Kerney remembered from Vietnam. Either Straley wasn't as sharp as he seemed, or Terrell had done one hell of an acting job.

Kerney approached the issue from a different angle. "How did Terrell wind up on the Trade Source board of directors?"

"I recommended him at his request," Straley said. "He was between diplomatic appointments at the time, and with his government and military background I thought he could serve the corporation well."

"In what ways?" Kerney asked.

"Trade Source was founded as a venture capital company looking to expand into South American media, publishing, print, and television markets. The Hispanic population is burgeoning, becoming more sophisticated, especially in large South American cities. That caught my interest as an investor. In Hamilton's prior diplomatic postings he'd worked closely with foreign officials who could open doors to overseas investors. We wanted to make sure each entry into a foreign market would have strong local appeal."

Sara picked up the thread. "From what I've learned, Trade Source doesn't have a strong media focus anymore," she said.

"Which is why I left the board," Straley said. "I'm a media man, always have been. Newspapers, magazines, television, the Internet, and radio stations interest me. That's where my corporate expansion goals lie."

"Why did Trade Source veer off in a different direction?" Sara asked.

"Hamilton brought a proposal to the board that had the strong backing of the Commerce, Treasury, and State Departments. They were interested in helping developing nations in South America establish a banking and financial technological infrastructure without using foreign aid appropriations. Trade Source was asked to provide the venture capital, identify subcontractors, and oversee the initiative under a memorandum of understanding that guaranteed reimbursement for all costs plus an equitable profit margin. I opposed it."

"Why?"

"It wasn't where I wanted the company to go, and I didn't think we had the resources to take on two major corporate initiatives simultaneously."

"How did it play out?" Kerney asked.

"Hamilton arranged important meetings between Trade Source corporate officers and ranking financial leaders and money managers in Peru, Venezuela, and Ecuador. Ultimately, Trade Source signed contracts to supply hardware and software products, plus provide technical assistance and training."

"Was Trade Source acting as an agent for a U.S. Government foreign aid package?" Kerney asked.

"You could look at it that way," Straley replied, "but it wouldn't be accurate. Using privatization strategies to achieve government goals has become commonplace on the federal level."

"Why did Trade Source buy APT Performa?" Kerney asked.

"As I understand it, that was done based on Hamilton's recommendation. I was off the board by then, but I heard that APT Performa had exactly what was needed to begin putting the necessary systems together."

"Do you know Clarence Thayer?" Kerney asked.

"Only by reputation. I understand he runs a tight ship and knows his business."

"What about SWAMI?" Kerney asked.

"That's another issue entirely. As I understand it, Thayer sold the company but kept the rights of certain proprietary inventions. SWAMI was one of those. It was at an early stage of development at the time and not much was made of it. From what I've read recently it's about to make Thayer and his outside investors very rich men."

"Do you know anything about Terrell's personal finances?" Sara asked.

"Hamilton lives comfortably," Straley said. "He's not rich by any means, although I know he'd like to be."

"What if he's found a way to become rich?"

Straley gave Sara a studied look. "Are you suggesting Hamilton may have held back what he knew about SWAMI from the board for a piece of the action from APT Performa?"

"Why not?" Sara replied. "A technological breakthrough like SWAMI is almost priceless. Granted, Terrell would have eventually made some profits through the stock he held as a board member if Trade Source had secured the rights to SWAMI. But what if he cut a sweetheart deal with Thayer to keep SWAMI off the negotiating table for a bigger piece of the pie?"

Straley cocked his head. "Hamilton has always wanted to be a major money player."

"Think about it," Sara said. "Terrell brought the APT Performa proposal to the Trade Source board, made the arrangements to bring various federal agencies to the table, and coordinated meetings with South American financial representatives. Did he do it solely for patriotic reasons?"

"I doubt it," Straley said, holding up a hand to stop further questions. "But what does any of this have to do with your contention that Scott Gatlin may not have murdered my daughter?"

"We think your daughter was killed because of what she knew," Kerney said, "not because of who she slept with. We believe she learned secrets about her husband's activities that may be directly related to Trade Source, APT Performa, and the SWAMI project."

"What do you think she knew?" Straley asked.

"First, let me give you some facts," Kerney said. He highlighted the major points, concentrating on the FBI cover-up of Phyllis Terrell's murder, her connection to Father Mitchell, the priest's probe into intelligence operations in South America, and Hamilton Terrell's involvement in the cover-up.

"These facts are fully documented?" Straley asked when Kerney stopped talking.

"They are."

"So, what did my daughter learn that got her killed?"

"That, we don't know," Kerney said. "But, one way or another it directly relates to your son-in-law."

"If it's a government secret, you're never going to know," Straley said. "Are you willing to share your documentation with me?"

"This isn't a news story, Mr. Straley," Sara said.

Straley looked at Sara straight on. "I know how the government can manipulate the media under the guise of national security to suit its own purposes, young lady. I have no intention of falling into that trap. But I want to look at your facts for myself before I decide what to do."

"What can you do?" Kerney asked.

"If Terrell played an active role in causing my daughter's death, as you've suggested, I will find a way to poison his reputation. Sometimes innuendo can ruin a career just a quickly as a front-page scandal headline."

"Perhaps something will show up in your mailbox from an anonymous source," Kerney said as he stood up.

"I'll keep my eye out for it, Chief Kerney."

*   *   *

Until Kerney and Sara Brannon left Santa Fe, Applewhite had worried about finding the right killing field. Since the hit had to be staged, icing Kerney at home wouldn't do. No matter how well orchestrated, neighbors might see things, remember little details, especially on a weekend, when people were at home.

Applewhite went high-speed mobile down the Interstate in Charlie Perry's car, putting the details into play on the radio. She had Charlie airborne. The pilot had instructions to maintain a holding pattern once he was in range. The men tailing Kerney were in Ramah, ten kilometers away from Proctor Straley's ranch, ready to follow Kerney as soon as he moved. She punched up images on her onboard laptop that gave her satellite visuals of the terrain, roads, vehicles, and structures along Kerney's route.

The area was bracketed by National Forest, Indian land, and the malpais, and had few permanent residents. A winter storm in the mountains had brought local traffic to a standstill.

Storm clouds masked a portion of the satellite visuals. Applewhite switched to a Global Positioning System that highlighted topography of the area. Defined by a prominent ridgeline, the uplift ran for a good sixty miles. A state road cut through it at the Continental Divide, dropped out of the mountains, and ran straight west for about fifteen miles through canyons, mesas, and frontage pasture land. The stretch of road would do nicely for a killing field.

Charlie's luggage was in the trunk, along with a wad of greenbacks and a bank confirmation of a six-figure deposit in an offshore account. The money could easily be traced back to Enrique DeLeon.

The fast-moving storm slammed into her east of Grants. She fought her way through it, breaking into sunshine and a slushy pavement. The chopper pilot radioed a diversion around the storm. She caught the turnoff to Ramah through the badlands just as the helicopter reported a twenty-minute ETA.

Past the village of San Rafael the highway was snowpacked with no traffic. As she entered the Zuni Mountains the road turned to snow-covered ice.

The chopper came into view out of the southwest. Applewhite asked for an LZ location. The pilot radioed he could offload at a clearing near the road to Paxton Springs.

"Give me a visual on traffic," Applewhite said.

"There's one four-by-four behind you, eight clicks back," the pilot replied. "Nothing's coming at you for a good twelve clicks, and it's slow moving all the way. The LZ is behind tree cover and out of sight from the highway."

"Copy that," Applewhite said.

She plowed off the pavement at the Paxton Springs turnoff through eight inches of snow, and bumped her way to the waiting chopper. The wash of the slow-moving propeller blades dusted snow off the tall pine trees, creating eddies that puffed and then disappeared in the wind.

Applewhite gave the pilot orders while two men in fatigues loaded a drugged, rubbery Charlie Perry into the backseat of the car.

The pilot nodded, put a hand to his headset, and said, "The target is moving."

"Let's do it," Applewhite replied.

Bobby Sloan lost sight of Applewhite on the curves through the mountains. When she'd switched to Perry's car in the APT Performa parking lot, he'd been forced to maintain visual contact. He put the Bronco into low four-wheel drive and pushed it to the max to make up ground. Wheels spun snow and tires whined as he hit ice. He pointed the Bronco down the middle of the road, fishtailing through curves, downshifting on short straightaways, until he made it through the pass and had a clean line of sight down the empty road. Nothing.

Where the hell was she? She couldn't have been moving that fast. With no homing devices on Charlie Perry's car, he had no way to track her.

A helicopter came out of the mountains, flying low, gaining altitude, moving toward Ramah. It changed course, came straight back at him, and flew overhead. He watched in the rearview mirror as it cleared the mountain and disappeared from view.

He slowed, made a cautious U-turn, and went looking for Applewhite. She had to be somewhere behind him. But where? He crawled along at ten miles an hour looking for car tracks off the road. At the Paxton Springs turnoff Applewhite's car almost sideswiped the Bronco as she slid onto the highway.

She careened by, steering into a slight spin before straightening the wheels. Bobby took a quick look, ducked his head, and kept moving in the opposite direction. When she was out of sight he pulled to the side of the road.

Applewhite had left Santa Fe alone, of that Sloan was certain. But he was just as certain he'd seen a head bob up in the backseat when she passed him.

He swung the Bronco around, hoping he hadn't been made, wondering what in the hell was going on.

The tape across his mouth didn't keep Charlie Perry from giggling. Although the blindfold kept him from seeing things, the helicopter ride had been exciting. For a while they'd gone up and down like a bumpy roller coaster with the blades thud, thud, thudding, and the wind swoosh, swoosh, swooshing outside. It had been lots of fun.

Now he was swishing along in a car. This was better than Disneyland, where his father had taken a picture of him pulling Donald Duck's tail.

Charlie tried to grin. The tape across his mouth made it impossible, his ankles and wrists were hurting a little bit, and he wished someone would take the blindfold off. He wondered if he'd done something bad, and what was going to happen next.

Muddy slush from the ranch road splatted the truck windshield. Kerney turned on the wipers while Sara weighed in with her take on the Straley interview. Hamilton Terrell had been the point man for the operation since day one. He'd married Phyllis Terrell to position himself favorably with Proctor Straley, and then used Straley to wangle his way onto the Trade Source board. After that it had been just a matter of swaying the board with the promise of a lot of easy money from the public coffers.

Kerney agreed it had all been a setup to mask SWAMI and set the stage for Terrell's secret trade mission. Both had to be tied together, otherwise all the killing made no sense. But proving anything still remained highly remote, getting to Terrell wouldn't be easy, and time was running out.

Most of the tire tracks on the snow-covered road gave out when they reached the Pine Hill Navajo Reservation cutoff. They passed the snow-tinged butte of El Moro National Monument. The powerful, beautiful presence of it made Sara want to stop and play tourist. She wistfully thought about asking Kerney to bring her down on a weekend jaunt, and quickly nixed the idea. There might be no weekend jaunts with Kerney if she didn't stay alert and focused.

The vehicle tracking Kerney reported in. He had a five-minute ETA to Applewhite's location. She asked about road traffic. No vehicles other than Kerney's were traveling east. She told the surveillance driver to keep it that way.

Applewhite had spotted Detective Sloan when she'd passed him at the Paxton Springs cutoff. She got confirmation from the chopper pilot that she was still being followed.

"Keep him out of my zone."

"Affirmative," the pilot said. "Are you authorizing deadly force?"

"Do whatever it takes," Applewhite said, as she eased to a stop along a straight stretch of road. "Is anything else moving toward me?"

"Negative," the pilot said.

"Close the road behind me," she said.

Applewhite staged a one-car accident. She drove the car at an angle off the road, turning the wheels to put it into a skid. She backed up and adjusted the car's position so that a raised front hood would keep Kerney from seeing in as he approached. She pulled Perry out of the backseat, put him behind the steering wheel, took off the blindfold, ripped the tape from his mouth, locked him inside the vehicle, and popped the hood.

Charlie gave her an insipid smile through the car window. She got a rifle and ammunition out of the trunk, moved over a fence into tree cover, and waited.

The cop in Kerney would force him to stop and investigate.

Taking him out would be another enjoyable hit. But the prospect of whacking Sara Brannon made Applewhite break into a big smile.

Bobby Sloan saw the helicopter land on the pavement and went cross-country through the trees to get around it. He caught a glimpse of the pilot watching him and talking rapidly into his headset as he bounced by. He ground the Bronco through a snowbank to get back on the road and the front wheels bottomed out in a ditch. He slammed the gearbox into reverse and the back tires screamed as he inched his way out.

Just as the rear wheels gripped solid, Sloan heard the chopper. He geared into low, took the ditch at an angle, and spun rubber down the road. Before he could make the curve, the chopper dropped down sideways in front of him. The door on the chopper slid open, and the windshield exploded in Sloan's face as he took fire.

He felt a nick on his neck as he gunned the Bronco back into the trees. The back window blew out and he could hear rounds slamming into the tailgate. He redlined the engine, bounced off a tree, topped a rise, and barreled down to the highway. He could see Applewhite's car in the distance and the tiny outline of a vehicle coming from the opposite direction.

He downshifted and waited for the chopper to come at him

again. Cold air whistled through the vehicle, freezing his face as he punched the accelerator. He felt tired, woozy, unable to focus. He looked down and saw his blood-soaked shirt. He put his hand up to his neck and felt wet spurts as his heart pumped his arteries empty.

Realizing he was a dead man, he tried to squeeze the wound closed anyway. His foot found the brake and the Bronco did a quick three-sixty before tilting on its side and spinning into a tree. Just before impact Bobby Sloan passed out.

Kerney saw the stranded car two hundred yards ahead and slowed. He touched the brake, scanned the vehicle for damage, and couldn't see any.

"What do you think?" he asked Sara.

"I can't tell from here."

He caught a flash of light at the edge of some trees off the south side of the road. He touched the brake again.

"I saw it," Sara said, opening the glove box. She grabbed Kerney's .38, checked the rounds in the cylinder, and emptied a box of ammunition in her coat pocket. "Do you think it's a setup?"

Kerney unsnapped his holster. "It may be nothing."

He upshifted, and tried to look inside the car. The raised hood obstructed his view. It was a late-model four-door Ford, just like the one Charlie Perry had been driving. His misgivings jumped ten notches.

"Get down," he snapped. "I'm going to ram it."

He gunned the engine, drove off the road, and hit the Ford at a slant. Airbags filled the cab, rounds blew holes in the passenger window and deflated them. He hit the gas pedal hard. Metal crinkled and snapped as he slammed the Ford further off the road. The truck lurched to a stop and Sara followed him out the driver's door and crouched with him behind the protection of a tire.

Rounds peppered the Ford, shattering glass. Kerney took a quick look inside and saw a body slumped awkwardly in the driver's seat.

Blood splatter stained the windshield. He sneaked another look at the trees, took fire, and spotted the shooter's position.

"There's a dead man in the car. The shooter is south of us, in the trees, half a click to the left about ten yards in. Look for the tree with the broken branch."

Sara got a fix on the location. "Give me covering fire," she said. "I'll go."

"You can't run that fast, Kerney." She moved away before he could stop her, snaking her way back to the truck.

Kerney followed her, ducked behind the open truck door, reached up, and cut away the deflated airbag from the steering wheel with a pocket knife.

"What are you doing?"

"I can drive faster than you can run," he said. "You cover me." He pulled out spare magazines and stuffed them in his back pocket.

"We both go," Sara said.

Kerney looked at her hard, ready to argue.

"We don't have time for this, Kerney," Sara snapped. "Take the right flank."

"Okay." He levered the driver seat back as far as it would go, crawled into it with his head below the windshield, and geared the engine into reverse. "Ready?"

Sara nodded and moved back to the car. A bullet took out another window in the Ford. Kerney hit the accelerator, raised up, spun the wheel, and headed for the wire stock fence, firing out the driver's-side window in the direction of the trees.

Sara ran zigzag around the trunk of the car to the fence line. Rounds dug into the snow inches away from her. Kerney rammed his way through the fence. Sara crawled under the wire, firing as she went. She got up and started running in a low crouch.

Kerney closed on the sniper's position. The front wheels dipped into a trench and the driver's-side mirror blew apart. He wheeled the truck, hit the brakes, and heard bullets dig into steel. He bailed out, looking for Sara. He saw only her tracks in the snow. He called to her and got no answer. He slammed in a fresh magazine, crawled under the truck, and scanned for any sight of her. A single rifle shot rang out.

"Sara," Kerney yelled.

He saw her rise up out of the trench a hundred feet away and start running for a tree. He emptied the magazine at the sniper and loaded another clip. Sara made it to cover and pointed at the tree closest to Kerney. She pulled off two rounds and kept firing while Kerney sprinted forward.

He slid headfirst behind the tree, emptied the magazine at the shooter's position, fed in another clip, and looked at Sara. She patted her chest and pointed ahead, signaling her next move. Kerney shook his head and watched helplessly as she reloaded and crawled away from cover. He pumped rounds and watched as she disappeared from sight into the grove.

Everything got quiet. The tree with the broken branch was dead ahead. He looked for movement. Every muscle in his body tensed as he searched for a hard target.

"It's clear," Sara called.

Kerney stayed zeroed in on the tree until Sara stepped out and waved him in. He found her standing over Applewhite's body. There was a bullet hole in her leg, but the killing shot had come from the rifle Applewhite had stuck in her mouth.

"Meet Elaine Cornell," Sara said. "She was hard core to the end. Let's get out of here."

They drove back to the Ford. The man in the front seat was Charlie Perry. He had a nasty hole in his left temple.

"So that's Charlie Perry," Sara said. "What's he doing here?"

"I think he was supposed to play patsy," Kerney said.

She reached inside the shattered car window, grabbed the microphone, and keyed it. "Listen up, you bastards," she said. "Elaine Cornell is dead, Agent Perry is dead. If you want more, bring it on."

She smiled sweetly at the incredulous look on Kerney's face and tossed the microphone inside the car. A helicopter came out of the forest and veered away. Sara's cell phone rang. She dug it out of an inside pocket.

"Maybe they're calling in their regrets," Kerney said. "Let's hope so."

Kerney waited impatiently, watched the chopper until it moved over the Zuni Mountains, then gave the truck a quick look-over. The bumper was crumpled, a headlight shattered, and the grill was pushed in. There were scratches on the hood and bullet holes in a front fender, door, and window.

"I've been ordered back to Fort Leavenworth," Sara said with amusement. She dropped the phone in a pocket and brushed snow off the front of her jeans. "The Pentagon wants a peacekeeping mission drawn up. Seems there's trouble brewing somewhere in Africa."

"Do you believe that?" Kerney asked as he checked the engine for damage. It seemed intact.

"Does that thing run?" Sara asked.

"It better."

Sara nodded in agreement. "It's not unusual for the school to prepare tactical plans and operational field doctrines for peace-keeping missions. Geopolitical assessments based on proposed strategic military deployments have to be factored in if the mission is going to succeed."

"Really?" Kerney said as he cut away the deflated passenger's-side airbag. The road was clear in both directions. "But do you believe it?"

"Why shouldn't I?" Sara said innocently. "Aren't you interested in geopolitics and military field doctrine?"

"I'm deeply interested. Tell me about it while I drive."

Sara slid onto the seat. "No, I'd just be babbling."

"Babble all you want," Kerney said as he pulled onto the high-way. "After what just happened, I need the distraction."

Sara prattled a little and Kerney asked stupid questions. Several miles down the road they found Bobby Sloan's body inside the Bronco and their survivors' euphoria vanished.

Chapter 14

In the courthouse basement Tim Ingram got word of Applewhite's screw-up and went into damage-control overdrive. He ordered the chopper pilot and the surveillance team on the scene to shut down the highway in both directions—nothing in, nothing out. Kerney and Sara Brannon were to be held in protective custody.

He called the commander at Kirtland Air Force Base, invoked a Defense Department intelligence directive, and ordered the immediate dispatch of a security forces unit and a munitions team to the Ramah highway. They were to relieve personnel on-site, secure the area, establish roadblocks, and remove all bodies and vehicles ASAP.

Helicopters took off with two combat control teams. Vehicles and heavy equipment rolled with munitions experts onboard.

By phone Ingram gave the base public-information officer a press release cover story. All news outlets were to be advised of an accident involving a military armament shipment on the Ramah highway during a heavy snow storm. Cleanup crews were en route. There was no danger to the public. Motorists were cautioned to detour around the area or expect long delays.

At computer consoles, team members sent top-secret encrypted messages to the White House and the Pentagon, conveyed satellite photographs of the failed hit to the Defense Intelligence Agency, forwarded Applewhite's recorded radio traffic to the National Security Agency, and transmitted Ingram's contingency plan to army intelligence.

Ingram fired off his own quick status report: assignment blown, nontarget police officer killed, field operative dead, containment teams en route, advise no further action. He ordered up an air force chopper, told the team to shut everything down, and hauled ass to the airport.

The Bronco had landed on its right side. The seat belt had kept Bobby Sloan's body from sliding down to the passenger window. Shards from the blown-out windshield glimmered in the dark blood pool that coated the glass. Weapons, flashlights, and equipment had broken loose from mounting racks and were strewn about the cab. Clipped to the windshield visor was a photograph of Bobby's wife, which he always carried with him as a good-luck charm.

Kerney reached through the windshield, pulled out Sloan's briefcase, and went through it with blood-sticky fingers. He found Bobby's surveillance log, tore it up, and watched as the wind scattered the pieces. He tossed the case back inside the vehicle and kept his eyes off Bobby's face as he yanked out the on-board laptop, stomped on it, and spun it into the trees out of sight.

"What are you doing?" Sara asked.

Heartsick, Kerney shook his head. "I don't know." He felt deflated, angry, helpless. He kicked a piece of the shattered laptop away, took a deep breath, and let it out slowly. "It's over. It ends right here."

He pulled out his cell phone. "I'm calling it in. Bobby, Applewhite, Perry—the whole stinking mess."

Sara stepped up to Kerney and gripped his arm to stop him. "Let's think this through."

Kerney didn't want to hear it. "We're outgunned, outmanned, and outmaneuvered."

"We've got company," Sara said.

He looked over his shoulder and tensed. Two men in camouflage fatigues came out of the woods carrying assault rifles. They crossed the road in a disciplined, perfect tandem, weapons at the ready.

Sara reached into her pocket and wrapped her hand around the .38. Kerney judged the distance to the nearest cover, snaked his hand inside his jacket, and grasped the semiautomatic.

One of the men called out, "Chief Kerney, Colonel Brannon, step away from each other and put your hands in the air where we can see them. Chief Kerney, slowly turn to face me. Do it now."

"What do you think?" Kerney whispered.

"We better do as they say," she whispered back.

"Do it now!" the man ordered.

"I'm sorry I got you into this," Kerney said as he turned and clasped his hands at the back of his neck.

Sara took her empty hands out of her pockets. "Let's see what these gentlemen want before you start apologizing."

Ingram flew over the westbound convoy on the Interstate. A troop transport, two flatbeds, an ambulance, a container truck, and a big-rig tow-truck were moving in close formation, led by a Hummer with flashing lights.

Ingram waited for his orders to come in by encrypted radio relay. If the removal sanction remained in effect, could he do it? Instructions came through to contain and suppress if possible. Ingram looked out the cockpit window and smiled.

In his headset Ingram caught chopper traffic as the two Special Ops teams arrived at the scene and blocked the highway. He listened to pilots bark off-load orders as team members dropped into intercept positions at the few dirt roads that fed onto the highway.

On approach he had the pilot make a run down the five-mile

containment area. They flew over the mountain pass roadblock, over Kerney and Sara Brannon under guard next to the Bronco, past the line of special-ops airmen guarding side roads, past Charlie Perry in the shot-up car, and on to the western roadblock.

Ingram ordered his chopper back to the Bronco. The pilot put the bird down on the highway. Ingram walked through deep snow to Kerney and Sara Brannon. Both were cuffed, hands at their backs. He had the cuffs removed and sent the guards out of earshot.

He looked at them for a long minute before speaking. Kerney's jaw muscles were torqued together. Sara Brannon's eyes questioned him, but she gave no sign of recognition.

"Shouldn't you be on your way back to Fort Leavenworth, Colonel?" Ingram asked.

"I was just leaving," Sara replied.

"That may still be possible," Ingram said. A cold wind blew against his neck. He turned up his collar. "But first, tell me what you know."

"I know one of my officers has just been murdered," Kerney replied sharply.

"Make this easy on yourself, Chief," Ingram said wearily. "I'll ask the questions. How did you ID me?"

Kerney stared hard at Ingram before replying. "You were named as the source who confirmed that Applewhite was FBI."

"Who passed on the information to you?"

"A friend of mine."

"Does he have a name?" Ingram asked sharply.

"Chief Baca of the state police."

"Did Chief Baca assist you in any other way?"

"No."

Ingram took in the answer without comment and glanced at the Bronco. "Why did you put a tail on Agent Applewhite?"

"Last night I discovered who you and Applewhite really are," Kerney said. "Once I knew she was operating covertly, I decided to have her watched."

"You suspected her?"

"Get real, Ingram," Kerney snapped. "The woman just tried to murder us, and I've got a dead officer your people killed inside the Bronco. Of course I suspected her."

Ingram stuffed his cold hands into his coat pockets. "Why did you visit Proctor Straley?"

"I wanted to find out if Applewhite had any connection to the Gatlin killing."

"And?" Ingram asked.

"Straley had no information. He accepts what he's been told."

"Who else besides Detective Sloan was helping you?"

Either Ingram didn't have a clue that he and Charlie Perry had also been under surveillance, or he was trying to give Kerney an out. "Nobody," Kerney said.

Ingram nodded as though Kerney had given the right answer. "Are you willing to walk away from this and not look back?"

"What will it take for us to do that?" Sara asked.

"All that you know about SWAMI can never be revealed, discussed, or made public. The same applies to your investigation into the Terrell-Mitchell homicides. You will state this in writing and sign a binding, confidential document. Should you choose to go public on either of these matters, you will both be arrested and charged with the illegal possession of government secrets and obstructing a federal investigation. At the very least it will end both of your careers."

"What else?" Kerney asked.

"You must turn over all information gathered during your probe, and stop any further investigation into the death of Randall Stewart. You will acknowledge as accurate and conclusive the FBI findings of the Phyllis Terrell homicide investigation."

Kerney eyed the Bronco. "How do you propose to make Bobby Sloan's murder go away?"

"Let's say that you asked Detective Sloan to meet with you in Ramah to participate in the Proctor Straley interview. Bad weather delayed his travel and an accident occurred involving a military munitions vehicle. Unfortunately, the detective was killed in the collision."

"You can make that scenario happen?" Kerney asked.

"In a very short time it will happen."

"What about Applewhite and Perry?" Kerney asked.

"They were never here," Ingram replied.

"What if we don't agree to your terms?" Sara asked.

"The scenario regarding Detective Sloan's death is flexible, Colonel," Ingram said. "Two more victims can easily be added, if necessary."

"Even if we walk now," Sara said, "what assurance do we have that your decision won't be overturned by a higher command authority?"

Ingram smiled thinly. "I believe you've been given some cause to trust me in this matter, Colonel."

"I have," Sara said, "but it's not you I'm worried about."

"Any further contemplated action will be based on my debriefing. I doubt you'll have any reason to worry."

"That's good enough for me," Sara said.

Ingram gave Sara a brief smile and turned to Kerney. "Do we have an agreement?"

Kerney nodded stiffly.

"Very well." Ingram switched his gaze back to Sara. "A word of caution, Colonel. When you return to Fort Leavenworth be very careful about what you do and say."

He motioned to the guards, who came forward and escorted Kerney and Sara to his helicopter. He heard the distant sound of the convoy on the road and walked to meet the lead vehicle. The Hummer stopped. He gave the officer his instructions, climbed into the chopper, and told the pilot to head for Santa Fe.

Kerney and Sara read and signed the binding agreement while Ingram looked on. At his cottage Kerney helped Ingram carry case material and evidence to his car. He watched Ingram arrange boxes neatly inside the trunk, and wondered why the rear license-plate lights were broken. He handed Ingram the last box filled with Father Mitchell's videotapes. Ingram stuck it in the trunk and closed the lid.

"Tell me one thing," Kerney said. "What started all the killing?"

Ingram hesitated and looked away. "A floppy disk."

"Stolen?"

"I didn't say that," Ingram got behind the wheel. "But think about your question, Kerney. Where did it all start?"

Kerney nodded. "Who was the triggerman?"

Ingram gave Kerney a tight smile. "Don't you mean trigger person?"

"I guess I do." Kerney smiled back.

"No more questions," Ingram said.

"When do I get my truck back?"

"Soon," Ingram said, cranking the engine.

After Ingram drove away, Kerney carefully checked cottage and grounds for wiretaps, bugs, and cameras. Everything apparently had been removed. Unwilling to risk the possibility he'd overlooked something, Kerney took Sara to the hotel in his police vehicle. At the reception desk he upgraded from the junior suite to an executive suite and tipped a porter to fetch Sara's luggage.

He told Sara what Ingram had said after the porter left the room. "Are you surprised?"

"That Ingram answered my question, yes. That it all leads back to Hamilton Terrell, not at all." Kerney checked his watch. "I figure we've got an hour to talk freely before they catch on that we've changed rooms. Why do you think Ingram let us off the hook?"

Sara sank onto the couch in the large, elegant sitting room. "He could have simply been following orders. It would've been stretching it to claim that a police chief, his wife, and a detective had all been killed in one traffic accident."

Kerney eased into an overstuffed chair. "Why did he warn you?"

"To ease his conscience. No, more than that, I think. He never asked for the message he sent me last night, and he didn't seem eager to kill us."

"So, do we abide by the terms of the agreement?" Kerney asked.

"Is there a way not to?"

"Ingram didn't get everything. Andy Baca and Sal Molina have a lot of documentation, and they're not bound by any constraints."

"To be sent to Straley?" Sara asked.

Kerney nodded.

"I say offer him something—not a lot—if he renews his promise to use it with discretion, and tell him he'll get more if he doesn't blow it. Just make sure you're not the one who puts it in Straley's hands."

"I think Andy would be willing to help out."

"So what's next?" Sara asked.

"When big brother stops watching us, we're going to live happily ever," Kerney said.

"That's a scary thought."

"Which part is scary?"

Sara laughed. "I'll reserve comment. Will you stay on as chief?"

"For two reasons. I want to finish what I've started with the department and see Hamilton Terrell taken down a peg or two. Bobby Sloan and the other victims deserve that much. What about you?"

Sara smiled and rubbed her stomach. "I'm having a baby. But before that I plan to graduate from the Command and General Staff College, preferably at the top of the class. Then I'll see."

"Are you thinking of leaving the army?"

"It's something we need to talk about." She patted the cushion. "Will you please come here and put your arms around me?"

Kerney moved to her. Sara turned so she could lean against his chest and snuggle in his arms.

Kerney kicked the sheets off and looked at the clock. He'd slept until eight. The look of anguish he'd seen on Lucy Sloan's face last night remained frozen in his mind.

Sara had stayed with him throughout the afternoon and evening, as he met with Andy Baca, Sal Molina, and Larry Otero, and then paid a visit to Bobby's widow. On the way to the airport last night they agreed to use e-mail sparingly, watch what they said on the telephone, and keep an eye out for anything suspicious. The need to be paranoid felt like an invisible wedge thrust into their lives.

He thought about his meeting with Andy, Sal, and Larry. They all took the news of Bobby's death hard, but agreed to keep the truth buried. Andy didn't have a problem with filtering information to Proctor Straley as long as Kerney set it up. They decided on what would be included in the first envelope. The taped hotel-room conversations between Applewhite and Perry, and Applewhite's phone calls to Terrell, would go out first. Andy would mail it if Kerney's contact with Straley result in a green light.

He dressed and went outside to get the Sunday paper. Sometime during the night his truck had been returned. It looked a mess. He opened the door to retrieve the key. On the seat were the tracking devices Molina and Sloan had planted on Applewhite and Ingram's cars.

It seemed that Ingram had done a lot more than simply ease his conscience. He'd have to tell Sara.

He drank a cup of coffee and read the paper. He found the phony fatal-accident story in the regional news section. The accident victim wasn't identified. Tomorrow it would become front-page news when Bobby Sloan's name was released to the press.

A sidebar national news article reported a helicopter accident at Kelly Air Force base in Texas. Two federal civilian employees had been killed, but the pilot had survived unharmed. Kerney figured that took care of Applewhite and Charlie Perry.

An international news headline caught Kerney's eye:

MEXICAN DRUG LORD ASSASSINATED

El Paso Texas: According to Mexican police, Enrique DeLeon, considered to be the most powerful drug lord in Juárez, was found shot to death at a remote location south of the city. Authorities speculated that DeLeon was killed by members of a rival drug gang. An unnamed police source said that "there is evidence to suggest that a meeting took place between DeLeon and unknown parties which resulted in the shooting," and also noted that "the killing was professionally done."

DeLeon's driver was also found murdered at the scene.

Maybe there was a silver lining at the end of a terrible week. DeLeon had tried to kill him once, and Kerney had often wondered when he would try again.

Kerney flipped to the business briefs section. A headline read:

LOCAL CEO TO INK SOUTH AMERICAN TRADE DEAL

Clarence Thayer, CEO of APT Performa, left Saturday for Caracas, Venezuela, to sign an agreement with banking officials from five Latin American countries. Under the pending agreement Thayer's company will install state-of-the-art computer security software based on research carried out at Sandia and Los Alamos National Laboratories. The countries involved are Colombia, Venezuela, Peru, Ecuador, and Panama.

"Our software tools will assist developing countries in managing liquid financial assets, resulting in improved fiscal accountability," Thayer said before flying to Venezuela.

In Washington a Commerce Department spokesman said the pending agreement will play an important role in helping Latin American countries actively participate in the global economy.

Kerney folded the paper and put it aside. Wallace Brooks had told him SWAMI was three months away from launch. Kerney wondered if some special features were being brought on-line early. If so, he could imagine rows of intelligence analysts drooling on their monitors as they waited expectantly for the data to roll in.

He dressed in his uniform, and went to work. He called the

mayor and city manager to inform them of Bobby Sloan's death. He wrote a memo to all personnel for distribution on Monday morning. By radio he spoke to the day-shift commander, gave her the word about Bobby, and asked to have the flag outside the building lowered to half-mast. He alerted the department's honor-guard commander and requested a full police escort to accompany Bobby's body back to Santa Fe. He made contact with the police chaplain and requested support service for Lucy Sloan. He telephoned every senior off-duty officer above the rank of sergeant and gave them the news.

Early in the afternoon he taped a black ribbon across his shield and called Proctor Straley from a shopping-mall pay phone.

Straley picked up.

"Do you remember our conversation yesterday?" Kerney asked.

"I do, and I'm glad you called," Straley said. "After you left it occurred to me that if a federal appointee, such as an ambassador, failed to disclose his financial holdings fully, that is a violation of the law."

"Do you propose to look into that possibility?" Kerney asked.

"If you keep your part of the bargain, I will," Straley said.

"In that case you'll receive something soon," Kerney said. "If you put it to use, more information will follow."

"Results may not come quickly," Straley said.

"I'm a patient man, Mr. Straley. Good luck and good hunting."

Kerney hung up. He passed by shoppers lining up at the food court, kids cruising in and out of the video arcade, and moviegoers buying tickets for the first matinee.

A wide-eyed child grabbed his mother's hand and pointed at him. "A policeman," the boy said excitedly.

Kerney smiled at the boy, crouched down, and shook his hand.

"I want to be a policeman," the boy said, beaming.

"I can tell you would make a very good policeman," Kerney said. Sara's pregnancy rushed through his mind. He thought about how much he was looking forward to raising a child. He'd never had that opportunity with Clayton.

"Yep, I would."

"You come and see me when you're a little older, and I'll give you a job," Kerney said.

The boy's eyes danced and he nodded seriously.

Kerney walked away feeling better than he had all day. He got back to headquarters to find Larry Otero waiting. He was dressed in his blues with a black ribbon taped across his shield.

"Swing-shift briefing is about to start," Larry said.

Kerney nodded. "We need everybody doing their jobs, Larry."

"They will, Chief. We've got good people."

Kerney walked down the stairs with Otero at his side. "Has a collection been started for flowers and some money for Bobby's wife?"

"It's under way, Chief."

Kerney stopped at the briefing room door. "You ready?"

Otero nodded.

Kerney walked into the room, where a group of silent men and women greeted him with downcast eyes.

About the Author

Michael McGarrity is the author of *Tularosa*, nominated for an Anthony Award, *Mexican Hat, Serpent Gate, Hermit's Peak*, and *The Judas Judge*. He is a former deputy sheriff for Santa Fe County, where he established the first Sex Crimes unit. He has also served as an instructor at the New Mexico Law Enforcement Academy and as an investigator for the New Mexico Public Defender's Office. He lives in Santa Fe.